Praise for *Unforgotten*

"Shepard Gray's riveting follow-up to *Unforgiven* centers on a deadly game of cat-and-mouse. Readers won't be able to resist the propulsive plotting. This begs to be read in one sitting."

Publishers Weekly

"Gray's latest Amish romantic suspense novel is a thoughtful exploration of themes of shame, empowerment, and forgiveness. This uplifting story of healing reminds readers that God's love and ⸺ ⸺ endures even within one's trauma and fear."

Booklist

Praise for *Unforgiven*

"A propulsive series opener. Gray's multifaceted narrative blends uneasy suspense, slow-burning romance, and community drama, all while leaving plenty of secrets yet to be uncovered. Readers will be eager to get their hands on the follow-up."

Publishers Weekly

"Shelley Shepard Gray pens a story of love, hate, and forgiveness that will touch readers' hearts and stay with them long after they finish the last page. Gray is a master storyteller who creates characters that are so alive they feel like good friends. My highest recommendation."

Nancy Mehl, author of the Ryland and St. Clair series

Books by Shelley Shepard Gray

A Season in Pinecraft

Her Heart's Desire
Her Only Wish
Her Secret Hope

Unforgiven
Unforgotten
Unshaken

UNSHAKEN

SHELLEY SHEPARD GRAY

Revell
a division of Baker Publishing Group
Grand Rapids, Michigan

Published by Revell
a division of Baker Publishing Group
Grand Rapids, Michigan
RevellBooks.com

Printed in the United States of America

Library of Congress Cataloging-in-Publication Data
Names: Gray, Shelley Shepard, author.
Title: Unshaken / Shelley Shepard Gray.
Description: Grand Rapids, Michigan : Revell, a division of Baker Publishing Group, 2025.
Identifiers: LCCN 2024044647 | ISBN 9780800746049 (paperback) | ISBN 9780800747107 (casebound) | ISBN 9781493450619 (ebook)
Subjects: LCGFT: Christian fiction. | Thrillers (Fiction) | Novels.
Classification: LCC PS3607.R3966 U57 2025 | DDC 813/.6—dc23/eng/20240920
LC record available at https://lccn.loc.gov/2024044647

Cover image of Amish woman by Laura Klynstra / BPG.

The author is represented by The Seymour Agency.

Baker Publishing Group publications use paper produced from sustainable forestry practices and postconsumer waste whenever possible.

25 26 27 28 29 30 31   7 6 5 4 3 2 1

To Susan and Frank,
who successfully pulled me out of
a bad case of writer's block late one night.
Neighbors like y'all are hard to find.

Anyone who belongs to Christ has become a new person. The old life is gone, a new life has begun!

2 Corinthians 5:17

Things turn out the best for those who make the best of the way things turn out.

Amish proverb

PROLOGUE

SOUTHERN OHIO
TUESDAY, MARCH 5

Today was the day. After weeks of hanging around the Broken Arrows, learning the way they did things, and earning their trust, Timothy Jones was finally going to get initiated.

Kane, his best friend in the gang and his appointed handler, had told him the news when Timothy had arrived to clean the clubhouse. After watching him pick up trash, clean toilets, and sweep the floors, Kane said that all he had to do was meet the dealer on the side of a junky-looking dollar store, inform him that the Broken Arrows wanted their money, and be just menacing enough for the guy to take him seriously. As soon as he got the money and the guy was out of sight, he would walk out to the parking lot, where Kane and several other members were going to be watching.

As soon as he handed off the two grand, he'd be in.

"This is the guy." Kane tapped his phone's screen a couple of times and then held it up for Timothy to see. The pic was

7

of a guy about five foot ten, skinny. Wearing loose green Army pants and a faded T-shirt. When Timothy upped the magnification, he got a pretty good look at his expression. He knew that blank, stoned look well.

Timothy felt a wave of distaste course through him. He hated drug addicts. "He looks strung out."

Kane snickered. "He likely is. Which is why he owes us so much cash."

Unease snaked down his spine. The addicts he knew didn't carry much money, if any. Any cash on hand quickly became their drug of choice. "What if he doesn't have the money? What do I do then?" The dealer might be skinny, but he was still bigger than Timothy. Even though he was eighteen, his height had stalled out at five foot seven. Was he supposed to beat him up in the parking lot?

Kane clasped his shoulder. "Buddy, of course he's not going to hand it over without incentive. That's why you're going to have this."

"This" was a gun. It was on the small side—nothing like the Glock Kane carried around. Timothy reached out and held it. It was solid and had a good weight to it.

His shoulders eased. He could handle this. At least, he thought so. A couple of the guys had taken him out to target practice two weeks ago. It had been the first time he'd ever handled a gun, but after an hour, they'd said he'd done okay.

Kane was studying him. His expression was hard. "What do you think? You good?"

There was only one answer. "Yeah. Sure."

Kane's stance relaxed. "Good. Good." Grinning, he said, "Just think, tonight we're gonna have a party using some of that money you bring in. We'll make you official and get you your own bottle of tequila. Maybe even find you a girl. It'll be great."

"Yeah," he said again. After Kane slapped him on the back, Timothy walked outside, lit a cigarette, and tried not to think about what he needed to do. Because the honest truth was that he didn't care about tequila or girls. The only thing that mattered to him was that after today, he'd finally belong somewhere. After years of living in foster care and only getting a plastic trash bag to move his things, he'd be surrounded by people who cared.

Plus, once he was a member of the Broken Arrows, he'd have some money. Maybe then Audrey would change her mind and give him the time of day again. She might not have wanted him in a gang, but he hoped she'd change her mind after seeing how much better he was as a full-fledged gang member.

That's what he needed to think about.

Because if he messed this up?

It would likely be bad. Really, really bad. He'd have nothing.

Exhaling a ring of smoke, he leaned back his head and closed his eyes. And hoped no one was around to see that his hand was shaking like a leaf.

1

Stephanie Miller didn't know much, but she knew one thing for sure and for certain. It had been a mistake to gasp. In the span of three seconds, the scary young Englisher who'd fired the gun turned. Their eyes met.

And then, right there in an empty lot at the side of the store, everything in her world changed. A new, awful tension filled the air.

Unable to keep the teenager's gaze, Stephanie looked down at the man who'd been shot. Blood pooled on the ground beneath his chest. But worse was that while the man's eyes were wide open, they were vacant.

He was dead.

It didn't make sense. Not the killing, not the fact that neither she nor the gunman was trying to help the poor man on the ground, not the fact that nearby was a silver sedan with a woman inside who was honking the horn. The sound of it seemed to reset Stephanie's head.

Shock turned to fear. Confusion became horror. All the disbelief Stephanie had wanted to hold tight faded into a new, stark clarity. One that was so bright, it was almost blinding. She'd witnessed a murder. She needed to get out of there. Scream. Go tell someone. But who? She didn't trust anyone. Not anymore. Especially not the police.

The gunman blinked.

She looked him in the eye. Silently begging him to disappear. To be a product of her imagination.

But of course he wasn't.

Then, as if in slow motion, he raised his right hand.

She cried out. Dropped the plastic shopping bag she'd clenched in her hands. Little by little, her brain finally started working again, sending frantic, garbled messages to her frozen limbs. She needed to run. Get away.

"No," he said in a harsh voice. "Stay there."

She could smell the sharp, metallic scent of fresh blood pooling on the ground. Staying there meant she'd soon be dead on the ground too.

Ignoring his orders, she started for the store's entrance. The clerk inside was a nice woman. Maybe she'd help her get away?

All of a sudden the silver sedan screeched to a stop right next to her.

Now what was happening? Was it someone else with a gun? She let out a piercing scream.

"Shut up!" the gunman yelled.

Focusing on him once again, she willed herself to stay silent just as the car's passenger door swung open.

"Get in!" the woman called out.

Peeking into the car, she noticed an older woman with brown hair and kind-looking eyes.

"Come on, honey," the woman said. "Please trust me."

Stephanie's legs felt as if cement had filled them. She was stuck. "N-nee."

"Get in or you're going to get killed too! Come on. Please!"

"Don't do it." The man clicked his gun.

He was pointing it at her. The choices seemed to swim in front of her eyes. The woman and the vehicle. The dollar store.

The scary guy. The gun.

"Now!" the woman yelled.

Meeting her eyes, Stephanie knew what was the best option.

The gun fired as she was getting in. She cried out just as the woman careened forward.

Suddenly all Stephanie was able to do was close the passenger side door.

The pain that skimmed her arm felt like burning ice. It took another few precious seconds for her to realize what had happened. Then, as a curious, wet warmth saturated her sleeve, she looked down at her arm. The elbow-length sleeve of her best blue dress was turning red.

She'd been shot. That man, nee, that teenaged boy, had shot her. Just like he'd shot that poor man on the ground.

"Hold on," the woman said as the car jumped forward and zigzagged out of the parking lot.

The woman turned right and then accelerated. Stephanie grabbed the door with her good hand as they flew down the road. Every so often, the woman changed lanes or passed a vehicle going too slow.

"That guy was part of a gang," the woman said as they continued to speed. "I've known him a long time and hoped and prayed that this day would never come. The man he shot and killed? I'm pretty sure it was part of his initiation."

Her words made no sense. Stephanie was also pretty sure

that she didn't care. All she wanted was to get out of the car and go to the hospital.

"I'm bleeding," she said.

The inside of the vehicle smelled like coffee and a hint of perfume. It wasn't unpleasing, but it did seem to symbolize the woman sitting beside her—and the differences between them. Stephanie had lived all her life in a sheltered environment. After her parents died, the police had picked her up and held her at the station until her aunt and uncle came to get her.

Ever since then, they'd supervised most of her days, which usually meant that she attended to her young cousins, did laundry, and cooked.

This woman, on the other hand, looked as if she'd lived a full life and rarely let anyone tell her what to do.

Stephanie was twenty-three and had been waiting for her ride home. She'd gone to the dollar store to buy a month's supply of necessities for herself. It was the only day of the month her aunt and uncle allowed her to mix among the English.

No, it was the only day of the month when she had a taste of freedom.

She doubted that the woman driving the car had any idea what that was like. She'd likely never thought twice about walking into a store.

As worry and stress settled in, she stared at the splotches of blood on her sleeve and apron. The blood had permeated the fabric. The stain wasn't going to come out. Her aunt was going to be so very mad at her for ruining her new dress.

She bit her lip. Felt tears form in her eyes as the pain radiating down her arm began to register. A stained dress was the least of her worries. They'd left behind a man on the ground. A dead man.

Stephanie lifted her chin and looked at the woman driving the car again. Saw that she was older than her. Maybe mid-thirties. She had dark brown hair that hung in a silky sheet around her shoulders and hazel eyes.

What was going on?

When the woman reached out a hand, Stephanie shied away from it and attempted to speak in a coherent manner. "N-nee." Frustrated, she reminded herself to speak English, not Deutsch. "I mean, I need to go home."

"You can't." Looking crestfallen, the woman said, "Listen, I know you don't know me. I know you're scared. But please try and trust me."

Trust her? Stephanie shook her head. "You don't understand. There's a man on the ground. I think he's dead. I need to go tell the lady at the store—"

"You don't," she interrupted. Looking more agitated, she lowered her voice. "Honey, I'm not joking. This is important. Really important. You need to come with me. We'll go talk to the police."

"Nee." Her reaction was guttural. Instinctive. The police were awful. Scary. They'd taken her from her home. Had told her that she couldn't even bring her dolls to keep her company. Told her that someone would get them later, said that she would be all right. But they'd lied. "No police."

"You witnessed a murder, honey. We have to talk to the police."

"No. No police."

The woman's expression pinched, like she didn't like nor understand what Stephanie was saying. Like she was going to ignore her wishes. As they came to a light, Stephanie glanced at the door's handle. As soon as they stopped, she'd get out. Run.

The lady pressed on the brake.

Now was her chance. She reached for the handle.

"No!" the lady screamed. Then, just as if the traffic light hadn't turned yellow, she pressed the gas pedal. The car accelerated, shot through the intersection. Cars honked. Tires screeched.

And then they were on their way again.

Feeling dizzy, Stephanie tried to take a breath. "No police. Please," she said. "Just let me go." This woman needed to release her. Leave her alone. Maybe she would if Stephanie screamed?

"Honey, please. Listen."

"Nee, *you* listen. No police. I hate them. *I hate them.*"

The woman muttered something under her breath. Looked in the rearview mirror. Then seemed to come to a conclusion. "All right, then. We'll go to plan B."

The woman wasn't making any sense. "Please. Let me go."

"I'm sorry, but I can't. If I don't get you someplace safe, that kid who had the gun is going to find you. Or one of the guys I spied nearby will." She tugged on Stephanie's wrist. "I promise, you're in danger."

"No. No, I don't know you. I have to go home. My aunt will be expecting me." She would likely punish Stephanie, but that would be the worst that happened. They didn't trust the police either.

The woman didn't respond. Instead, she seemed to tighten her grip on the steering wheel and accelerated. Five minutes passed. Ten.

Her arm throbbed as the leaking wound continued to stain her dress.

When the woman finally parked behind an old building, her hands were shaking. "Honey, my name is Bev Anderson. I'm a social worker. One of my former kids, one of the foster kids I used to be in charge of, was the one who shot you. I know him."

Stephanie tried to keep up. "You . . . you're his friend?"

"No. I mean, yes." Looking even more shaken up, Bev said, "I mean, I used to be his friend. At least, I tried to be." Staring off into space, she added, "Timothy had a lot going against him, but I thought there was a chance that I could help him." Her voice broke. "But now . . . well, I think I've lost him. He killed a man and he shot you."

"I still don't know why."

"You were a witness. When he gets picked up, Timothy will be headed to prison for a good long while."

Stephanie felt bile rise in her throat. "I don't know what happened. I was standing off to the side of the store like I always do, waiting for my driver to pick me up. I didn't think anyone was around, there never is. But then . . . there they were. And the man was shaking his head and saying no. And then . . . then, I saw him. I saw your Timothy raise his gun. I saw the man on the ground. I saw all the blood on the pavement."

"Oh, honey. That must have been horrific." Bev closed her eyes. "Oh my word. I'm so sorry! Here you are in pain, and I'm not doing a thing for you. Roll up your sleeve, would you? I've got a pretty decent first aid kit in the back. Hopefully all we'll need to do is put on a butterfly for now and then later—"

No way did she want this woman to doctor her arm. She shook her head. "Nee. Stop! I want to go home. My arm is burning."

"I'm sorry, but that's not a good idea."

"Why not?" Everything this woman was saying might be true, but she had been living Amish, not in a closet. She knew how things worked.

"Honey, what's your name?" Bev asked as she leaned in between the two front seats and started fishing around for the kit.

"Stephanie."

"Stephanie is a pretty name. It suits you. Ah, here it is." Bev pulled out an insulated tote bag and settled it on her lap. Turning to face her again, Bev frowned. "You haven't rolled up your sleeve. Come on now. We can't stay here too long."

"You don't understand. I want—"

Bev cut her off. "Stephanie, I know you're scared but we have to patch you up, and I need to figure out what to do next."

"There is no 'next.' I want you to drop me off at my house."

Bev shook her head. "I'm sorry, but I can't. You're a witness to a murder. You would be able to describe the entire event in detail to the police. Timothy and the gang are not going to want that to happen."

Slowly what Bev meant began to sink in, but on its heels was the panic that always surrounded any thoughts about the police. "I won't say anything. I don't want to talk to anyone."

"I'm afraid that doesn't matter." Her voice became even more intense. "While the rest of the world might simply describe you as an Amish girl in a blue dress, Timothy won't. He's seen you up close. He'll look beyond your prayer covering and remember your auburn hair. He won't just see a girl with no makeup on. He'll be able to describe your blue eyes. He knows you're slim and on the tall side. He knows that you're a pretty thing and probably what . . . twenty-one?"

"Twenty-three."

"Right. There aren't a lot of girls who look like you, Stephanie. You're stunning. The fact that you're Amish makes you even more memorable. I'm afraid you're going to be very easy to find."

"But I live—"

Bev talked over her yet again. "You live right outside of Peebles, don't you? In the Amish settlement there?"

"Jah."

"See, everyone knows about the Amish community there. There's a good number of families, but it's not all that big. It won't be difficult for anyone in that gang to discover where you live. And Timothy or his handler will find you there, Stephanie. They won't give up until you've been silenced."

Silenced?

Bev took a deep breath as she opened up the first aid kit. "Here's why Timothy is going to move heaven and earth in order to find you. If you testify, Timothy is going to get sent to prison for a very long time. He's going to be tried as an adult because he's eighteen. He knows this. I have a feeling the gang members who were lurking around know this too. They know if he's arrested, he's going to talk. The police will force him to tell them every secret he knows about the Broken Arrows. The gang isn't going to want that to happen."

For sure, Timothy's future looked grim, but he had done a very bad thing. "I . . . I just want to go home."

"I know, but that's not an option until the police have him in custody. Now, hold still. I'm going to see how bad you were injured. Then, once we get you patched up, we're going to decide what to do next."

Just as Stephanie turned so that Bev could look at her arm, Bev's cell phone rang again.

Glancing at the screen, she murmured, "I need to get this. It's my cop friend."

"I don't want to talk to him!"

"I understand. Please, trust me."

Stephanie felt yet another trickle of fear slide through her. If Bev kept her promise, maybe everything would be taken care of and she could go home.

"Will, hey. What's up?"

All of the ease in the woman's body seemed to leak out of her as she listened to her friend. "Will, actually, I happened to be in the parking lot when that took place. Yes, I know I should have called you. But, um, you see, I was on my way to help an Amish girl I know. She was in trouble."

Stephanie couldn't help it, she started shaking. Even though Bev was telling her friend a lie, it was very possible that she was only saying such things because Stephanie was sitting beside her.

Eventually, Bev was going to break her promise and hand Stephanie over to the cop. Old memories clashed with new fears, mixing together, churning up old hurts. Against her will, tears started to fall.

Beside her, Bev was listening on her phone. She took a deep breath. Looked Stephanie's way. Concern filled her eyes.

After a few more seconds, she seemed to interrupt her friend. "Will, uh, I'm sorry, but that can't happen. Yes. Yes, I understand, but there are some other circumstances . . ." Looking frazzled, she said, "Listen, couldn't you get your clues from the victim? From his ID or something?"

There was a new, far more worried expression on her face as she listened closely to Will.

Still trying not to completely fall apart, Stephanie pursed her lips.

"I understand. No. Ah yes. Listen, I'll keep in touch. Yes, I promise, if I remember anything constructive, I'll call right away. Yeah. Yes. I understand." After yet another few seconds, she murmured, "Thanks."

When she disconnected, Bev stared out the window. Swallowed. Then seemed to come to a decision. "Stephanie, Will called me because he knows I was trying to find a way to reconnect with some of the boys in the gang. He called to tell me about the shooting. After we talked—you heard what I said—he had some news to share."

"What is it?"

"I'm sorry, but there's no easy way to tell you this." Turning to face her, she said, "The body of the man you saw murdered is gone."

"What do you mean? He wasn't dead after all?"

"No, he was dead. It means that the gang carted him off. They're going to do their best to keep this murder under wraps. Prevent it from getting solved."

Releasing a ragged sigh, Stephanie said, "So that means I can go home? It's over?"

"No, honey. It means that if you're sure you don't want to talk to the police, then I'm going to have to find you someplace safe for a spell. Do you want to change your mind?"

"No."

"Are you sure? If I call him back, I could explain things to Will. Why, I bet he'd even let me stay with you during the interview. Or I could get your family."

"Nee!" She didn't trust Bev not to go back on her word, and involving her aunt and uncle would only make things worse.

Long, interminable seconds passed as they stared at each other. Stephanie knew she was trembling, but she didn't back down. There was no way she'd ever go into a police station ever again. Never.

Finally, Bev released her breath. "All right, then. In that case, you're going to need to hide."

"Hide?"

"I know. I know. You have questions. I know you're scared too. I don't blame you one bit. But this is what we're going to do. I'm going to patch you up and then call my brother."

"Your brother?" What in the world did he have to do with this mess?

"Yes. He's down in Crittenden County. That's in Kentucky."

"Kentucky." She knew she sounded like an echoing robot, but nothing Bev was saying made sense.

"Southern Kentucky. I'll feel better once I get you under his protection." She smiled encouragingly then.

Stephanie did not return that smile. This woman might have saved her life, but that didn't mean Stephanie completely trusted her. They were strangers.

Bev's look of encouragement slowly faded into worry. "What's on your mind?"

Oh, a lot of things—starting with witnessing a murder and ending with being forced to run away with a wound in her arm. "I just wish that I'd never gone to the dollar store today. If I hadn't left *mei haus*, I wouldn't be in this mess."

"I'm sure you do wish that."

Bev's words and tone sounded trite, and they fueled a rush of anger. "You're acting as if what has just happened is nothing."

Bev turned to face her more fully. Her expression was devoid of any gentleness or humor. In its place was something hard, almost defiant. "Stephanie, you listen to me. I know what you've been through is traumatic. I know you're scared to death. I know you don't trust me and that running doesn't make anything seem better. But I'm going to tell you the best piece of advice I can give. I've told it to countless children under my care." She took a deep breath. "Wishing for things to be different doesn't help. Hoping that things will be better in the morning doesn't mean that things will be."

Her voice hardened. "What is happening right now is your new reality. You have a choice to make, and that's to either accept what is happening and survive, or to cry and complain. I'm not saying that crying and complaining aren't justified. But honey, it's not going to make things better. Do you understand?"

"Jah." She'd already learned that lesson a long time ago.

"Good. Now let's take care of your arm so we can get you on your way."

Stephanie kept her silence as Bev gently removed two straight pins from her dress and carefully eased down the fabric to uncover her shoulder.

She felt exposed but hardly cared. Her arm hurt, her nerves were frayed, and she was fairly sure that Bev's words were the awful truth.

It didn't matter how much she wished things were different, they weren't going to magically change. She was hurt, she was in danger, and she was on the run.

Nothing was going to be just fine ever again.

2

Everything had been set in motion the moment Stephanie had realized that she had no choice but to do what Bev Anderson wanted.

While Stephanie had sipped the water Bev gave her and tried to get her bearings, Bev called her brother. Her voice was both wheedling and bossy. In mere minutes, she seemed to have enlisted him in her plan to hide Stephanie. Though it all sounded rather convoluted, Stephanie had been too afraid to voice her opinion.

Next thing she knew, they were at a supercenter parking lot, and Stephanie was under strict orders to stay hidden. Bev even made her take off her white *kapp* and put her hair into a ponytail.

Within fifteen minutes, Bev had returned with a suitcase, backpack, and two shopping bags full of English clothes. Not wanting to chance anyone seeing an Amish girl changing clothes in a public restroom, Bev made Stephanie change into jeans and a long-sleeved T-shirt in her car.

Soon after, Stephanie was given detailed plans about what to do next. Which left her where she was now—on a bus pulling into a station in Nashville, Tennessee.

Once the bus parked and the driver opened the door, Stephanie was going to be on the clock. She was going to have twenty minutes to get off the bus, locate her bag, and navigate her way through the throng of people until she found the escalator.

Then, after she somehow managed to get herself and her bag on that thing without breaking her neck, she was supposed to go directly outside.

Once outside, she needed to open up her new backpack, pull out the cheap pay-by-the-minute cell phone Bev had bought her, and call Hardy. Hardy was Bev's younger brother and the man who would drive her to Crittenden County. His boss had a place where she could stay in the center of Marion.

Bev had told her all these instructions multiple times. While she'd been driving. As Stephanie had been changing clothes. When she'd been sitting in the back seat removing tags and placing her new items inside the suitcase.

Bev had repeated the directions so many times that Stephanie imagined she could recite them in her sleep. Bev had made it all sound so easy. A piece of cake.

Stephanie knew this journey was anything but that.

She liked cake. She liked it a lot.

But never had she had to go through so many obstacles to have that first bite.

Instead, she was pretty sure that anything that could go wrong was going to. There were too many things out of her control.

Experience told her that it was hard to count on too many people. There was always someone who lied or didn't follow through on their promises.

Jah. She knew all about people who didn't follow through on their promises. Hating that her thoughts turned once again to the police officers who'd taken her to her aunt and uncle, Stephanie forced her mind to concentrate on the present. If she allowed herself to drift back into the years after her parents' car accident, she would disappear into the shadowy world of depression again.

She'd come too far to return to that place.

This, this journey should be her only focus now. And she'd overcome hard things before and survived. She could survive this ordeal too.

After all, she had no choice. All she had to do was stay strong and keep focused.

"Miss? Are you getting off or heading down to Chattanooga?"

"Hmm?" She looked to her right. Realized the quiet woman who'd been sitting in the seat next to her was waiting on her to move.

"This is Nashville, dear. Didn't you say this was where you were getting off?"

"Oh. Yes. This is my stop." That was true. So why was she having such a hard time moving?

"Mine too." The tightening of the woman's jaw practically screamed that she was seconds away from losing patience.

"Sorry," Stephanie mumbled as she grabbed her purse and got to her feet. Aware that the clock was ticking, she scooted out to the bus's aisle and stepped forward.

"Wait!"

Fear prickling at the base of her neck, she turned.

"Don't you need this?"

Her new backpack hung from the woman's hand.

"Danke," she whispered as she quickly grabbed it. Right as she realized that she'd forgotten to speak English.

When the woman frowned, no doubt trying to connect the woman dressed in jeans and a ponytail with Pennsylvania Dutch, Stephanie felt her hands begin to shake.

How could she be so stupid? It was a sign. Another example of why she was not going to survive. She might not even be able to find this Hardy. Bev had warned her to only speak English. No matter what. She'd already messed up.

Gott, help me, she silently prayed over and over as she followed the rest of the passengers down the aisle and eventually climbed down the steps of the bus. *Please help me*, she continued. *It's real obvious I'm not going to be able to do this on my own.*

Of course she heard no reply. But maybe He had been listening, because she found her suitcase easily. It also wasn't difficult to locate the escalator leading upstairs to the main exit.

Now all she had to do was follow everyone else onto the thing. Quickly.

Everything inside herself protested. She'd never been one to rush. Not when she was a little girl and not as an adult. She would do her chores well but never all that fast. She often had the highest marks on her tests in school, but she was usually the last to turn her paper in. Her friend Jenny had called her maddening—usually because she'd always been the one to have to wait for her.

After her parents died and she'd moved in with her aunt and uncle, Stephanie had tried to do things at a faster pace, but the results had been dismal. She got confused and forgot things. At last, even her aunt had agreed that Stephanie needed to remain the person she was. A slow and methodical one.

Biting the inside of her lip, Stephanie watched carefully as the three people directly in front of her stepped on the moving stairs, then after adjusting her backpack's straps on her shoulders, she stepped forward. Her right hand gripped the rail while she pulled her suitcase behind her. Amazingly—or maybe it really was God's grace—she didn't fall and was even able to step off the contraption without knocking into anyone.

If she ever made it to Marion, Stephanie decided to give herself a little cheer about that. She'd done real good on that moving staircase, especially since it was the first time in her life that she'd been on one.

Her momentary burst of happiness fled as she spied the electronic screen on the wall. The clock was still ticking.

She now had less than ten minutes to follow the last of Bev's directions.

She needed to get to the exit, stand on the sidewalk, pull out her cell phone, and call Hardy. At least Bev had already programed the number in her phone. All she had to do was tap on his name. She'd practiced that during the drive too.

Swallowing hard, she ran a hand along the seam of her new jeans. The soft fabric gave her the courage to ignore the continuous stream of doubts running through her head and walk through the automatic sliding glass doors. She looked like everyone else now. No one was giving her a second look. Or, if they were, it was not because she looked Amish but likely because she couldn't hide how nervous she was.

Immediately, she stepped into chaos. Cars lined the street. Other vehicles honked impatiently. Travelers dragged suitcases much like hers while staring at their phones. Children darted among anyone stopped for too long. A pair of homeless men were sitting against the terminal's concrete wall holding signs. When she paused to read one, someone knocked into her back. She stumbled.

At least another two minutes had passed.

Her breath caught as she scanned the area and looked for a safe place to stand and place her phone call. Bev had told her that Hardy was honest and kind but punctual. He wasn't going to be very patient with her if she dallied.

Stephanie hadn't had the nerve to ask why.

Was this Hardy man really so busy that he didn't believe in giving anyone the benefit of extra time? Even someone who was completely out of her element?

Maybe he was or maybe he wasn't. It didn't matter.

After carefully moving to a recently vacated spot next to the curb, Stephanie pulled her phone out of her purse, tapped the name on the screen, and held it up to her ear. Just like she'd practiced. It rang once.

"Stephanie, you ready?" The voice was heavy and deep, like each word had been pulled from his chest.

"Jah. I mean, yes." Hating that she'd once again forgot herself, she sighed. "Sorry. I mean, is this Hardy?"

"Nobody else is going to answer my phone, girl. So, you ready?"

"Yes. I'm standing outside. I mean, I'm standing near the curb and some sliding glass doors." Remembering what Bev had said, she added, "I have on a pair of blue jeans, a long-sleeved white T-shirt, and black tennis shoes. Oh, and I have long, dark auburn hair."

"I see you." A grain of amusement entered his voice. "I couldn't miss you if I tried. Now stay put, and I'll be right there. I'm driving a black pickup truck and have on a black baseball cap."

He was here. She hadn't gotten there too late. She'd done

it. "Okay," she said before she realized he'd already disconnected.

Quickly stuffing her phone in one of her back pockets, Stephanie took a deep breath.

She was now in Nashville. The temperature was warmer than in Cincinnati. The nighttime sky was cloudy and the air was thick with humidity. Looking into the distance, she spied a faint line of dark clouds. A storm was coming. A fierce one, she reckoned.

She wondered if she knew that because she'd grown up on a farm or if people in all walks of life knew such things.

All thought of rain and humidity fled as the biggest black truck she'd ever seen in her life pulled up to the curb. While she stood there, a man who easily looked like he could wrestle a bull and come out the winner hopped out of the truck's cab. Eyes fastened on her, he strode forward.

"Hey, Stephanie."

He had a thick scar on his face, making his serious expression look almost fierce. To her shame, she couldn't help but stare.

When he held out his hand, she flinched.

If he noticed her rude behavior, he didn't seem upset. Still staring at her face, he spoke again. "I'm Hardy and you're okay." His voice had deepened into a low drawl. All the slight traces of amusement had vanished. In its place was a seriousness and something that felt like patience.

The way her father used to speak to her when she'd complain that most of the kids ignored her on the playground.

The memory of her kind father formed a lump in her throat. Even after all this time, his loss made her want to cry. No way was she going to do that. Forcing herself to once again push his memory to the back of her mind, she exhaled. Attempted to get her bearings. "Um," she uttered.

Her mind had gone walking. She was so rattled that she'd already forgotten what she was going to say. Boy, she was such an idiot. "I mean—"

Hardy cut her off. "Don't worry about it none. But we gotta go, yeah?"

She noticed then he had hazel eyes and thick, dark lashes. Just like his sister.

Worry filled his gaze. "Come on now, girl. Don't shut down. Not yet."

Not yet. Why did that time frame make things seem worse? Memories from the last eight hours burned her mind. The things she saw. The promises she'd made to herself to stay strong in order to survive. Why did they all suddenly seem so far away and out of reach?

"Steph. Stephanie."

She flinched. "Yes?"

"I know you're scared, but you've gotta trust me."

"I . . ."

Impatience flared in his eyes before he tamped it down. "Hand me your backpack."

She didn't want to touch him. Didn't want to trust him. Saliva was forming in the back of her throat. She was going to either throw up, choke, or pass out. But she shook her backpack off her shoulders and handed it to him.

Somehow, he managed to pull the suitcase from her grip. "Breathe, and get in." He pointed to a silver step on the side of his vehicle. "That's a running board. Use it to get yourself up. But do it now, okay?"

At last, she inhaled. "Okay," she whispered.

He obviously didn't hear her. He was securing her suitcase in the back seat of his truck.

She opened up the passenger door, grasped the seat with one hand and a little gray bar with the other, stepped on the running board, and pulled herself in.

"Close your door," Hardy said as he closed his.

"Where's my backpack?"

"I put it right behind you. It's safe. Just like you. Yeah?"

"Yes."

"Good. That's real good. Now, I just texted Bev. She knows I've got you. You're safe now."

Was she really? It seemed like with every mile, things were getting scarier, not easier. "What will happen now? Do I not need to worry about Timothy anymore?"

"We'll discuss it in a sec. For now, we've got to go."

There was the reminder about time again. Forcing herself to stop thinking so much, she followed his directions. The backpack was now sitting on the floor behind her seat and the passenger door was closed. She'd done it.

"Seat belt. Come on now, pull it out and strap yourself in."

She'd forgotten! Pulling on the black belt, she fastened the buckle just as he pulled out of the parking lot.

Hardy didn't say a word as he switched lanes, switched again, and then turned left at a light.

She gripped the sides of her leather seat as he turned, picked up speed, and then merged with traffic on the highway. Only then did she realize she was sitting on her phone. After darting a glance at Hardy and debating a couple of minutes, Stephanie shifted, pulled the phone out of her pocket, and held it on her lap.

He glanced her way. "Don't call anyone. Not yet."

"I won't." Swallowing again, she added, "I mean, I was

going to put it in my backpack, but I forgot it was in the back seat."

"Ah." He seemed to be waiting for her to say something else, but she had no idea what she should say.

Because she didn't know how to act. Not right now. Not around a man like him. All the drivers she'd ever ridden with had been older. Less demanding. None of them had ever driven a giant truck like this either. Because she'd never been in another state before.

Because no matter how much Bev had told her that Hardy was a man she could trust, Stephanie didn't completely believe it. And why should she, anyway? Bev had been a stranger too.

"Try to relax, yeah?" he murmured in a gentler tone. "We've got a little bit of a drive ahead of us."

Turning around, she reached her backpack, unzipped the front compartment, and put her phone inside. Just as she was about to zip it back up, she spied the light blue slip of paper Beverly had given her before they'd said goodbye. It had her name and phone number on it. Just in case she wanted to talk.

About what, Stephanie didn't know.

About how scared and lost she felt? Or how badly the wound in her arm felt even now?

She still felt out of sorts, and her thoughts continued to dive. Maybe Bev would like to chat about how shaken Stephanie had been by the sight of the man on the ground, or mere moments later, when her dress's sleeve had been stained with blood?

She wrinkled her nose. It was doubtful that she'd ever completely forget how the blood's sharp, metallic scent had seemed to engulf her.

Nee, she did not want to speak to Bev about what happened. She wished she would never have to think about it again.

But even if she wasn't on the run, Stephanie was pretty sure that no matter how hard she tried to forget that experience, she never would. The mind was a funny thing, she reckoned. Holding some memories tight while removing others in seconds. She had no idea why she could remember every second of the worst moment of her life but couldn't seem to remember what she'd had for breakfast yesterday.

Shaking, she quickly pulled the zipper back up and sat straight again.

Hardy glanced her way. "You doing all right? You look like you just saw a ghost or something."

"I'm fine. I, uh, just saw something that sparked a memory I wanted to forget."

"Hmm. You think zipping it away is going to do the trick?"

"No," she said honestly. "I don't think it's going to help me much at all."

To her surprise, he laughed, the sound deep and rough. "Yeah, I didn't think so. Hiding my bad doesn't help me much either. Lord knows I've tried."

Stephanie folded her arms across her chest. Thought about that. She figured Hardy was right. Ignoring a reminder of the crime she'd seen wasn't going to help her much at all.

No matter what she did, she was never going to forget that, until eight hours ago, she'd been in a different world. And even though she hadn't been exactly happy, she'd known what to expect. There was comfort in that, she decided. At least there was in comparison to her current situation— which was that she was heading toward the southwest corner of Kentucky in the care of a very large man in a very large truck.

She really hoped he was as trustworthy as Bev claimed he was.

She might have been able to breathe easier if she could forget the other piece of sage advice the older woman had given her—that hoping and wishing didn't help much.

Bev had been right. Sometimes all wishing and hoping did was make a person feel worse. More alone.

She'd learned that truth over and over again.

3

All good. Don't worry.

Reading her brother's text one more time, Beverly breathed a sigh of relief. Hardy had her. Stephanie would be safe now.

The wait for her brother's text had felt interminable. But that was on her, not him. She'd been too much on edge, continually reminding herself of everything that could go wrong. Stephanie was a very sheltered young woman. She'd likely been in shock too. Bev had worried that Stephanie would forget all the instructions mere minutes after boarding the bus.

Bev, on the other hand, hadn't been able to think of anything else.

After making sure that Stephanie was safely on the bus, Beverly had gotten back in her car and headed home. She lived in a townhouse in a new development in Milford. It was close enough to her office in Batavia to make a short commute yet far enough away to give her some space from most of her clients.

She loved her work, but there was no denying that social

work was hard. Having a heavy caseload of children in the foster care system felt like the toughest job of all.

Getting a little distance from the clients she served was the only way to stay sane. Or, at the very least, to be able to sleep at night.

Unfortunately, even after getting inside her immaculate, organized space, Bev felt at loose ends. Now that she wasn't in the moment, now that the image of Stephanie's hurt expression wasn't fresh in her brain, she felt ashamed. It felt wrong for her to be sitting in her comfortable home after sending Stephanie away on the bus.

She'd also been thinking about Timothy. He'd been such a sweet, hurt boy when they'd first met. He'd touched her heart so deeply that she'd even considered fostering him herself. After reminding herself about all the other kids she was responsible for, Bev had told herself that he was going to be better off with a family.

He hadn't been, though. Not really. Some of the homes weren't all that great, and eventually Timothy had stopped believing that his life would get better.

And now he'd killed a man.

By now they would've sent an officer out to look for Timothy Jones. After they talked, Will had promised to stay away from Stephanie's aunt and uncle's house. That would keep her family safe for a little while.

So everything was going to get handled. More or less.

Still feeling uneasy, she opened up her laptop, booted up her computer, and wrote a detailed report about what happened. Will would want it, and she was going to need that documentation for herself.

An hour later, she closed her computer. She hadn't done too much, but she did feel better. She decided to write some more notes—these just for herself. There were several teens she should visit soon. She knew of a couple of boys who were on the brink of following in Timothy's footsteps.

Timothy's story could be just the ammunition she needed to scare them straight. At least for a little while longer.

So those were good things. Good things in spite of the fact that she'd probably just made a bunch of very bad choices. For the first time, she'd taken a situation into her own hands and hid a witness.

She should be full of regrets.

So far, she didn't have a single one. The fact was that she'd lost several kids to that gang. The Broken Arrows had just enough money and power to do reckless things. Dangerous things. Wrong things.

The police might be able to watch for Timothy, but chances were slim that they'd find him easily. The Arrows had connections with other gangs and with folks in Appalachia. It wouldn't be difficult for him to disappear. And right now, there wasn't any reason for the cops to protect Stephanie. Not until they found the body.

In the meantime, someone in the gang would've found her. That auburn hair of hers was too striking to forget. She'd been standing too close and would be able to not only identify Timothy but describe in detail what she saw.

She knew Stephanie wouldn't stand a chance the moment the head of the Arrows learned what Timothy had done. She didn't know Stuart—he'd never been in the foster system—but she had been aware of who he was for some time. Stuart, or "Stew" as he was known, would stop at nothing to keep himself safe.

She might have lost Timothy to the gang, but she was

going to do everything she could to save one sweet Amish girl.

She fell asleep on her couch. When the first glimpse of light shining through her open shades woke her up, Beverly knew it was time to face a new day.

It was also time to visit Stephanie's family.

She chose a modest outfit of loose-fitting slacks and an equally loose top in dark navy. She pulled her shoulder-length hair into a neat ponytail at the back of her neck and headed out to Peebles.

Eventually she turned right and began following her phone's directions to the address Stephanie had given her. After passing more than one buggy and several fields of sheep, she navigated the final narrow, hilly roads to Stephanie's aunt and uncle's house.

It was a tidy white clapboard house with a small arrangement of shrubs near the front door.

No doubt by now they would be worried sick. Bev knew it would have been best if she'd visited Mark and Jo Miller as soon as she dropped Stephanie off at the bus station. But she hadn't been able to do it. She'd had a strange, uncomfortable feeling hanging over her head all afternoon. It made no sense, but she couldn't seem to quite abandon the feeling that she was being followed.

It was ridiculous.

Or . . . maybe it wasn't.

She now knew five of the Broken Arrows members. Once, most of those boys had been sweet and had gazed at her with big eyes. She'd placed them in foster homes, visited them, talked to their teachers, and tried to develop a rapport.

But the months passed and their lives never changed— some bounced back and forth between their parents and foster homes while others had simply moved locations every year or two. The boys' expectations had faded. They didn't believe in Santa Claus and they didn't believe in having a future.

Eventually, they didn't even believe in her. Because she'd failed them. If Stew or Timothy knew it was her car that Stephanie had gotten into, then she would be their link to the girl. Which meant the worst could still happen, no matter how much she tried to prevent it. Lots of things happened that shouldn't.

Getting out of her sedan, she tried to pull herself together. It was past time.

The door opened, startling her.

A dour-looking Amish man about her height stared at her. When he spoke, his voice was surprisingly mild. "May I help you? Are you lost?"

"I'm not lost, but I hope you can help me. I'm looking for Mr. and Mrs. Miller."

"I'm Mark Miller." He didn't step forward or smile.

"Mr. Miller, my name is Bev Anderson. I'd like to speak with you and your wife, if I may."

"Why do you need to talk to us? You aren't here to sell us anything, are you?"

"No. Not at all." She tried to smile.

He did not. All he did was continue to gaze at her with suspicion.

Bev supposed she couldn't blame him. So far, all she'd done was park in their driveway and ask to speak to them. "I'm sorry, I meant to say that I wanted to speak to you both about Stephanie. Your niece."

Again, to her surprise, the somewhat skeletal-looking man didn't move. "What about Stephanie?"

"Well, I'm sure you must be worried sick after she went into town to go to the dollar store yesterday and never returned."

Mark Miller stared hard at her for a long moment. So long that Bev even wondered if he was going to allow her inside. Just as she was about to turn around, he inclined his head. "Jah, Stephanie did go to the dollar store and never came home again. We haven't heard from her neither."

"I have some answers for you."

A line formed between his brows. "Well, then. I reckon you'd best come in."

He turned and walked back into the house.

Seeing that he hadn't closed the door completely, Bev took it as a sign that she was supposed to follow.

Goose bumps formed on her arms, much like the ones that showed up when she was investigating a report that a teacher or minister had filed. It was as if her body knew before her head when she was walking into a bad situation.

Pushing aside a sense of foreboding, Bev entered a dark living room. A lone kerosene lamp was lit in the corner of a sparsely decorated space. She'd been in several Amish homes over the years. Two families in the area sometimes fostered babies when there was an urgent need.

Those families had always been kind. And while their houses were Plain, the feeling inside was anything but grim. Instead, she'd often felt a lively warmth that was contagious. She'd never had a moment's worry when those families were caring for babies. They would be loved and cared for.

Bev knew that she would never feel that same sense of peace in this house.

Feeling almost panicked, she scanned the area for books

or a project. Knitting needles. A basket of toys. Even a desk with letters or a deck of cards. Anything that would give her a better feeling about the home. Anything to show that a functioning family lived on the premises and that Stephanie was an integral part of it.

But instead, all she found was Mark and his wife standing still and silent.

No doubt they were wondering why she wasn't getting to the point of her visit.

"I apologize," Bev said with what she hoped was an embarrassed and not irritated smile. "It took a second for my eyes to adjust."

"You may have a seat on the couch," Mark said.

"Thank you." Looking up at the woman, she smiled slightly. "Hi. My name is Beverly Anderson. I'm a social worker."

The woman frowned. "What has Stephanie done?"

On the way over, Bev had debated about how much to tell Mark and Jo Miller. She didn't want to share too much, mainly because she didn't think it was safe for them to know too much. There was a chance that someone from the Arrows would somehow figure out who Stephanie was and decide to make a house call.

However, the couple did deserve to know some modicum of the truth. Though they might be keeping their true feelings hidden, they had to be worried sick about their niece.

Weighing her words, she said, "I met Stephanie when I was in the dollar store parking lot yesterday. She . . . well, she got into some trouble."

Jo frowned. "What sort of trouble?"

"Actually, she isn't in trouble. It's more that she saw something disturbing." Bev felt her cheeks heat. She really was a terrible liar. Clearing her throat, she continued, "I'm afraid she might have witnessed a crime."

"What kind of crime?" Mark asked.

"She, ah . . . well, I believe Stephanie saw a man get attacked." In a way, that was the truth.

"Why didn't she come home?" Jo asked.

Bev figured that was a legitimate question. Unfortunately, she didn't have a good answer for that. "She was so rattled, I invited her to spend time with my parents." Yep, the lies kept coming, and each one sounded more outlandish than the last. They'd sounded far more believable in her head.

Jo's eyebrows rose. "Why?"

"Well, she was afraid of what she saw and what might happen if someone followed her home. She doesn't want to place you in danger. We visited for a while, and next thing I knew, we were on my phone and talking to my parents and they bought her a bus ticket to come stay with them."

"Without asking us for permission?" Jo turned to her husband. "I do not understand why she would do such a thing. She knows she must abide by our rules."

With a sinking feeling, Bev knew the lies were going to have to continue. "Stephanie was worried you would be upset. But, like I said, she didn't want to do anything that might put you in danger." When Jo still looked confused, she added, "I think Stephanie was worried that you would want her to stay. And that might have made it unsafe for your children."

"She still should have returned home," Jo said. "We expect her to help with Charity, Hope, and Evan. And with the laundry."

"I see." Well, she was starting to see a lot about Stephanie's life in this house. Here, she'd done her best to convey that Stephanie was worried about their safety, but her aunt seemed more concerned about her niece shirking her duties. "I'm sure the children will miss her company."

Jo didn't reply.

Glowering at Beverly, Mark Miller stood up. "None of your story sounds believable. I think that Stephanie is involved in something sinful. So sinful that you don't even want to tell us."

Before Beverly could get a word in edgewise, Mark folded his arms over his chest and turned to his wife. "I warned you that no good would come from us allowing her to go to the store once a month. It is obvious now that she wasn't going there for only her shampoo and candy."

Bev stood up as well. "I don't believe your niece was there to get into trouble. She doesn't seem to be the type of young woman who would do something like that."

"I didn't think you knew her," Jo said.

"I don't. I mean, not very well."

"I find that difficult to believe. Why would a stranger help her?" Mark said as he walked to the door. "Please leave."

Bev glanced at his wife, looking for an ounce of compassion or worry. Instead, Jo was sitting quietly with her hands neatly folded on her lap. She looked almost bored.

For some reason, that bothered Bev more than the uncle's bluster.

Still determined to alleviate their worries, she said, "Before I leave, I want to make sure you have a way to get information. Do you have a telephone number?"

Mark shook his head. "We have no telephone."

"I mean, perhaps you have a phone shanty? Or you know someone who has a number in case of emergencies? When I hear something from Stephanie, I could let you know. I'm sure you'll be worried about her."

"When you hear something from my niece who is recovering from a shock at your parents' home? Who somehow boarded a bus without any of her belongings?" His eyes got colder. "Please see yourself out."

She walked to the door but paused before exiting. "If I do hear something about her that I think you'll need to know, I'll come back."

Neither of the Millers said a word.

Feeling both relieved to be away from the dour couple and a bit embarrassed, Bev walked down the front steps and got in her car. But before she drove away, she spied three children peeking at her through one of the upstairs windows. Their expressions were somber. Stephanie had lived there. In that dark, silent house with her sullen aunt and uncle.

And suddenly Beverly had a much better understanding of why Stephanie hadn't put up more than a token fight about leaving her home.

It was because she currently didn't have much of a home to return to. She wasn't so very different than many of the children Bev had removed from homes over the years. Or, from the teenagers living in foster care. Most of those had already come to terms that no one wanted to adopt them. They were only biding their time until they were eighteen.

Stephanie wasn't even all that different from the way Bev and Hardy had been when they were living in the projects in St. Louis. The place they lived had become only a placeholder. Only a spot to reside in until they were old enough or something better came along.

She prayed for Stephanie and Hardy the whole way home. Wished them an easy journey and hoped that her tough-looking and gruff brother would unbend enough so that he wouldn't scare the poor girl half to death.

Only when she arrived back home did she pray for herself and ask for guidance.

She'd learned that doing the right thing didn't always make one feel better. Sometimes it brought on a bunch of new worries and doubts and insecurities.

She needed to talk to Hardy.

4

Hardy Anderson had grown up in public housing, entered the Army at eighteen, and spent six years living around the country and surviving two deployments. He'd seen a lot, both very good and very bad. Until ten minutes ago, he'd thought he'd seen it all and that nothing could surprise him anymore.

He'd been wrong.

He'd never met anyone like Stephanie Miller.

As he drove down the stretch of highway, he felt the girl's attention on him once again. She was shy but observant. So very quiet.

He couldn't believe Bev had sent her to him. The poor thing would likely be more comfortable with twenty other people his sister knew. But maybe that didn't matter. For all his life, he'd always done what his sister asked of him. It was the least he could do.

When he felt the girl's gaze on him again, he decided to say something. "You okay?"

"Yes," she said after a brief pause.

What did that mean? Had she been afraid to admit that she needed something? Searching for ideas, he found only one that made any sense. "Do you need to go to the bathroom?"

"No."

She sounded horrified that he'd mentioned it at all. It would be kind of cute if they weren't going to be in his truck for at least another two hours. "Are you sure? If you need to go, we can stop. I know of a couple of places where not too many people frequent. They're clean too." Bev always loved a clean bathroom.

"I do not need to stop. Or, um, use the toilet."

"Okay. If you do, tell me. But give me some warning, yeah?"

When she didn't reply, he glanced her way again. She'd closed her eyes.

All right then. Reluctant to turn on the radio—she was so skittish he figured his usual preference of Southern rock would rattle her—Hardy allowed his thoughts to drift again.

Back to another time. Back to when he and Bev used to dream about getting in a vehicle and going anywhere.

They'd always been sure that anywhere else would be better than where they'd been.

Though he and his sister had grown up in public housing, he'd somehow still grown up believing in the power of the human spirit to overcome almost anything, even though he witnessed the depravity that hid in some people's souls. His mom worked several jobs in order for them to have everything they needed—and then partied in her extra time.

In school, he and Bev had taken different paths. His sister had worked as hard in school as their mother did in life. Because of that, she'd earned every teacher's respect and support. She'd graduated near the top of her class and gotten a scholarship to college.

He had not done any of that. He'd never been close to failing in school, but he sure hadn't ever been a scholarship candidate either. If they'd gone somewhere different, he might have been able to excel in athletics and gotten ahead that way. But their school didn't have an athletics program; the focus was solidly on academics.

When he turned eighteen the beginning of his senior year, he knew he was going to need the help of the United States Armed Forces to move forward.

The sergeant he interviewed with had practically held his hand as he'd guided him through the physical and written tests. Then, after he joined up, the man had kept close tabs on him, reminding Hardy constantly of the better future that was in store for him. Holding on to that dream kept him on track those last few months of high school.

That had been so long ago.

Feeling the girl's gaze on him once again, he coughed. Not wanting to talk about bathroom breaks again, he tried another conversational thread. Something else obvious that maybe, if talked about openly, would ease her mind. "I know you can see that scar on my face. The doc tried his best to sew it clean, but what could he do? He was in a tent in the sandbox."

She didn't say a word.

Feeling more awkward, he added, "It's just a scar from being in a war zone overseas. That's all. I mean, I know I don't look like much, but you don't need to be scared of me."

"I'm not."

He laughed softly, mainly because she sounded so hesitant. "You sure about that?"

"As sure as I can be, I suppose. After all, you are a stranger."

"That is true."

"Besides, your sister told me you were a good man."

He couldn't help responding to that. "Bev said that?"

"Jah. She said you were a hero in the military."

"I was no hero, but I was in the military. I served in the Army."

"In Kentucky?"

"Oh no. I was stationed all over." Glad she was finally speaking to him, he smiled slightly. "I went wherever I was told to go."

"Mmm."

When she turned away, obviously content to end their brief conversation, his thoughts returned to his past. About how those six years in uniform had taken a punk kid and turned him into a man.

There, he'd trained in combat, mechanics, and self-defense. He'd learned to get along, and he'd learned to listen and keep his mouth shut.

Once he'd been armed with those skills, he'd moved up the ranks. Soon, he had new recruits reporting to him. His orders were to make soldiers out of them. Usually, he succeeded in that.

He'd been deployed, earned his sergeant's rank, and was then deployed again, where he'd met his lieutenant. Carter Russell.

"Where are we going again?" Stephanie asked.

"My boss is a wealthy man. He owns a lot of property in the southern part of the state. I'm going to put you at one of those properties."

"What's your boss's name?"

"Carter. His name is Carter Russell. I doubt you'll meet him, but if you had the opportunity, you'd like him a lot. Most people do." Carter was not only rich, he was also easy-going and friendly. Those were good qualities in life, though they had given him a rough road when he'd first been in the Army.

"You like him, don't you?"

"I do consider him to be a friend, but it's more than that. I owe him a lot."

When Hardy had been discharged, Carter offered him a different kind of future. A future in the country, where there were horses and trees and peace. Where he would work for both Carter and the Russell trust but not be told what to do every hour of the day.

Now, he lived on the Russell property. A two-thousand-acre cattle ranch that had been owned by the Russells for several generations. Carter had been a late-in-life baby. His father had passed when he was still in the Army, and his mother was spending her last years with a niece in Jupiter, Florida. Carter spent half his time on the ranch and the other half in Cincinnati, overseeing a variety of holdings run by his family's trust.

When they met, Hardy had just made sergeant and Carter had been a fresh-from-college second lieutenant. He'd been as green as the spring grass.

Most everyone had written him off. Hardy had learned that Carter was smarter than he looked, though. He was some kind of mathematical genius, and Hardy reckoned that the higher-ups were just putting the guy through his paces until they stuck him in a cubicle in the Pentagon and asked him to use that big brain to help solve a hundred logistical and financial problems.

That had happened. Eventually.

But until then, Hardy had taken it upon himself to protect the guy. He'd gotten adept at advising Carter with a nod or a sideways glance. And Carter, to his credit, had shown that he'd not only been blessed with a big brain but also a good dose of common sense. The kid had watched him closely and learned quickly.

Before long, Carter wasn't quite so green, most everyone had stopped hazing him, and a major had taken notice of Carter Russell's big brain.

Eventually Carter had been transferred to DC. But before he left, he'd become a good enough friend to wonder what Hardy was going to do when he got out.

And that's how Hardy had ended up on the Russells' property. There, he oversaw security, supervised a half dozen men, maintained vehicles, watched over the massive main house and guest cabins, and pretty much did whatever the Russell family asked him to.

It was a quiet job. A lot of times, it was a lonely one, but he didn't mind. He knew the family counted on him, and they paid him enough to have a pretty cushy life. So much more than he'd ever dreamed he'd have growing up in the projects.

Hardy looked over at Stephanie. When Beverly had called him and explained the situation, Hardy had instantly gotten on board. It wasn't just Carter who'd taken care of him—he owed his sister a lot too. And he knew some of the people she'd worked with over the years—well, they had nothing to lose and a lot of time to devote to making sure they stayed out of prison.

From what Bev told him, the Amish girl was on the run for her life. She absolutely was going to need a protector because sometimes a person's family just wasn't enough.

Especially when the Broken Arrows gang was involved.

A year ago, when his sister had first told him about the

gang that had recently formed on the outskirts of Appalachia, he'd been tempted to roll his eyes. A bunch of bored small-town teenagers wreaking havoc didn't scare him.

Not after the evil he'd witnessed overseas.

But of late, Bev's stories had started to sound more worrisome. The gang had become organized, aligned themselves with some bigger gangs who were affiliated with the drug trade, and were recruiting members right and left, especially some of Bev's lost boys. The foster kids who had so little and even less of a future.

It was obvious that his sister had reached her limit. The gang might have gotten ahold of some of her boys, but she wasn't about to let them have an Amish girl too.

So he was Stephanie's new protector. No matter what.

He didn't mind taking on that role either. He might not know many Amish people, but he'd had plenty of practice looking out for other folks. If he could keep Carter alive in the middle of the sandbox, chances were pretty good that he could do the same for this woman.

She might be in danger, and he was good at fighting.

If she needed to disappear, he could pull her into one of the many cabins on the property, and no one would be the wiser. The ranch had two thousand acres, every bit of the perimeter surrounded by electric barbed wire.

There were also only two ways in or out of the property, and both were manned 24-7. That guard station also had a camera on the main house and the main barn and would let out a signal if any of the fencing was breached.

It was a whole lot safer than most places she could have gone. He instinctively knew Carter would approve of it too.

All Hardy had to do was hope this girl wouldn't get so

freaked out by the sight of him that she took off running before he had time to get her to trust him.

That was a legitimate worry too. The sizable scar on his face, courtesy of a pair of insurgents, made a person want to keep their distance.

He didn't even like looking at himself in the mirror.

5

Stephanie reckoned that they'd been on the road for about ninety minutes. During this time, Hardy remained relatively silent, For the most part, she was too. She wasn't used to speaking with Englishers, and certainly not men like Hardy. After their brief conversation about him being in the Army and his boss, she'd stopped asking him questions.

After that, the only time he'd initiated conversation was when he'd asked if she cared for a bottle of water, a granola bar, or a bag of pretzels. She'd refused it all.

Though she was forced to accept his ride, Stephanie thought it was a little greedy to accept a stranger's food too. Besides, she still felt squeamish inside. When she wasn't thinking about getting shot, her mind kept replaying the way the poor man had been bleeding on the ground. She wasn't sure if she'd ever be able to think about that without feeling sick.

However, when her stomach started to cramp, it reminded her that it had been a very long time since she'd eaten.

She was beginning to think that an empty stomach was making her feel worse instead of better.

Now the silence was starting to pull at her something awful. As a light rain started to fall, every doubt and worry that she'd entertained began talking in her head.

Maybe conversation wasn't a bad idea after all.

"Is your last name Anderson too?"

Hardy cast her a sideways glance. "Yeah." After a beat, he added, "I'm Bev's brother, remember?"

"I didn't forget. I . . . well, I didn't know if she'd gotten married and had a different name."

"Nope. She's never married. Neither of us has. Why do you ask?"

Because she hadn't thought of anything else to talk about. She shrugged. "I was just curious. I don't know why I asked."

"Well. I can't deny that our last name is fairly unremarkable. Anderson is a pretty common name."

"Not where I'm from."

"You're Amish, right? Bev told me."

"Yes."

"How many brothers and sisters do you have?"

"None."

"Really?"

"Really. My parents . . . well, my mother said the midwife told her that she couldn't have any more children."

"I'm sorry."

She shrugged. "I can't say that there's anything to be sorry about. I didn't know any different. Now, when I look back about everything that's happened, I think the Lord had a plan."

"Why is that?" he asked as he clicked on the windshield wipers to a faster speed. "Do you like it being just the three of you?"

She clenched her fingers together as she considered how to answer. "I did like it, but that's in the past. My parents died when their driver got in a car accident."

He frowned. "I'm sorry to hear that."

"Thank you. I had to move from Holmes County to where I live now. With my aunt and uncle." Unable to help herself, she added, "And their three children."

"I see. It's good that they took you in."

"Yes. I'm grateful for their kindness."

Hardy scoffed. "No need to be grateful. I'm sure they wanted to, right? I mean, family is everything."

"Do you truly believe that?"

"Of course."

"But you and your sister have chosen to live so far apart from each other."

"I can't deny that. She and I do live far apart, but we have for a long time. Bev went to college at the University of Cincinnati, I joined the Army. While I served, she took a social worker position at the same place she interned. That became her home and mine became the Army."

Though she didn't doubt that he'd done well in the Army, she didn't think it could be a substitute for a home. Not that she was going to tell him that. "Hmm."

He waved his right hand in the air. "Anyway, now we're used to it. It was expected, anyway."

"Why is that?"

"Our home life wasn't great. Though our mom tried her best, Bev and I didn't want to follow in her footsteps. Getting away was a goal for a while."

"You achieved it, ain't so?"

"Yeah." He frowned. "Sorry, I didn't mean to share so much with you. You've got enough going on without having to hear my history."

"I'm glad you shared. I like learning more about you. Did you leave the Army after your face got hurt?"

"Yeah. Carter Russell was an officer in my unit. We worked

a lot together. When it was time to get out, he offered me a job here at his ranch."

"That was nice of him."

"That's a fact."

"Hardy, could I have one of those granola bars now?"

"Sure. Go fish it out of that sack. Get whatever you want."

Reaching between the seats, she found the sack, pulled out a couple of bars, and picked the one that had peanut butter in it. "Do you want one too?"

"Sure. Any of them is good."

After handing him his, she unwrapped hers and took a first bite. The salty-sweet taste of the granola and peanut butter gave her a much-needed jolt. She'd been foolish to wait so long to eat.

Beside her, Hardy ate his in three giant bites. He crumpled the wrapper and stuffed it in a space in his door. It was strange, but his actions amused her. Not a bit of him was delicate or dainty.

As silence between them wore on, she thought about leaving everything she'd known after her parents' accident. She thought about the Lord placing Bev in her life just when she needed someone the most. Thought about Bev and Hardy Anderson settling in someplace different from their hometown. She thought about how Hardy didn't think of that as a bad thing—he'd simply accepted it and moved on. He'd acclimated.

Could that happen to her? Was the Anderson way her future? Her stomach clenched. What if this strange journey she was on was God's will? "Do you think I'll ever get to go back to my aunt and uncle's house? Do you think it will ever be safe for me to return?"

"I imagine so. The police are involved. Chances are good that they'll find and arrest the man you saw."

"I hope you're right."

"Me too." He continued to talk in low, measured tones. "But we both know I wasn't there. You were."

"Yes."

"Now Bev's the one who's going to keep us informed. All I'm doing is what my sister asked me to do. That's it."

"Oh." She shouldn't have been surprised. So why was she a little disappointed that he sounded so disconnected?

"You should call her after you get settled. She'll give you advice and tell you what she thinks."

She leaned back against the seat, uncomfortable with all that was being unsaid. She felt as if the two of them were having mental conversations interspersed with the words flowing between them.

"I'm still shaken up," she said in a quiet voice.

"I'd be surprised if you weren't. Witnessing a murder is a horrible thing."

"I'm also still afraid. I'm afraid that Bev's warnings were right," she confided. "I'm worried that maybe someone from that gang knows I got on that bus."

"You'd be foolish not to be worried. Timothy saw you get in a car. That means there's a trail. All sorts of things could happen."

Hardy's blunt comment spurred a bark of laughter from her throat. "You don't mince words, do ya?"

"Not about this." He frowned as he darted in between a set of slower-moving cars on the three-lane highway, going right, then left, zigzagging through traffic just as a light rain started to fall.

Though the truck didn't swerve, and Hardy didn't seem too perturbed, she held on to the edge of her seat. When the traffic pattern seemed to slow, she relaxed, until she heard him mutter under his breath.

He jerked on the steering wheel as he glanced in the rear-view mirror and crossed lanes again.

"What's wrong?" she called out.

He ignored her. All his concentration was on whatever he seemed to see behind them.

Still gripping her seat, she turned, trying to find who was there.

"Don't. Don't turn around. And whatever happens next, don't do anything stupid. Okay?"

Stupid? What was she going to do? She was locked in a speeding truck that was going faster than she knew was possible.

She refrained from pointing that out, though, as his frown turned into a full glower and tension radiated from him. As if sensing their mood, the rain began to pelt the truck, turning into a storm. Lightning crashed overhead as they swerved, barely making the exit ramp amid a clatter of horns and screeching brakes.

"I don't understand. What's happening?"

"It looks like all those worst-case scenarios I was throwing out there came to fruition. You've been found, sweetheart."

He zipped forward, turned right. Turned right again as the rain continued to pour down on them.

He reached for his phone, clicked a button, and started talking into it. "Hey, it's me. I'm going to be bringing someone back to the ranch. They'll stay in one of the cabins. Tell the other guys that they need to be alert. There could be trouble." Pause. "Positive." Another pause. "Yeah. I'll be in touch."

He clicked off his phone, tossed it in the space under the

console, and turned left, left again, and then veered to the right on a narrow road.

"Hardy, where are we going?" she asked in the firmest voice that she was capable of.

"Somewhere new," he bit out. "And no, I am not going to tell you anything more. Let me concentrate on getting you to where we're going in one piece."

Stephanie gripped the edge of her seat again, this time not to hold on for dear life but to still her shaking hands.

Everything had gone from bad to worse, and it seemed as if it wasn't going to get better any time soon.

Lord, I know You hear my prayers, she called out to Him silently. *What have I done to make You ignore me?*

But she felt nothing but tension. It walked hand in hand with fear and desolation.

No, with fear, desolation—and a new strength she hadn't been aware she possessed.

Letting out a gasp of breath, she surmised that that might be enough.

6

So many things had gone wrong during the last twelve hours, it was impossible to count them all. With a feeling of unease, Timothy Jones eased his vehicle farther into the shadows behind a fast-food restaurant he'd just gone inside.

He figured he'd done a pretty good job of scaring the Amish girl and whoever was driving her. Hopefully she was scared so badly that she wouldn't want to go home. Maybe they'd keep driving for days. They'd end up going so far away that it wouldn't be possible for him to ever find them. If that happened, he'd be so relieved.

He really didn't want to kill anyone else.

Thinking about how he wished he'd never joined a gang to begin with, he ate the last of his burger. Tracking the girl all this time had been exhausting. He'd give just about anything to pass out. Instead, he was procrastinating on what he was supposed to do, which was call Kane with an update.

He didn't want to do it, though. Not yet. Not ever. Kane was going to be ticked that he hadn't been able to get ahold of the girl, and now he had no idea where she was. Kane wasn't going to care one whit about him being in an old Buick in a torrential rainstorm. Or that he had no idea what he was doing. It was pretty much a certainty that Kane was going to freak out on him. Threaten bad things.

Which was why his phone was still in his pocket.

It might be for a while longer too. At the moment, the only thing that he wanted to do was enjoy a couple of minutes to breathe. And he needed a cigarette. Maybe if he had a smoke, he'd stop running scared and be able to figure out what he was going to do tomorrow—well, today.

If he survived that long.

He honestly wouldn't put it past the gang to have someone following him. They didn't trust him. Not anymore.

Timothy's fingers shook as he pulled out the carton of Reds and his lighter. It took two tries to get the flame to catch. At last, he could inhale the combo of fortifying nicotine and tobacco.

Man, he hated being addicted to the stuff.

When he was little, his momma used to warn him about the "cancer sticks" that seemed to constantly be in her right hand. "Don't do this, Timothy," she'd say. "Folks act like all sorts of things are worse, but I don't know anyone who got off these things easily. They're addictive and bad for you. They cost an arm and a leg too."

That hadn't stopped her from buying the cartons, though. Just like her words of wisdom hadn't stopped her from doing a lot of things she shouldn't.

In the end, it wasn't the cancer that had gotten her anyway. It had been the needle in her arm.

Or maybe it had been a dozen other things that had piled on until her body had finally given up.

All he'd known was that one day she'd been alive, skinny, and barely getting out of bed, and then the next day the police had been pulling him out of school to tell him that a neighbor had discovered that his momma had passed away that morning.

Inhaling deep, he tried to hold the warm smoke in his chest. But it, like most things, had to come to an end. He exhaled, forcing the smoke out. Breathed in a mouthful of clean, sweet air.

And allowed himself to remember the first time he'd met Bev. Miss Anderson.

She'd walked in through his front door in slouchy pants and a baggy shirt. Her ugly-as-sin canvas tote bag she always carried had been stuffed to the gills.

But she'd looked at him and smiled.

For one sweet second, Timothy had thought that everything was going to be all right. He was going to go to a better house. There was going to be food on the table. Maybe he'd get some clothes that fit.

But even if he didn't have all those things, he'd have Bev.

Some of his dreams had come true. Well, every now and then they had. He'd spent the next four years living in foster care. Some of the houses were all right. Some were worse than the place he'd lived with his mother. All of them, however, had been temporary.

Which had been the worst part.

Timothy reckoned that it did something to a child's spirit when he realized that he couldn't count on much in life. Not even the bad stuff.

By the time he was twelve, though, he knew better than to care about cancer. Lots of kids didn't make it to eighteen. Besides, he'd had plenty of other things to worry about. Mainly how to not get beat up in the halls at school.

Now he was eighteen, and in the last twelve hours, he'd

essentially become an idiot. After almost a year of doing grunt work and gaining trust and showing up, he'd finally gotten noticed by Stew. Kane had handed him a .22 and told him it was time to prove himself.

Timothy had been given a job. At last. All he had to do was go up to the dealer in the dollar store parking lot and scare him a bit. Use a little pressure to get the money he owed the Arrows. Kane had smiled, slapped him on the back, and told him that it was going to be easy.

Holding the gun in his hand had felt good, but there'd still been a little part of him that was scared. Sure, he'd shot a gun before, but that had just been in a field. All he'd had to do was hit a tree and work on his aim.

When he'd driven into the parking lot of the dollar store, he'd been sweating like it was a hundred degrees outside instead of fifty. Kane had assured him that what he was about to do was no big deal and that he'd be nearby but staying out of sight. Just in case something went wrong.

The guy who owed them money was going to have it on him and was probably going to be so freaking scared that he'd give it to him right away.

Within a couple of seconds, though, it became apparent that Kane had been wrong. Real wrong. The guy wasn't scared to death and started laughing when Timothy asked for the money. Then he turned away.

That was when Timothy realized that everything was going to go wrong. His job would leave without paying, and Timothy would never be able to go home without the money.

Next thing Timothy knew, he was trying real hard to sound mean and tough. But his hand was shaking, and he essentially lost his mind.

Because he pulled the trigger and watched as the guy's shirt filled with blood.

Then, just when he was sure nothing could be worse, an Amish girl showed up. A red-headed, blue-eyed Amish girl who looked at him directly in the face. And then, instead of running out of sight, she just stood there. Practically giving him no choice.

He'd gotten so spooked, he'd stood frozen for a second, right until a car had come barreling in between him and the girl. The passenger door had opened, the driver had yelled, and he'd freaked out. Because he'd recognized that voice.

He would have known it anywhere because Bev Anderson had once been everything to him. His first crush. His big sister, his dream mother. The woman he'd put on a pedestal and given superhero powers. No matter how bad things had been for him, he'd believed that somehow, someway Bev would make his life better.

But she never had.

Then, there she was again, jumping into his life. But this time she wasn't on his side. Instead of coming to rescue him, she was there for someone else.

It made him so mad he lifted the gun again.

And his stupid finger pressed down on that trigger and sent out another bullet. Practically the next second, Kane shoved Timothy into his van so they could figure out what was happening to the Amish girl. As he drove, he chewed Timothy out, berating him for killing the guy.

Afraid of the consequences, Timothy didn't attempt to defend himself and focused more on keeping sight of the car they were following.

He didn't give Kane any information about the driver,

though. It might not make sense, but he didn't want anything to happen to Bev.

After they'd followed the car to the bus station, Kane went out and bribed the ticket agent to tell him where the girl was headed. After getting the bus's arrival time for Nashville, he'd checked in with Stew.

Instead of ordering Timothy to stay at the bus station, Stew told Kane to take Timothy back to Batavia. Timothy was supposed to get himself together, get his car, and wait for the Amish girl to get off the bus in Nashville.

The bus was going to make several stops before arriving there. After checking the bus's schedule again, Timothy parked outside his old girlfriend Audrey's neighborhood. To the exact spot where they used to make out before he had to get her home by curfew.

Man, he'd loved her. Still loved her. Even though she broke up with him when he joined the Arrows.

Then Kane's call brought him back to the present. "Timothy, some of the guys picked up the body when we left, but they couldn't find the money he owed us. Where is it?"

"I don't know."

"Did you take it? Are you trying to pull something over us?"

"No. I never got any money."

"Well, it wasn't on him. What happened to it?"

"Kane, I don't know! Maybe someone else took it."

"You're trying to blame someone else in the gang?"

Timothy could feel sweat pouring off of him, but he had to stand up for himself. "Kane, I told you the truth. I never got any money."

"This is serious, man. Stew's about to pull a gun on you himself. You're in really big trouble with the Arrows. You need to get on Stew's good side again or he's going to give the cops your name when they start asking around." He snapped his fingers. "Next thing you know, those cops are going to interrogate you."

"I can handle them."

"No, you can't." Kane's voice dripped with derision. "They'll find a way to make you talk. And then, after you squeal, they're going to come after us."

Timothy hated that Kane thought so little of him. Hated that he'd actually thought of the guy as his best friend. Hurt and disappointment colored his next words. "I'm already down here to scare the girl. Isn't that enough?"

"It might have been if you had the money. Since you don't, you're going to have to make sure that witness never says a word to the cops." He took a breath. "You're going to have to silence the girl—and soon."

Everything inside of him froze. "What do you mean?"

Kane's voice lowered. "Just what I said. Silence her, Tim."

Kane was ordering him to kill her. Kill an innocent woman. Now that he realized Kane had never really been his friend, Timothy no longer felt the need to hold his tongue.

Not completely, anyway. "Kane. She's Amish. And she looked scared to death. She's not going to do anything."

"She might have looked scared, but if that woman hadn't pulled her into her car, she would've marched right inside that dollar store and told the manager everything she knew. She could still do that. Find that girl and shut her up."

"And then? Then, if I do all that, what happens to me then?"

"And then, if you take care of that Amish girl quickly, we might let you live. Where are you now?"

"Nowhere. Just, ah, driving around."

"You're going to need a burner phone. And then you need to toss yours. Call me once you have it and I'll let you know if anything happens back home."

Home. That was a joke. "How long have I got?"

"If you don't get this wrapped up in a few days, it won't be good. Hopefully you can at least understand that."

"I got it."

"Good."

Timothy was staring at his phone's screen. "But . . . but what should I do about the gun after it's done? Should I toss it?" It would have his fingerprints all over it.

"No. Not until you check in."

"But—"

"Man, what else do I have to tell you? Get going and follow my orders."

After Kane hung up, Timothy realized he had half a tank of gas and fifty or sixty bucks in his pocket.

He started driving again.

And here he was somewhere in the middle of Kentucky. He pulled over at a gas station, bought a pack of smokes and the burner phone. Thought about calling Audrey. Just to give her his new phone number.

Then he remembered that she probably wouldn't answer the phone. When he'd told her that he was going to join the Arrows no matter what, she'd said he was dead to her. Bitterness coursed through him as he realized her words might very likely come true.

Now, here he was, driving again. Thinking about that truck. Thinking about how Bev had helped that Amish girl.

Then, at long last, Timothy remembered a conversation he'd had with Bev years ago. He'd been complaining about his future. About how he had no idea what he was going to do with his life.

Bev had stared at him in worry, then began to tell Timothy all about her younger brother, Hardy. About how he was a big, strong guy but hadn't always been that way. But he'd entered the Army and done real well for himself. So well, that he'd even gotten to be friends with an officer who'd hired him after they both got out.

Bev's brother, Hardy, was now working on a huge ranch in Crittenden County. It was a place so big and secure that if somebody wanted to, they could hide out there.

Back when she'd told him that story, he'd laughed. Who in the world would want to hide out on a big ranch in southern Kentucky?

He now had a pretty good idea who.

7

s the rain drenched their world and lightning crashed around them, Hardy allowed himself to only focus on one thing, and that was getting the woman sitting next to him to safety.

Stephanie looked half frozen in fright, scared of him, nervous about the way he was driving, and was obviously not a fan of raging thunderstorms in the middle of the night.

All he could afford to care about was that she was alive. If she was breathing next to him, he was doing his job.

Which, come to think of it, he hadn't heard her even so much as gasp in quite a while.

"You okay?" he murmured.

"I don't know."

"Take a deep breath, okay? Just keep breathing."

He almost smiled when she did just that. "Good job."

To his surprise, she let out a small, shy laugh. "You almost sound like you're used to things like this."

"I wouldn't say that," he replied as he took a curve, slowing as the entrance to the Russell property neared. "I have been through some things, though. I can keep you safe." She looked doubtful as he slowed, then her eyes widened when he drew to a stop in front of the guardhouse. All visitors had to check in before whoever was on duty opened the black electronic gate a few feet beyond.

"Where are we?"

"We're at the Russell Ranch. You're not going to be safe enough in Marion, Stephanie. You need to be someplace more secure," he said as he rolled down the window and pressed a button. A loud buzz sounded, followed by Foster's signature rasp. "Name."

"Foster, hey. It's Hardy."

"Hardy? I didn't think you were going to be back on the property until tomorrow."

"I know, but the situation's changed. I'm coming in."

There was another buzz as the gate opened. He drove the truck through the gate. After the gate shut behind him, he stopped to talk to the guard on duty. "I'm about to call Carter, but I want you to meet Stephanie. She's going to be staying in one of the cabins on the property."

As expected, Foster's voice turned even more serious. "Mr. Russell know about this?"

"That's not your concern. I'll call him in a while. We're coming in hot, though. I need to get her on through."

"I'd think about cabin three. It's stocked."

"Sounds good." He nodded to Foster through the window of the booth, and as they left the guardhouse, Hardy reached for Stephanie's hand. "Almost there, Stephanie. Hang in just a little bit more for me, okay?"

"Okay."

"Good job." He squeezed her hand gently. "When that gate is closed behind us, we're as safe as we can be."

"You sound so sure."

"I am. The Russell Ranch security is second to none.

Everyone on staff takes it seriously. Someone mans the gate 24-7. If it's not Foster at the controls, it's one of the other two people Carter has on staff. In addition, there are cameras stationed along the perimeter and around the main house and some of the outer buildings. They can be viewed from both the guard booth and in the basement of Carter's house. No one is going to get on this property without us knowing." He tapped the brakes, hoping the knowledge would give her a sense of relief.

But by the look in her eyes, it didn't help one bit.

"I don't know what's going to happen now," she whispered. "Do you?"

There was no way he was going to lie to her. "No."

"What is cabin three?"

"It's exactly what it sounds like. A cabin on the property. There will be some food there. A shower. A bed so you can catch some sleep."

"What about you? Where will you be?"

"I'll be in one of the cabins nearby," he said as he drove down the lane and over a cattle guard, and then took the right fork in the road.

Feeling the wariness emanating from her, he added, "I've promised to look out for you. I promised my sister. I'm also putting my boss and good friend in the thick of this mess that you're in. I don't do any of that lightly. Do you understand?"

"Jah."

She wasn't looking at him, though. Instead, she had folded her arms around her chest and was looking down at her lap. She'd curved in around herself. As if she was afraid to let anyone in. Even the person who'd just sworn to keep her safe. "Hey, I know this is hard. You're dressed like an Eng-lisher, you're far from your family and running scared. But

Stephanie, if you are willing to do anything at all, I hope you'll be willing to take a chance on me. I only want to help you. You don't have a thing to fear from me."

She said nothing as he slowed their speed into a crawl, the crunch of the gravel under the tires mixed with the sound of the pouring rain against the truck's cab.

When she released a ragged breath, an unknown need to help her made him start talking. If for no other reason than to fill the void that was beginning to feel soul sucking in the truck's cab. "The Russell Ranch stretches across the hills and valleys of southern Crittenden County. There's a main house, three barns, an employees' guesthouse, and a number of small cabins spread out across the area. Like I told you before, the entire area is surrounded by a fence that is both barbed and electric. Both entrances are gated, illuminated, and continually monitored. One has a full-time guard. In addition, the Marion police and the county sheriff's department are on speed dial. I can't think of a safer place for you to be."

He felt rather than saw her skepticism. "Do you have any questions?"

"Nee."

They passed another cabin, then headed down a small, sloped hill until they came upon a bend on the left. Five minutes later, he pulled into the driveway of cabin three.

The cabin was illuminated. Even in the dark, it looked as pretty as a picture. Near the road was a small mailbox. It was mainly for show. When Carter had some of his fancy guests in town, he'd sometimes have his assistant make a small goody basket to welcome them. Just below the mailbox was a lockbox with the cabin's key.

"Wait here a second," he said as he climbed down from

the cab and punched in the code on the lockbox. When a key fell into his hand, he felt another burst of satisfaction. Once again, every control and safety protocol put into place was working properly.

Getting back in, he said, "Stephanie, when we park, I want you to stay in the cab until I come around and help you down." She nodded. Minutes later, he did exactly what he'd said he would. "Here. Take my hand," he said after opening her door.

When she slid her hand into his, he felt a zing of tenderness wrap through him. She looked so innocent and scared. Taking care not to grip her hand too tight, he guided her to the ground, grabbed her backpack and small suitcase, and walked her to the door. Instinct had him placing himself between the world and Stephanie.

After opening the door, he turned on the lights, then closed and secured the door behind them. "We're here."

Stephanie looked around with wide eyes. "Oh! It's pretty."

"I've always thought so too. They're all small. Usually folks only stay here a night or two. There's a bedroom, bathroom, small living area, and a kitchenette. We'll get what you need for food, but there should be a few things here already."

"Where will you be?"

"I'll be close. Like I told you, I'll be in the next cabin over."

She didn't look relieved by that in the slightest. "But I'll be here."

"Yes. You're safe, Stephanie. I swear on everything I hold dear that that's the truth. No one's going to get on this property without me knowing."

"Oh. All right."

She didn't sound relieved, though. If anything, she sounded even more worried. That didn't set real well with him, but he didn't know what else to say. It wasn't like he'd made these plans. All he was doing was trying to help Bev out.

He wasn't without compassion, though. "Hey, try not to worry. I know you're scared and hurting, but you're going to be okay now."

Stephanie was facing him with wide eyes filled with pain, and it seemed like an overwhelming sense of loss was emanating from her body. "Nee," she said in a tone filled with emotion. "I am not going to be okay anytime soon."

As much as he ached to prove her wrong, Hardy knew that he was no fortune teller. He sure wasn't privy to all she'd gone through in the last day.

So, she might be right after all.

But what could he say to that? His sister had asked for his help, and now he knew Stephanie was in danger. He couldn't change the past and he couldn't change her present situation. Not without some planning and some help.

"How about I show you where you can rest, then?" He turned and walked toward a pair of doors just beyond the kitchenette. "The bedroom is down this way," he said. He knew she was right behind him.

After all, there was nowhere else to go.

8

She'd been so scared the night before. Even though everything that Hardy had said made sense, she'd almost begged him to stay with her. No—it was more than that. She'd been tempted to cling to him like a vine. All the events over the last day and night had been too much. The murder. The way Bev had appeared out of nowhere. Going with Bev, changing into these English clothes, getting on the bus, driving through the rain, getting tailed, and finally being deposited in a tiny cabin in a strange place.

Curved around every one of these moments was a constant ring of fear that hung on to every thought and movement. It had been a heavy burden, tinged by exhaustion. When Hardy had walked out, she'd begun to cry. Next thing she knew she'd fallen on the bed and sobbed into the pillows, crying for everything that had happened and for all the prayers that weren't answered.

Eventually she'd quieted enough to wash her face and put on the long white nightgown Bev had bought her. Next thing she knew, she'd woken up with the sun.

The new day brought with it a ray of hope. She still had

no idea what was going to happen next, but her world didn't seem so desperate and bleak.

Pleased to be enjoying a better outlook, she got out of bed, stretched, and decided to take note of her surroundings. The little cabin was so very pretty. And now that it wasn't raining and the sun was shining through the windows, she realized there was more to see than she'd previously thought. She put on the thick terry cloth robe that was hanging in the bedroom closet and decided to explore.

Stephanie supposed if she walked into a storybook and added bells and whistles and a fancy fireplace, she'd end up in a cabin just like this. It truly looked like something in a children's story, with the gleaming hardwood floors, brightly woven rag rugs, and the tan suede couch.

Caressing the seat cushion, she whistled low. What type of person would have such a creation in just a guest cabin? A very rich one, she supposed.

Walking into the kitchenette, she ran her fingers over the smooth granite countertops, eyed the electric oven's smooth black surface, and admired the bright white cabinets. To her amazement, the refrigerator was stocked with bottles of water, soda, juice, and beer. An inspection into the small pantry revealed crackers, cans of soup and chili, as well as several boxes of pasta and cereal.

Now even more curious, she hurried to the bathroom's open doorway. Now that she wasn't bleary-eyed with exhaustion, she noticed that it had sparkling beige tiles, white walls, a shower, two sinks, and the most gorgeous bathtub she'd ever seen. It looked like a modern remake of a cast-iron tub and was black on the outside and gleaming white on the inside. The faucet was fancy and chrome and there was even a little emerald-green table beside it filled with containers of bubble bath and salts.

"Hardy dropped me into a princess haus," she murmured. "A tiny, fancy princess haus."

Unable to stop herself, she turned on the tub and felt the cool water turn warm within a minute. If she set the stopper, she could be soaking in that tub in no time at all. Allowing herself to imagine the decadence, she smiled. It would be so good to soak her aching muscles, wash her hair, and then put back on the fluffy white robe that she was finding to be completely comfortable and cozy.

Soaking in that tub would surely be an amazing way to start or end a day.

So different from her life back at home, which began before dawn, continued with dishes and the henhouse, and lingered for hours as she tended to her cousins, did laundry, and fought boredom.

The bed she'd slept in was large and comfortable. The room was clean and bright. She'd had soft sheets and blankets and a comforter. It was so peaceful.

Back home, her bedroom was only a curtained section of the basement. She had a small cot and an old wooden crate as a bedside table. Her only source of light was the flashlight that she rested on the crate. She'd had to buy her own batteries for it, so she was always worried about using the flashlight too much.

She'd almost forgotten what it felt like to sleep on a real bed.

"Nee," she told herself. "You mustn't find fault with everything you've been given. Aunt Jo and Uncle Mark are good people to take you in the way they did. If they hadn't, you might have had to grow up in a foster home."

Her words were true, but they didn't help to make her feel as grateful as she'd hoped they would. But maybe that was the problem. Gratitude and happiness didn't always walk hand in hand.

And then, just like that, her reality returned. She was not a princess living in a tiny cabin with a stocked refrigerator and pantry.

All she was, was Stephanie. A twenty-three-year-old woman who still spent her days trying to repay her relatives for doing something they should have wanted to do in the first place.

She was not on vacation either. She was on the run from a terrible young man who thought nothing of killing innocent people.

And who had decided to kill her too.

All at once, the complete terror that she'd been feeling enveloped her again. She turned to the mirror and looked at herself. Under that nightgown and robe was a lump on her arm from the hasty bandages Bev had put on to staunch the blood. Her hair was hanging down, part of it still tied in a ponytail.

And then there were her eyes and face. She looked haunted and afraid. Because she was both of those things.

Because she was all alone in a cabin somewhere in Kentucky. Because the only person she knew right now was a rather gruff, large man who excelled in ordering her about.

Who also happened to be very handsome and had clasped her hand when they were driving by the guard's station. Who'd gone out of his way to reassure her that she was safe and that he would protect her.

So maybe he hadn't been that bad, after all. But even if that was the case, she had no idea when she was going to see him again. She wasn't even sure if she was allowed to open the cabin door. She was stuck in this princess cabin.

And suddenly it didn't seem so wonderful after all.

Tears filled her eyes again, and though her instinct was to stop them, swipe her eyes, and pretend that she was fine, she didn't have the energy.

Plus, maybe she should go ahead and cry. Again. She had a lot to cry about, after all. Holding it inside wasn't going to help her much.

And then, just as she was about to give herself permission to fall apart . . . she did. This time she fell apart on the cold floor of a very, very fine bathroom. She sank to her knees, curled up into a ball, and cried big, loud tears. That made it hard to breathe and even harder to pretend the last day never happened.

She hadn't cried like that in ages. Not since her parents had died in a car accident and the police had come to the house and taken her.

Hating the memory, of the way they'd ignored her questions and wouldn't let her take anything with her, Stephanie found herself trembling again. She'd been beyond scared. She'd been confused and petrified.

Things had only gotten worse from there. The policemen had brought her to the police station. First, she'd been told to sit in a chair. Later, she'd been put in an empty room. She'd been given a glass of water but had been too afraid to sip it.

Eventually, she'd learned that her father's older brother Mark and his wife Jo had been willing to take her in. She'd been told that she was lucky. That she should feel grateful.

But all she'd felt was confused and alone.

Aunt Jo was a devout and faithful woman. And had more

morals than her brother-in-law. Stephanie knew that because Aunt Jo had told her so more than once.

Actually, she told her at least once a month. Right about the time when Stephanie had overslept or forgotten a chore.

Or gone for a walk.

Which now seemed very tame compared to what she'd been going through since she'd first seen the gunman.

As the consequences of the day kept piling on, she kept crying until she was exhausted. She'd even reached out to wipe her face with part of the roll of toilet paper because standing up to get a real tissue from the chrome dispenser was just too much trouble.

And then the door opened with a bang, scaring her half to death.

Stephanie did the only thing she could do. She screamed.

She ran to the front room in time to see a man—slim, wiry-looking, and in his mid-forties—raise his hands as he came to an abrupt halt inside the doorway. "Hey! Sorry! I didn't mean for the door to open. Hardy asked me to bring some things for you. I was going to leave them on the porch, then decided to make sure your door was locked. I didn't expect the darn wind to pick up like we were in the middle of Kansas."

She had no idea what he was talking about, but two things had penetrated her head. One was that his hands were raised like he was in the middle of a bank robbery. The second was that he'd said Hardy's name.

She was shaking like a leaf but somehow managed to pull herself together. "You know Hardy?"

"I sure do," he said slowly as he lowered his hands. "I work for him."

"What do you mean?"

"Hardy Anderson answers directly to Mr. Russell, but everyone else who steps foot on this ranch works for Hardy. Sometimes I'm in the guard shack, other times I'm working with the horses, and today I'm running errands." Still moving slowly, he pointed to the porch. "Like I said, I brought you a couple of things."

"I'm sorry I screamed."

His expression flattened. "I'd be upset if you didn't, Miss. You shouldn't have to worry about doors flying open because some fool hand made a mistake." Standing almost at attention, he said, "I really am sorry about that."

This man looked like the opposite of a fool hand. He looked like he could scare just about anyone with one dark look. "What's your name?"

"My name's Crenshaw, Miss."

"Crenshaw?"

He nodded. "That's my last name. My first name is Jamie, but I haven't answered to that since I was about twelve." He swallowed. "Listen, I'm going to leave you now. Would you like me to bring in the bags? It's starting to rain a bit. I can set them right here on the floor." He pointed to a spot next to his feet. "Or I can go on out, close the door, and you can retrieve them at your leisure."

"You may bring them in. If you don't mind."

"It's my pleasure." He turned around, gathered the two bags in one hand, and then placed them on the ground in the exact spot he'd told her he would.

"Thank you."

He looked pained. "Lock the door when I leave, you hear me? You need to keep safe."

"I will." She was puzzled by how adamant he was acting.

She'd thought she would be perfectly safe on the ranch. Wasn't that why she was there?

"Good." And with that final word, he turned, walked out, and closed the door behind him.

After she saw his truck pull out and drive off, she locked the door like Crenshaw suggested. And then, in spite of everything, she found herself smiling. The man had certainly been right. He didn't seem like a "Jamie" at all.

9

Timothy's world just kept getting darker. He was exhausted, almost out of money again, and just when he'd finally calmed down about his failure to stop the girl and her driver, a cop had come out of nowhere and pulled him over for speeding.

Only by the grace of God had he been able to talk himself out of a ticket. It was still morning, and sheets of rain falling from the sky had made continuing on almost impossible.

When he had dipped into a gas station for more smokes and the phone, he'd caught sight of himself in the counter's reflection. It wasn't a good look. Timothy looked like crap. He knew the reason—because he hadn't slept in the last twenty-four hours.

He couldn't continue on for much longer.

Exhausted and in need of a shower and a couple of hours of sleep, he drove out toward Paducah and checked into the cheapest motel he could find.

The clerk had looked down his nose at him but had given him a room easily enough. And though the bathroom didn't even have a bar of soap, the water coming out of the shower had been hot. Scalding enough to burn off the stench of smoke on his skin and the feeling of dread and fear that clung to his very being.

After collapsing into bed, he'd fallen into a deep sleep. He was dreaming about Audrey wearing one of her favorite little sundresses when his phone started ringing.

After it disconnected, it started ringing again almost immediately. Then again. Timothy realized then that he no longer had a choice. If he ever wanted to go home to Batavia, Ohio, again, he was going to have to face the gang. They weren't going to go away, and they sure weren't ever going to give up.

Mentally coaching himself for the conversation to come, he hurried to connect. "Yeah?"

"Where you at?"

It was Kane. Timothy relaxed slightly. It wasn't Stew. "Hey. Sorry about not answering earlier."

"You should be sorry. You seem to have already forgotten my warnings. You need to get smarter, Timothy, because you've been ignoring my texts too."

"Sorry," he said again. He didn't offer an excuse, because what could he say?

"Don't tell me sorry. Tell me that it's all good," he added in an impatient tone. "Is it done yet?"

Timothy could practically feel the blood leaving his face. Feeling dizzy, he leaned back against the wall and did his best to try to keep his voice even. "No."

"Why not?"

"I found them on the highway. I tried to run them off the road, but the rain was something awful. It was hard to see five feet in front of me. And then later the sheriff pulled me over."

"How did that happen?"

Timothy flinched. "I was speeding. But I talked my way out

of it," he said quickly. "I didn't get a ticket or anything." He swallowed, hoping and praying that Kane would respond in a more positive way and they could start talking again. Like the way they used to, back when he'd been sure they were friends.

"But they got your driver's license, yeah?"

"They just checked it. That's all. Like I said, all I got was a warning."

"But they know you're there, man. How could you be so stupid?"

"I had to stop for the sheriff, Kane."

"This is bad, Tim. I'm not happy."

"Well, I ain't either." Before he thought the better of it, he said, "I didn't mean for any of this to happen. I didn't mean to lose the money or kill that guy or get a witness."

"Your excuses are getting boring, Timothy. Some of the guys are even starting to wonder what to do with you."

What did that even mean? "Oh."

"Worse, because you're so stupid, I'm going to have to see Stew today and tell him about your latest screwup. He ain't going to be happy."

His mouth felt like cotton had been lodged in it. "I know he's not, but I'll figure something out."

Kane kept talking. "Of course, now at least he's found something to occupy himself with until you get back."

"What does that mean?"

"Oh, nothing special. Or should I say no one special? It's just a pretty girl that you used to know." Kane chuckled. "I guess you used to know her real well, huh? Like, didn't she used to be your girl once?"

"Audrey doesn't have a thing to do with this."

"She might not, but she's involved now, Timothy. Stew's decided she might be of use."

The words came out before he could stop himself. "You need to leave her alone."

"Don't worry. Nobody's done anything but say hello. For now."

"What does that mean?"

"It means that Stew's kind of thinking that one of us should start spending a little time with her. Until you get back, that is."

Envisioning how scared Audrey would be, he blurted, "I'll come back today if Stew will leave her alone."

Kane sighed. "But you can't, Timothy. Because you haven't done anything that we asked you to. And now you've even managed to let a sheriff know your business."

"But—"

"Don't interrupt, Tim. That's rude." His voice dropped as he began to speak with exaggerated patience. "Here's what you're going to do, buddy. You're going to sit tight and lay low for a spell. Don't get pulled over and don't you leave Crittenden County."

"What about Audrey?"

"Audrey's good. I know you're worried about the gang messing with her, but I've decided to look out for that sweet thing. You won't need to worry about Stew bothering her none."

Audrey had met Kane once. Timothy had taken her out for a burger at one of the newer, popular restaurants that had recently opened near the mall. He hadn't thought the food was anything special, but he had enjoyed watching Audrey's pleasure. He drank two Cokes while she'd told him all about her classes at the college. She was so smart, and he'd loved that about her. Part of him had figured that if a smart girl like Audrey liked him, then he must be worth something.

Kane had shown up just after he'd surprised her with a little silver necklace. It hadn't been much, but it had been pretty. She'd been looking at Timothy like he'd hung the moon, right until Kane sat down and joined them. He'd flirted with Audrey, and she hadn't liked that one bit.

Timothy hadn't either—even when Kane had pulled out a wad of cash and paid for their meal. Later that night, Audrey asked him about Kane and the rest of the guys in the Arrows. When he told her that the gang wasn't any of her business, she'd gotten upset.

Which once again illustrated that she'd always been a hundred times smarter than him.

Returning to the phone call, Timothy didn't even try to temper his voice. "Don't hurt her."

"One of these days you're going to realize that nothing you want counts anymore." His voice lowered, sounding cold. Detached. "You don't count. You're a waste of space. You better start hoping and praying that you finally do something that's worthwhile."

The call ended before Timothy could say another word. Which was just as well. He was so freaked out, he'd been about to start begging the guy for all sorts of stuff.

Tossing the phone on the bed, he pressed his palms to his eyes. Tried to get ahold of himself. Tried to think of a way out. But nothing was sticking in his head besides Kane's words.

"You're a waste of space."

It rattled around in his head like a punch-drunk hummingbird. Flitting from his past to his future.

Seeking relief, he stared at the empty wall and the scars on the wallpaper where the television had been removed.

He needed to think about something else. Something that

didn't involve death, destruction, or Audrey. Just as he was drawing a blank, he spied a Bible on the nightstand. One of those Gideon ones.

He had nothing to do and nowhere to go.

Right now, the only thing he had going on in his head was a mess of regrets and bad decisions that seemed to continually put themselves on replay.

He needed something else to do. Something that might take a while.

Figuring at the very least it would make him fall asleep, he flipped the Bible open. Went to some pages titled Mark and started reading.

10

It was midmorning, and so far, Hardy still had no clue about what to do with Stephanie.

He'd hated to leave her alone the night before. She'd looked near tears when he'd walked out the door. The only thing that had stopped him from turning around was how innocent and sheltered she was.

Oh, he would've never done anything. He would have kept his distance, been respectful, and slept on her couch. But still, he sensed that even those things would've been too much for her to take.

When he'd entered cabin number two, he'd forced himself to take a hot shower and fall into bed. Leaving her had been the right thing, and a childhood living in the projects had taught him that doing the right thing was rarely the easiest. Most of the time it was frustrating and difficult.

Early that morning Carter had returned his call. On a positive note, Carter was all for Hardy offering Stephanie a place to stay. He was also fine with her staying as long as she needed to. He'd told Hardy to give Foster or Crenshaw a list of any necessities she might need. One of them would go out and get them.

But beyond that? He hadn't said much. Not even when Hardy had relayed that he was worried about Stephanie being there for an indefinite period of time.

All Carter had said was that he had faith in him.

Frustrated by that conversation and the fact that Carter was supposedly too busy to give him some direction about how to take care of an Amish girl hiding on his property, Hardy paced the length of the small living room. Wondering if it was too early to check on Stephanie. Debating if he should call one of the deputies or the sheriff, just to keep them in the loop.

Still not sure what would be the right thing to do, he decided to call up his sister. Bev had gotten him into this mess. As far as he was concerned, she could be the one to figure a way to get him out.

He breathed a sigh of relief when she answered on the first ring.

"Hardy?"

"Yep, it's me."

"Oh, thank the Lord. I was waiting to hear you'd arrived safely. You could've been calling me with updates, you know."

"I was a little busy." Which was pretty much the understatement of the year.

"How did she like the apartment in Marion? Did she seem okay when you left her?"

"About that . . ."

"Yes?"

"There's been a change in plans. We're at the ranch."

"Ranch? Carter's ranch?"

"Yep. She's settled in one of the cabins on the property."

"Why did you make that call?"

Reluctant to worry his sister even more, he said, "I thought she'd be safer here." Plus, no way did he want Stephanie to feel like she was all alone.

"Wow. I'm surprised Carter let you do that."

Deciding that there was no reason to tell her that he'd essentially informed Carter after he'd made the decision, Hardy murmured, "I'm grateful." Wishing he'd handled everything better, Hardy started pacing again. "Don't worry. Everything's okay. But I better get going—"

"No. Wait. Don't hang up. Tell me about Stephanie. Is she okay? How's her arm? Is she scared to death? You've been nice to her, right?"

Amused by her rapid-fire questions but used to them, he answered her in the order she'd asked. "She's okay. I'm not sure about her arm. I'm pretty sure she's scared, but that's to be expected, I guess. She wasn't complaining about it. And yeah, I was all right." Thinking of how gruff he'd been most of the time, he added, "I'll try to be nicer when I see her again."

"Hardy. Really?"

"Don't give me grief. I've been trying to keep her safe and I'm doing that."

"Fine," she muttered after a few seconds.

He wondered why she'd paused. Was it because she was still worried about Stephanie or because the girl was living on Carter's ranch? Bev had always been a little skittish about all things Carter Russell.

"You don't sound like it's fine."

"Sorry. You know I'm flipping out. I'm the one who sent her to you. It was a knee-jerk reaction. I didn't stop and think of the consequences. Not really. Now, though, all I'm doing is imagining what she must feel like, living in a cabin by herself on that ranch."

"I'm in the cabin next to her. She's not alone."

"What are you going to do now?"

"No, what are you going to do? What's happening with the police in Batavia?"

"You know it's not a big police department."

She sounded frustrated, and he didn't blame her. Because she'd been a social worker in the county for years, she had a better idea than most about how overworked the police department was. "I gave them my statement, so they've got a lot to work with. Until they find the body, I really want to keep Stephanie hidden. Plus, I don't think she's going to allow much of an interview. She's either afraid of the police or distrusts them. Maybe both."

"She might not have a choice in the matter."

"I agree, but I'd rather not put her through any more trauma if I can help it." Bev sighed. "And judging from the brief conversation I had with her aunt and uncle, I'm gonna guess that she wouldn't have been safe there either."

"Well, yeah. They're Amish, Bev. They won't have an arsenal in their living room."

"Stop. It's more than that. Her aunt and uncle weren't very nice. All they seemed to care about was that she wasn't going to be there to do her chores."

"It's too bad she's living there."

"I agree. But what can she do? She's a sweet, unmarried Amish girl."

"I hear you." In most cases, surely a twenty-three-year-old woman was more than capable of taking care of herself. When he'd entered the military, he figured most eighteen-year-old girls could do a better job with life than he could.

But this one? Stephanie seemed too sheltered and too sweet to handle most things. Even if she was street-smart, they were dealing with a gang.

"In any case, thanks to you, the girl is no longer your responsibility. She's mine."

"Well, thank goodness she is. At least you have military experience. You can protect her."

"I'm not a bodyguard service, Beverly. I have a job, with Carter."

"Who's also former military."

"He's in Cincinnati, Bev." Besides, Carter was a lot of things, but Hardy wasn't sure that he'd be worth much if gang members showed up.

"Well, I bet he'll come join you once he hears what's going on."

"Don't worry. I'm going to reach out to Sheriff Johnson and inform him about the situation."

"Roger that."

He grinned. "You should've gone into the service instead of my boss. You would've made a better officer than Carter."

"I doubt that." She chuckled. "But any qualities I had would have vanished the minute I realized that I was going to have to ignore people hurting in order to do my job."

Even though he knew she'd been attempting to make a joke, her generalization about responsibilities in the military stung. "Bev, we never looked the other way when people were hurting," he corrected in a soft tone. "We went places no one else wanted to go."

"I'm so sorry. You're right. I was just—"

"I know you didn't mean anything by it. I guess . . . well, I guess my ties to the Army are still strong."

"As they should be." Sounding even more flustered, she said, "I promise I'll be more sensitive."

"You're fine." Remembering some of the downtrodden places he'd been deployed, where it was difficult to place the mission ahead of the villagers' needs, Hardy added, "You aren't altogether wrong. There were times when I did have to ignore one person's needs in order to serve the greater good. I reckon God puts each of us in the place where He sees fit."

"I think so too. God doesn't make mistakes. That's one of the reasons why I'm so determined to help Stephanie. There has to be a reason why I was in that parking lot at that moment, Hardy."

"I hear you." And he had heard her words, loud and clear. It reminded him that the Lord probably had a hand getting him involved as well. He might not want to be Stephanie's protector, but he wasn't going to stop protecting her until she was safe and sound.

Which reminded him that it was time for him to go pay her a visit. "I gotta go. I'll be in touch."

"All right. Thanks."

"And Bev?"

"Hmm?"

"Be careful, all right?"

"You be careful too, Hardy. I'll be praying for you."

Disconnecting the call, he stared at the blank screen for a moment. Thought about how hard life could be. At times, it felt like all it took was one misunderstanding or one misplaced quip to bring out a world of hurt.

He needed to remember that and do a little bit of praying of his own. Praying for patience would be a good place to start. Feeling as if everything had settled inside him again, Hardy hopped in his truck and headed toward the sheriff's office before he was tempted to check on Stephanie first.

He arrived at the unassuming brick building ten minutes later. As always, Courtney, the department's receptionist and all-around fix-it person, greeted him the moment he walked through the door.

"Hardy Anderson, long time no see. How are you?"

"Better now that I see your smile," he teased. Courtney was a little older than him and almost as hardened by life. Over the years they'd developed a fun, almost sibling-like relationship. Her husband Blake was a good man but gruff and quiet. Hardy always thought that Courtney needed to be a receptionist just so she could have some conversation during the day. "How are things going around here?"

"They're going."

"Is Billy around?"

"Yep. You're in luck. He just got in from a smile and shake with some folks out in Paducah," she said as she stood up. "I'll go let him know you're here."

"Thanks."

Instead of taking a seat, he leaned against the wall, taking in the tidy reception area and the two hallways. One led to the offices, bathroom, and kitchenette while the other led to holding cells, interrogation rooms, and a first aid station.

"Hey, Hardy," Sheriff Johnson said as he walked out in a pair of jeans, boots, and a uniform shirt.

"Billy."

After they shook hands, the sheriff turned toward his office. "Come on back."

"Yes, sir."

The man's office was spotless as usual. His desk looked freshly polished, the rug on the floor recently vacuumed, and his computer and phone sat side by side. The only two things belying the man's penchant for minimalism were a framed photograph of his wife Kristie and a child's drawing of a family in a frame right beside it.

"What's going on?" Billy asked when they sat down.

"I've got a situation." As succinctly as he could, Hardy relayed what had been going on with Stephanie since the day before. As he talked, the sheriff's expression went from interest to incredulousness to concern.

When Hardy finished, the sheriff leaned back in his chair with a sigh. "You know, every time I start to think that things around here are going to calm down, something unexpectedly weird happens."

"Drug dealing isn't exactly a rarity around here," Hardy said. There wasn't a big drug population, but there had been more than one incident with meth and heroin over the years. He was no lawman, but even he knew that no place was safe from the opioid or drug epidemic.

"That's true. But out-of-town dealers and gang members hunting down an Amish eyewitness? That's a new one."

"I reckon so." He stood up. "Anyway, I wanted to give you a heads-up."

"I'm going to need to speak to Stephanie."

"I figured as much. When?"

"Now would be a good time."

Hardy had expected that. But he wasn't willing to heap yet another surprise onto Stephanie's slim shoulders. A person could only take so much. "Could you give me an hour or two? I want to prep her a bit. I haven't seen her since last night. I'm afraid she's scared. Plus, my sister said she's not fond of cops."

"A lot of Amish shy away from the police. She'll be all right."

"I hear you, but I think there's more going on than that. If I spring you on her, she's going to get rattled."

Billy glanced at the clock. "An hour, then. Who's at the guard shack at the front gate today?"

"Crenshaw."

Humor lit Billy's eyes. It was no wonder. Crenshaw was a prickly guy. He was about as friendly as a drill sergeant meeting a new recruit.

"Tell him I'm stopping by for a spell, okay?" he asked.

"Will do."

"Appreciated."

Feeling better, Hardy gestured toward the child's drawing. "I like your new artwork."

Turning to the picture, Billy's face was transformed with a pleased smile. "My niece Tiffany drew that for me."

"She captured your bald head real good."

He laughed. "I told my wife that I looked like an egg with arms and legs. She told me that Tiffany captured my appearance to a T."

"I'm just glad she didn't decide to draw me," Hardy quipped as he walked out the door. After tipping his ball cap to Courtney, he headed back out into the chilly morning.

And wondered if he should maybe stop at the market for a few more things for Stephanie. Maybe a puzzle or some ice cream and a couple of sweatshirts or something.

The girl didn't have much, and she was likely to be around for a while.

Because few things ever went as planned.

11

After she and her brother ended their call, Bev stared at her phone's blank screen. Obviously, she found no clues there, but she wished some kind of sign would've popped up.

She really needed to try to figure out what to do next.

Now that a little bit of time had passed, she realized that reaching out to her brother had been instinctive. It had been born out of years and years of counting on him for almost everything. To put it simply, Hardy was the most capable person she knew. He'd always been that way too. Even when they were kids, he'd somehow been able to take care of everything. She might have been the older sibling and the honor roll student, but he'd been the one who'd been amazing in life.

Even their clueless, exasperating mother had known that Hardy could take care of their life better than she could. When he reached middle school, he started asking for part of her paycheck so they'd have food to eat and heat in the apartment. And she gave it to him.

Now, he was bigger and stronger than most and had a wealth of military experience. Bev would never tell him such a thing, but he'd always kind of reminded her of one of those heroes in disaster movies. There was always someone who knew what to do and how to get it done. Who didn't shy away from bad guys or hesitate when it came to helping someone weaker than himself. In her mind, Hardy was practically invincible.

But she still felt a little guilty for roping him into this mess. And now his boss was embroiled in it too.

Her brother's tough, rough exterior was the opposite of the man he worked for. Actually, the man was far different than almost every man Bev had ever dated.

Which made it even more confusing that she had a crush on his boss. Carter Russell was very, very wealthy. Rich-as-sin wealthy. He was also a little bit spoiled because he'd never had to go without.

Carter had an athletic build but a far slimmer one than her brother's. It was more like a tennis physique to Hardy's football/wrestler build. Carter was also charming, southern, and had impeccable manners. Whenever they talked, he looked directly at her. Like she was more than an average-looking woman who'd not only never had a piece of designer clothing but wouldn't be able to even name one.

"Listen to you, girl," she chastised herself. "You've only chatted with the guy a couple of times a year. There's no reason for you to have a crush on him the size of Mount Rushmore."

The comparison was goofy. Carter was absolutely not presidential and he wasn't larger than life. But man, was he memorable. The last time she'd seen him had been at a charity event his family was hosting. She'd attended with Hardy and had been perfectly willing to blend into the background while her brother relaxed enough to converse with the Russells' associates.

But then Carter had sought her out and even cajoled her to dance with him one time. He'd been in a tuxedo, had a bit of scruff on his cheeks, and had gazed at her like she was special.

And though he treated everyone that way, she'd been mesmerized. Everything about him, from his dark brown eyes to his boyish features to his flyaway, a-little-too-long light brown hair appealed to her. So did his kindness.

She met so many intellectuals, soft do-gooders, and just plain bad people in her line of work, it felt as if everyone she came across had an angle that had nothing to do with helping others but instead with helping themselves. Carter, on the other hand, just went about his day making money and riding horses and whatever else he did . . . but amazingly touched a lot of lives in the process. She'd almost begun to believe that men like him didn't actually exist.

And . . . here she was again, wasting valuable time out of her day fantasizing about a man who likely never thought twice about her when their paths didn't cross. She needed to get it together.

Especially because she needed to call him. He might not take her call, but she needed to make sure she thanked him for helping Stephanie.

Taking a deep breath, she swiped until she found the contacts icon and then searched for his name. Because yes, Carter Russell was in her contacts even though they'd only had a couple dozen conversations over the years.

Before she could lose her nerve, she clicked on his name. After only one ring, he answered. "Hello?"

"Carter, this is Beverly Anderson."

"Bev?"

"Yes. You know, Hardy's sister?" And yes, she'd just sounded like she was fifteen and calling her first crush.

He chuckled low and deep. "Beverly, did you really think I wouldn't know who you were?"

"It's been a while, and you're a busy man. And um, you might not remember me."

"I remember everything about you." He paused. "Including the fact that you're usually running about a hundred miles an hour and helping at least two children at the same time. What's going on? Do you need something?"

"Oh . . . no. But um, I did want to thank you for helping Stephanie."

"Stephanie . . ."

"The Amish girl I asked Hardy to help me out with. She's staying in one of your cabins, right?"

Sounding a little guarded, he said, "Bev, it's real thoughtful of you to reach out and all, but I can't take any credit for putting her up. Hardy brought her to the ranch last night and then he informed me about it."

"But it is okay with you, right?"

"Of course."

Bev was starting to feel a little foolish for calling. "Oh. Well, okay."

He chuckled. "Beverly Anderson, I sure hope we have the occasion to see each other soon."

"That would be nice. Um, are you in Cincinnati right now?"

Maybe she could ask him to lunch as a thank-you.

"I'm sorry to say that I'm not. I was, but I'm actually in Florence right now."

She'd called him, and he was across the world. "I have a feeling you're talking about Florence, Italy, and not Florence, Kentucky," she teased. That was a common joke. The small city just on the other side of the Ohio River was a place where she and Hardy always called each other when they were on the road mainly because of the gigantic water tower that proclaimed "Florence, Y'all."

"Now I can't say that I would hate that . . . but I really am in Florence, Kentucky. I was in Cincy, but then decided that I'd better head down to the ranch too. Hardy might need some help."

"Oh. Well, um, yes. I bet he'll appreciate that."

"Listen, I've got an idea. No pressure, but how would you feel about heading down there too?"

"You'd like me to drive down to your ranch?"

"I would. After talking to Hardy, I'm thinking that this girl might need something more than just to stay hidden."

"I know my brother was going to reach out to the sheriff."

"Yeah, I know. And safety is important. But to be honest, Beverly, that's not what's got me worried."

"What's wrong?"

"I could be worrying for nothing, but this is an Amish girl. She's living in one of my cabins all alone. I don't have any female ranch hands or people on my security team down there. Maybe I should, I don't know. But all I know is that she's a sheltered woman among a lot of rough men." He paused. "No offense to your brother."

"None taken."

"Do you see what I'm getting at? She needs someone there who she feels comfortable with."

"I admit that I'm female, but she and I don't really know each other, Carter."

"Yeah, but if you don't show up, then the only person she's ever going to see is Hardy."

"Hardy would never hurt her," she blurted.

"I know that. Come on. I know him as well as you do."

"You're right. I'm . . . I'm sorry."

"But see, while you and I both know that Hardy would sooner cut off his ear than harm a single hair on that girl's head, Stephanie doesn't. And that's what counts, right?"

"Right. I mean, you're right."

"I'm even more of a stranger to her. Plus, Hardy is going to need to be on patrol. She'll be by herself a lot."

"You want me to go down to keep her company."

"It's your call, Bev. But . . ."

"But . . . it was also my idea to send her to Hardy." And the truth was that it hadn't been right for her to call Hardy, pop her on a bus, and then check with him every now and then to make sure she was all right. That wasn't good enough. Not for Stephanie. Not for Hardy. And, it seemed, not even for Carter.

"Yeah. What do you say?" he asked, his drawl turning even more slow and irresistible. "Can you get away?"

"I want to. It might take me a day or two. I have a couple of kids who I need to meet with."

"I understand."

There was something in his voice that felt a bit like a cattle prod. It poked and gave her a jolt in the right direction. It wasn't going to be enough for her to just do a little bit. In this case, she needed to step up and help Stephanie. Help Hardy too.

It was the right thing to do.

And, if by chance, she was able to see Carter Russell every now and then, since she would be staying on his ranch, that would be an added bonus.

Sure, it was a slightly embarrassing, selfish bonus. But no one would ever have to know. Would they?

"Carter, I can probably get away in a couple of days. I

know it's not as soon as I should go, but some of my kids are really at risk. I can't just leave them."

"If you can't come down, I understand."

"No, I'm coming. I just need a bit of time."

"Are you sure? I'm guessing Stephanie would feel a lot better with you around, but all those kiddos you work with need you too."

"On your ranch is where I want to be, Carter." She winced. Because she'd really just admitted way too much.

"I can't tell you how pleased I am to hear you say that, Beverly. I'll see you in a few days. Will you promise to call me when you're on your way? I'll be worried until I know you're safe on the ranch."

"I promise." If her voice sounded a little breathless, she hoped he'd never know the reason why.

Some things just needed to be kept private.

12

After she'd had her mini breakdown with Crenshaw, Stephanie pulled herself together. Sure, she was in the middle of the scariest situation of her life, but that didn't mean she could go around screaming at ranch hands.

After unpacking the bags, which included some fruit, a block of cheese, and some milk and orange juice, she'd taken a bath. When she was finally clean, she'd made herself a sandwich, sat down at the small table, and peered out the window.

The clouds were still heavy in the sky, but it looked as if the rain had stopped for the time being. A pair of cardinals were perched on a tree branch. Nearby was a bird feeder that was half empty.

Seeing the pair of bright red birds felt like a good sign. Someone had once claimed that cardinals were signs that someone in heaven was looking out for her. She'd always thought that a bit too fanciful, but now, as she watched the pair, Stephanie allowed herself to imagine that they'd been sent by her parents.

Just to remind her that she was never completely alone.

After she'd cleaned up her plate, she spent some time

wondering what to do with herself. She wasn't used to having any free time. Yet again, she reflected on her life with Mark and Jo. They'd taken her in, given her a place to sleep, and fed her three meals a day.

Not once had either of them lifted a hand to her. They'd also allowed her to do some chores at Miss Jean's house next door. That small job had given her not only a few hours of independence from time to time, but the ability to have some money all to herself—which she'd used once a month to buy her own necessities. There were lots of single women her age who still had to give any money they made to their parents.

So, she was grateful for that.

But Stephanie would never say that life with her aunt and uncle had been easy or carefree. Or happy.

Usually, it was depressing. She was always reminded of their charity and felt obligated to help with her two nieces and nephew and the chores around the house as much as possible. She loved those children and didn't mind helping with chores, but she was also aware that she didn't have a choice. Taking a day off or refusing to clean a bathroom or mop the floor wasn't an option. Because imagining a different life was both painful and useless, she'd tried her best to focus on the present and be grateful.

But that didn't mean that she hadn't longed for more than a few minutes to rest and relax from time to time.

After she tired of watching the birds, she decided to explore the cabin a bit more. There was a small bookcase with about thirty or so books inside. Pleased to find something to take her mind off things, she perused the titles, stacking a couple of choices on the coffee table. To her surprise, one of the hardcover books was actually a photo album. The cover was dark leather. She opened it, curious to see if anything was inside.

And realized that it was almost filled. Just as she was about to return it to the shelf, she noticed that one of the men in the pictures was the man who'd driven her to this very cabin last night. Hardy. It was a different version of him, however. This Hardy was in a military uniform and wearing sunglasses. His arm was tossed over a pair of other soldiers. All three of them were grinning in the way that men were apt to do. As if they had the world on a string and it was their right and expectation.

The idea of such cocky confidence should have repelled her, but instead it made her grin. Maybe it was because she'd seen some men in her church community wear the same expressions after they'd put up a barn.

Even though Mark and Jo used to take pains to remind her that their tight-knit circle was better than the outside world, those same full-of-themselves grins were reminders that the Amish weren't all that much different than their English counterparts. Not all the time.

After smiling at that stroll down memory lane, Stephanie flipped the page to look at a few more pictures. Discovered that not every soldier was a man; a few of them were women. They looked just as tough as the men by their side too. As she studied the photographs more carefully, she realized that some of the photos had been taken in the desert.

To her surprise, the soldiers in the photos didn't look as if they were hot, but how could that be? Wasn't the desert always warm? Maybe not. She wondered where in the world they'd been. What had that experience been like? Life changing? Horrific? Just sandy?

"You think too much, Steph," she chastised herself. "What does it matter?"

She supposed it didn't.

Two sharp raps interrupted her thoughts and made her heart race. Until she remembered that the last person to show up had been Crenshaw, and he'd apologized for scaring her.

He'd also reminded her to lock the door, since it seemed as if the door didn't always click shut in a secure way. Even more importantly to her, even though he'd looked a bit scary, the man had been kind and polite.

She needed to get a handle on herself. If it was a gang member on the other side of the door, he probably wouldn't be knocking. She was pretty sure he'd break down her door and then shoot her. Again.

Peeking through the peephole in the door, she saw Hardy looking back at her.

"It's just me, Stephanie," he said in his deep, raspy voice.

She flipped the dead bolt and opened the door. Tried to think of something to say but couldn't, so she decided to remain silent.

He did a scan of her face and body as he strode inside, both of his hands loaded with bags. "How you doing?" Still studying her, he said, "Your eyes are a little swollen. Have you been crying?"

"I have." Seeing no need to tell him about how all the events had finally caught up with her, she shrugged. "The tears were needed. I'm fine now."

After studying her for a few more moments, his concern seemed to ease. "I reckon you were entitled to a few tears. My momma used to say the same thing."

"Does she not say it anymore?"

"I suppose she would, if she could. But she's not around. She passed away ages ago." He folded his hands behind his back. A pose reminiscent of the photographs she'd seen. "I guess we have something in common."

"I guess so." She stared right back at him. Actually, she took a moment to study his face. Realized that she hardly noticed his scar anymore. Allowed herself to wonder if his mother's passing still made his heart ache.

Hardy was still standing next to the open door. His expression didn't exactly turn wistful, but a change did occur. Some of the jagged edges of his countenance seemed to smooth.

"Do you ever wonder why we got to experience death at such a young age?" His voice had turned soft. Almost as if he wasn't talking to her, simply thinking out loud.

But still, she answered. "Yes." She had indeed wondered why both of her parents had died when most everyone else's lived until they were old and gray. She wondered why she'd had to experience a lot of things, like living with a pair of relatives who weren't affectionate or loving.

Or even the most recent experience. Sometimes it was difficult to wrap her head around the fact that she'd walked into the middle of gang activity when all she'd been doing was buying a few treats for herself.

Another second passed as they stared at each other. Then, with a frown, Hardy shook his head slightly. "Sorry. I don't know where that came from." He held up the collection of plastic grocery bags in his hand. "I brought you a couple more things and wanted to talk to you about something."

"All right." She held out her hands for them, but he shook his head.

"No, let's go into the kitchen. A couple of the items need to go in the freezer."

She followed him the short distance, curious as to what he'd brought.

Looking pleased with himself, he set the bags on the table. "Go on, now. Take a peek. But open the white bag first."

She reached for the closest and gaped at what was inside. More clothes. She glanced up at him.

Hardy looked a bit uncomfortable. "I thought you might need some shirts and sweats that won't swim on you." When she pulled out what looked like a package of underwear, her face burned with embarrassment.

"Look, I know this is awkward, but I wanted to make sure you had what you needed. Besides, I was in the Army and around plenty of women in uniform in close quarters. We all learned real quick not to get too attached to privacy."

"I see." She opened the next bag to find a pair of tennis shoes, two books, and a thousand-piece jigsaw puzzle. The puzzle was of a group of dogs dressed up like cowboys. She couldn't help but giggle.

This time he was the one who looked a little awkward. "I wouldn't have picked such a dopey picture. Like I said, there weren't a lot of choices."

"It was very kind of you to think of me." He'd obviously paid for it all too. "The puzzle and books will keep me busy. I am grateful for the clothes as well."

He waved his hand toward the remaining bags. "Go on now. There's more."

Realizing that one of them was cold, she dove into it like a child on Christmas morning. Then, she embarrassed herself further by squealing at the sight of not one but two containers of ice cream.

"I guess you like ice cream?"

"Oh, jah. But who doesn't?"

The corners of his lips turned up. "I reckon you have a point. So, there's rocky road and vanilla. Do you like either?"

"I like both." The truth was her aunt hadn't been much of a fan of desserts of any sort. And when she had brought them out, Stephanie expected to be the last served. On more than one occasion there hadn't been anything left by the time it was her turn.

Once again, Stephanie promised herself that when she was on her own one day, she would strive to be far more giving to others around her.

Unaware of the direction of her thoughts, Hardy's lips turned up again. "I like both of those flavors too. One has everything, the other is just simple goodness."

"Indeed."

Also in the bag was a frozen pizza and a bag of potato chips. And a deck of playing cards. "Cards too?"

Hardy looked away, as if he was embarrassed. "Spending a bunch of hours alone is hard. Time goes slow. It's good to have something to fill the time."

"All of this will do the job."

"Good."

"Would you like a cup of coffee or something?" She felt silly, offering a beverage in a kitchen that wasn't hers, but she was anxious to do something for him.

"You know what? Yeah. That would be great."

She stood in front of the contraption. "I'm afraid you'll have to show me how this works."

"Oh. Sure. It's a Keurig."

That meant nothing to her, but she actively watched him fill the water holder, push a button, and put a little container into the top.

"This is called a K-Cup." He pointed to the tops of the ones resting in a basket. "See the different flavors?"

"I do now."

"So, you pop it in, close the latch, press the button, and put a cup underneath," he said as he demonstrated each movement.

When coffee started coming out, he said, "Pick out a pod, Stephanie. You're going to do the next one."

A minute later, she was doing just that. And grinning.

Until she noticed Hardy was staring at the open photo album she'd left in the center of the coffee table. "Man, I haven't seen these in a while. Where did you find this book?"

She pointed to the bookcase. "I was looking for something to read and pulled it out. When I opened the cover, I couldn't resist looking at the photographs."

He looked at them, and suddenly Stephanie worried she'd just done yet another thing she wasn't supposed to.

She froze.

With shaking hands, she carried her coffee cup to the table. "I'm so sorry, Hardy." Looking him in the eye, she added, "I have no excuse for doing this except that I was curious. I haven't had the opportunity to see too many photos. Plus, I was looking for anything to take my mind off what's been going on." She moved her hurt arm a bit.

Hardy's expression softened. "Hey—it's okay. I'm not mad. But we need to talk about some things."

"Okay."

"The sheriff is going to stop by. I don't know what he can do—the shooting was in another state and all—but I think it's good that we keep him informed. Don't you?"

"No."

"No?"

"I . . . I mean, I don't know much," she blurted. "Talking to him won't help."

"I told him that was probably the case," Hardy replied

in an easy tone. "However, there's still a chance you might remember something about the driver of that vehicle that I didn't."

Feeling more worried, she shook her head. "Nee. I never saw the driver. When you told me not to turn around, I didn't. I don't want to talk to him."

As if she hadn't said a word, Hardy said, "The sheriff's name is Billy Johnson. Sheriff Johnson. He's a good man."

"A lot of police don't listen to the Amish."

"I don't know why that happened where you're from, but here, that couldn't be further from the truth. He'll listen to you."

"But—"

"Stephanie, Bev told me that you don't like the police. I'm sorry about that. I'm sorry that you're mixed up in this whole situation. None of it is easy. But refusing to speak to Sheriff Johnson isn't going to make things easier. It might even make things harder in the long run. You need to speak to him."

"Do you promise that he won't take me to the police station?"

"I promise. He's coming to visit you here. To visit us." When she scanned his face, he added, "I promise."

"All right." She tried to make peace with that, then figured it didn't matter if she was at peace or not. After all, she didn't have much choice.

"One more thing."

"Yes?"

"I think I had better take a look at your wound."

"Now?"

"Well, yes. You need it seen to. Plus, it looks like it might be paining you some."

"It is. A little bit." But did she want him to examine her

wound? No, she did not. "But I'm sure it is fine. There's no need for you to look."

"I'll be gentle."

He would also be standing very close to her. Touching her arm. Already wondering what his fingertips would feel like, Stephanie felt her skin heat. "There's no need for you to examine me."

"How about this: I'll look at the wound, we'll talk to Sheriff Johnson, and then we'll celebrate by eating a pizza and having ice cream. What do you say?"

"Fine." Stephanie thought Hardy was going above and beyond what Bev had probably intended. So far, he'd driven her around, hid her on his friend's ranch, spoken to the authorities, shopped for her at a couple of stores, and was now planning to eat pizza with her too. She wasn't going to have to spend the rest of the day staring out the window, watching birds, and reliving the terrible man's actions, or being scared that he was going to show up at her doorstep.

"So . . . you ready to do this?"

No. She needed a moment. She picked up the three sacks. "Jah. Let me put these away first. I'll be right back."

"Take your time. I'm not going anywhere."

Hardy would never have any idea how glad she was about that.

13

Hardy had a memory that he held close. It was strong and clear. Even after all this time, it still managed to pinch a bit.

The moment was when he was seven and just started riding the school bus. Though Bev usually rode too, a teacher had volunteered to tutor her before school on some advanced math, since she was so smart and far above the rest of the kids in her class.

On that day, the first time he rode the bus without his big sister looking out for him, he learned there were territories on it. Certain people had certain seats. They were claimed and he couldn't change that.

And he knew that because he found out the hard way. He sat in the wrong seat, Darryl got in his face and screamed at him. Called him names. Threatened to hurt Bev.

And finally spit on him. It was wrong and humiliating. But even worse was the fact that no one did a thing.

Not even the bus driver.

After Hardy stood up, grabbed his backpack, and hurried to his designated new spot, he spent the rest of the bus ride trying not to cry.

He'd also done some thinking and decided to make some changes in his life. First, there was no way he was going to go through the indignity of being bullied and humiliated in front of people again.

When the bus driver stopped at school and everyone got up, he felt frozen in his spot. What he really wanted was to sit on that seat and have the bus driver take him back home. Facing his mother's confusion was better than walking into school and living in fear of who he might run into in the halls.

"Kid, you need to get up," the driver called out.

He shuffled his books again.

"Hey. Hardy, right?"

He looked up and then up some more. There was Edward. He was a sixth grader who lived in his apartment building. He was tough and huge. No one messed with him.

"You hear me?"

Finally meeting Edward's eye, he nodded. "Yeah."

"Then come on. You've got to get up and out."

He had no choice. He stood up. Tried not to shake as he felt the full weight of Edward's stare. To his surprise, Edward stayed by his side as they walked off the bus and down the walkway into the school.

As they walked, Edward talked. "Here's the thing with guys like Darryl, Hardy. They're always going to be around. You're gonna have to deal with them on the bus and in the street and when you're a whole lot older too. That's because they ain't got nothing else, right?" When Hardy had nodded, Edward continued. "You're going to do something better though. I know it."

"How come you know?"

"I just do."

"I don't want him spitting on me again."

"Don't worry about it. He's not going to do a thing to you ever again. I'll take care of it. And then, one day real soon, you'll take care of it too." He bent down slightly to look Hardy in the eye. "You hear me?"

"Yeah."

He slapped him on the shoulder. "Good."

When Hardy had gotten his first look at Stephanie in the bus station, he'd been reminded of that moment. She'd been alone and scared and hurt. Just like he had been. She needed a protector.

Now, as he waited for her to get done changing, Hardy allowed himself to accept the fact that he wanted to be her protector for a good long while.

Since it was taking her a minute, Hardy went into the kitchen and put away the items he'd brought in. When he spied the box of crackers Crenshaw had brought earlier, he gritted his teeth. The only reason Crenshaw still had a job on Russell Ranch was because he called Hardy up and shared what he'd done.

The man made no excuses and apologized for his mistake. And then he waited for Hardy to do what was necessary.

There wasn't anything to do, however. Stephanie didn't seem to be worse for wear. In addition, the flub had given Crenshaw the opportunity to speak with her. Though the man always looked as if he was two steps away from a prison break, he now was completely loyal to the girl.

That was a good thing.

"Here I am," she said, bringing his attention back to the present.

There she was. Dressed in her jeans and now a white T-shirt. He couldn't deny that she looked sweet. He also happened to notice that she looked a little flushed. Was she feverish? Man, he hoped not. The last thing he wanted was to leave the ranch with her for medical help.

He waggled his fingers. "Come here, Steph."

When she stopped in front of him under the bright flores-cent kitchen light, he brushed his hand across her forehead.

"What are you doing? It's my upper arm that's hurt."

"I know. I was checking to see if you had a fever."

"I don't. I'm not sick, Hardy."

There was something about the way she said his name, husky, slightly lilted, that threaded an awareness through him. He liked it. It triggered another round of protective-ness inside of him. And, yes, awareness of her. She was a pretty woman, and she was beginning to occupy most of his thoughts.

Including imagining them in a different situation. One in which she wasn't scared half out of her mind and he wasn't armed in case he had to hurt someone in order to protect her. A situation where they were standing close together, but she wasn't looking at him through a lens of fear and worry.

In his imagination, the look lodged firmly in her blue eyes was awareness. Of him as a man. Her man.

If she was looking at him that way, well, then it would only be the natural thing to pull her into his arms, pressed close. Close enough for her lips to open in a gasp.

Giving him the opportunity to lean down and finally taste those lips . . .

Which he really shouldn't ever do.

Grimacing, Hardy told himself to lock down that fan-tasy. It was not only never going to happen, it was just plain wrong.

She was frightened. Innocent. She was Amish.

He hadn't been frightened nor innocent since he was seven years old.

Nothing that just passed through his mind was good. It shouldn't have happened, and he needed to make sure he wouldn't think such things again.

He needed to be better.

"Let's go to the bathroom so I can take a look at that arm."

"It doesn't hurt all that bad." As if the thought of being next to him in such a tight space worried her, she frowned. "I can deal with it myself."

"I doubt it. I've got a pretty good feeling that what's under that bandage is going to need to be cleaned. I don't want to do it here in the kitchen."

"Fine." She turned and went back down the short hall.

He stayed on her heels. When he had her by the sink, he reached for her sleeve but realized he wasn't going to be able to clean the wound well.

If she was a soldier in his unit, he would tell her what the problem was, and the woman would likely just pull the garment off. It wouldn't be a big deal. Half the women had gone running in sports bras anyway. Of course, all he would care about was if the woman's arm was healthy enough to aim a gun.

This? Well, this was a different story.

"What's wrong?" she asked.

"I . . . well, I was just wondering how I was going to be able to clean your wound properly. The sleeves are kind of long. Do you have anything with a short sleeve?"

"It's still pretty cool. I think it's just sweatshirts and long sleeves. I can go check . . ."

Realizing that he had a black undershirt on, the kind his

mother used to call a wife beater, he pulled off his shirt and then the wife beater too.

She gasped. "Hardy, what are you doing?"

"Giving you something to wear." He handed her his undershirt. "Here. It's gonna be big, but it should keep you covered enough."

"Nee. I'm not going to wear your shirt."

He noticed she was staring at his bare chest like it was as ugly as his face.

Realizing that he had a number of scars on it too, he pulled his long-sleeved tee back on. "Sorry about that. Now, change, and I'll be right back."

She was holding his shirt to her chest but looked frozen stiff. "Hardy, I don't think—"

"I know this is awkward and uncomfortable but it's the best we can do right now. I don't have any other articles of clothing to give you, and the only other idea I've got is for you to wrap a towel around yourself." Seeing her horrified look, he nodded. "I didn't think that would fly either."

He was tempted to touch her. Just a pat. A reassuring stroke of her arm. Anything to soothe her. But he figured there was a pretty good chance that his effort at comfort would backfire on them too. Instead, he settled for using his words. He lowered his voice. "Listen, Stephanie. I know this is yet another hard thing you're being asked to do in a slew of hard and difficult things. But I'm all we've got right now. There ain't another female nearby. All I want to do is help you, right?"

"I . . . I mean, yes. Or . . . right."

Relieved, he nodded. "Good. Now let's get this taken care of. The sheriff's going to be here shortly. Don't faint on me now."

"I am not going to faint."

Stephanie not only looked affronted, but her protest had lit a fire in her eyes, giving Hardy a hint of the girl she was when no one was looking.

He couldn't help but stare, wondering if that was who she'd been when she was a little girl.

When their eyes met again, she inhaled. And then she closed the door in his face.

It was no less than he deserved. But boy, did it almost make him grin.

14

Hardy Anderson's knit shirt looked ridiculous on her. It was also far too big and in danger of showing more of herself than she ever wanted Hardy to see—and especially not under the bright fluorescent light. She looked pale and small and awkward.

She sincerely hoped that no one else would ever find out what she was about to do.

But first she actually had to do it.

Feeling like she might as well treat the moment like the proverbial ripping off a Band-Aid, she opened the door. "I'm ready now." She looked down at the floor. Bracing herself to feel Hardy's eyes skim over all her bare skin.

"Finally," he said.

She lifted her chin. "What?"

"Nothing. Except that it took you long enough. I had recruits undress, shower, and get dressed again in less time than it took you to put on that shirt," he said as he bent down and opened a cabinet door.

"I canna believe that you're criticizing me."

"I'm not criticizing you. All I'm doing is pointing out that we're on a time crunch here. You took your time."

"I did not." When he raised his eyebrows, she harumphed. "Really. I wasn't that bad. Plus, I'm injured."

He smiled. "Exactly."

Only then did she realize that he'd riled her up on purpose—just so she'd stop being so shy and let him see to her arm. It was a sweet thing to do.

But no way would she tell him that right now. "For someone who was supposedly so quick and fierce in the Army, you sure complain a lot."

His eyes warmed. "Some might say I have a reason for that." Putting the first aid box on the top of the toilet lid, he said, "It's a little cramped in here, isn't it?"

Since that was obvious but it was his choice to change her bandage there, she kept her mouth shut.

"Here. I've got an idea."

Next thing she knew, he was picking her up and setting her on the counter. And before she could let him know that that was very inappropriate, he got out some small scissors from the kit and started to carefully remove the bandage. In some places the bandage stuck to her skin. It pinched. And, yes, it hurt too. She pursed her lips to keep from crying out.

He noticed. "You okay, honey?"

His hands were gentle. Far more tender than she would've believed he was capable of. "I'm okay."

"Almost done now." After tossing another portion of the soiled bandage in the trash, he frowned. "There's just one more piece . . . got it."

Stephanie turned her head until she could see her wound in the mirror's reflection. It was bigger than she'd imagined and caked with dried blood. It also looked a bit angry. Unable to help herself, she winced. "It doesn't look too good."

"No, it doesn't, but your skin isn't too warm. I don't think an infection has settled in. Yet."

"Yet?"

As if weighing his words, he paused before nodding. "I think it needs to be cleaned. Thoroughly."

"Are you sure?" That sounded painful.

"I'm afraid so." He ran a finger along the swollen skin. "I'm worried that it's not clean enough. Bev told me that she did what she could, but that you two were in her Corolla and in a big hurry."

"We were both really rattled."

A muscle in his face twitched. "I should've checked it last night. I'm sorry."

"No need to apologize. I couldn't have handled one more thing last night."

Meeting her gaze in the reflection, he asked, "Will you trust me to help you?"

His question was so earnest, Stephanie almost laughed. So far, all she'd done was trust him. And there were so many things she'd trusted him for without any real reason to do so. Now, here he was, going above and beyond for her, yet still taking the time to ask her opinion. She didn't have much experience with people in her life going to such great extents to see to her needs.

"Steph?"

He was still waiting. Her mouth went dry. "Jah, Hardy. I will trust you."

Hardy seemed pleased as he turned on the faucet. "I'll be right back. I'm going to get a bowl while the water heats."

When he returned with a plastic bowl and two clean dish-cloths, he studied her face. "Are you worried? I promise that I'll be as gentle as I can."

"No, it's not that."

"Then what's going on?"

"Oh, I was just thinking about how trust is a funny thing. I ended up here because I trusted your sister. Even though she was a complete stranger."

"Beverly is good people. You were right to trust her," he added as he opened up a bottle that he'd placed in the bowl. After he poured a bit inside, he held the bowl under the faucet.

When the bowl was back on the counter, Stephanie said, "I'm glad I trusted Bev. It's just that I don't have a lot of people in my life who are willing to go to such great lengths for me."

"I wish you did." He dipped the corner of one of the cloths into the hot mixture.

"Me too. It just hit me that if I hadn't trusted Bev, I would still be back in Adams County at my aunt and uncle's house. I guess I'd be sitting at home right now wondering when that man was going to show up and being scared to death."

"Would you have told your family?"

Feeling him brush the warm cloth on the area around her skin, she shook her head. "No."

"Really?"

"They . . . well, they would've found a way to twist it into my mistake. They would've reminded me that if I had stayed home, none of this would have happened."

Dabbing at her arm, he frowned. "It doesn't work that way. You can't stay home round the clock because you don't want anything bad to happen."

"They believe something very different. At least in my case." As she watched him continue to dip the cloth into the warm liquid and then dab at her wound, she tried to think of something else. Unfortunately, if she wasn't thinking about the pain, she was thinking about Hardy.

Neither was helping her situation.

"Tell me about being Amish."

Surprised, she looked his way. "What do you want to know?"

"Anything. I know some Amish around here but not well enough to be invited into their homes. How is your home different?"

That startled a laugh from her. "How is it not? First of all, there's no electricity."

"How do you cook?"

"Gas or propane. The haus is also far more plain inside than this cabin."

"What do you mean?"

"I mean that there are few things on the walls. Far fewer tools in the kitchen. Far less of everything."

"I guess your bedroom is pretty basic too."

"You could say that." No way was she going to describe her curtained area in the basement.

A look of regret filled his eyes. "You know what? I should apologize. I'm making it sound as if your home is somehow lacking because it doesn't have a bunch of bells and whistles." When she giggled, he stared. "What did I say that was funny?"

"Nothing. Not really. It's just that I was thinking that an Amish house probably does have bells and whistles. It's the television and radio and computers that we lack. Ain't so?"

He chuckled under his breath. "I guess so." He seemed to think about that for a while as he gently swabbed at her wound. His ministering hurt, and blood began to ooze from the opening.

Feeling a little sick, she looked away and stared at his face instead. Those hazel eyes. Not quite green, not quite brown. She was mesmerized.

It might have been her imagination, but it seemed like he was giving equal attention to her expression and the wound.

He truly cared about her. He didn't want to cause her pain.

"I think we're good now." He waved his hand over her arm, attempting to dry the area before reapplying a bandage. "Are you in a lot of pain? I can get you an ibuprofen."

"I don't need a pill. Just, um, to put back on my own clothes."

"Oh. Of course." Before she could tell him that she could hop off the counter unassisted, his hands were once again curved around her waist. Right after that, he was steadying her on her feet. "There you go."

"Danke." When he didn't move, she cleared her throat. "I need you to leave, Hardy. So I can get changed."

His eyes widened for a second before he seemed to regain his composure. "Sorry. Um, just leave everything out. When you're done changing, I'll go in there and clean up."

"That isn't necessary. I can do that."

"Fine. What do you say we have that pizza now, before the sheriff arrives?"

"You may bake the pizza, Hardy." Just to mess with him, she lifted her chin a bit. Hoping to appear a little bit princess-like.

He stilled, then his eyes warmed. "Your wish is my command, ma'am."

When they shared a smile, Stephanie realized that something special had passed between them. Something pure and honest and good and real. It was sweet and reassuring and perfect.

She just wasn't sure what that meant.

15

Even though she'd told Carter that she would head down to Crittenden County soon, Bev wondered if she'd spoken too quickly. "Soon" was going to have to be later instead of sooner. As much as she believed that she should help her brother with Stephanie, Bev was just as committed to her foster kids, and it was going to take some time to rearrange her schedule so she could take a few personal days.

Bev felt bad about the delay, but it couldn't be helped.

Though Stephanie was no doubt scared and in danger, she was also a grown woman. In addition, she had Hardy looking after her, which meant a lot. Hardy could not only handle just about anything that came up, he was also a born caretaker. Even if he and Stephanie didn't get along or never exchanged more than a few words at a time, Hardy would still look out for her and keep her safe.

Beverly couldn't say the same thing about all of the children in her caseload.

The simple truth of the matter was that not all foster homes were ideal and not all foster kids were easy to care for. It wasn't their fault. Most of them had been through some terrible ordeals.

But they did have one constant in their lives, and that was her. She found it harder and harder to leave them for any length of time.

Especially Justin Emmerson, who was causing trouble again.

Sitting on one of the swings in his foster family's backyard, Bev contemplated the number of ways she could bring up his latest outburst without him completely shutting down. It was surprising that even after ten years of working with children in the system, she still wasn't always sure of the best way to help.

Looking at Justin out of the corner of her eye, she reflected that it was probably not all that surprising after all. The twelve-year-old had been through a lot in his short life, and his experiences were like no one else's. There was no way she'd ever push him to conform completely. No matter how hard he—or anyone caring for him—tried, he wasn't ever going to act like an "average" kid.

As she thought about all of those things, Bev continued to let the silence surround them. Justin had enjoyed far too few moments of peace in his life.

But maybe this wasn't the best way to handle things today. He was looking increasingly agitated.

"Are you ever going to say something, Ms. Anderson?"

Hmm. Usually, he insisted on calling her Bev. She smiled at him. "Yes."

He kicked the patch of dirt under his feet. "Well, then?"

"I've been trying to think of the best way to get started."

He almost flinched. But he covered up the movement with lightning speed. "To do what? Tell me that I'm about to get kicked out of here?" His voice was filled with bitterness.

And, yes, more than a little bit of pain.

Boy, that made her heart hurt. If she wasn't his social worker and wasn't so worried about losing their fragile connection, she would have hurried to his side and given him a hug.

But Justin had issues with being touched.

So, she did the next best thing. She crouched in front of him, so they were not only eye to eye but he was even a little bit taller than her.

It was all positioning, she guessed, but he needed that. There were too many people in Justin's life who had power over him. His awful parents. The string of mediocre foster families. The teachers who cared but didn't have the skills or the time to truly be there for him.

And now, the gang members who were beginning to reach out to him. They were telling him the things he wanted to hear—but they scared him too.

The Broken Arrows were what had brought her to the house.

"Justin, you are not about to be kicked out of here."

"Yeah, right."

"I'm serious. The Hendersons like you. They like having you here."

The boy didn't say a word, but something new entered his expression. He shut it down before she could decipher it.

So she continued. "I'm telling you the truth. You know I wouldn't lie about that."

"What are you here for, then?"

"I think we should talk about yesterday. About what happened at school."

His posture slumped. "I already talked to the principal."

"I know."

"How come you know? Did he call you?"

"Yep. And so did the Hendersons."

His expression practically burned with hurt. "And what did all of you decide I should do?"

"Believe it or not, we talked a lot about what we could do. The principal and I agreed that we need to help you figure out ways to deal with those boys." Mr. Cousins, the principal, had confirmed what she'd guessed—that a couple of those boys were hanging around some of the gang members and no doubt trying to gain their respect.

Justin stared at her with those amazing pale green eyes of his. Eyes that girls were going to get lost in. Eyes that one day someone special was going to fall in love with.

If he lived that long.

As the moment continued, Justin looked as if he wanted to memorize every feature on Bev's face. Then he surged to his feet.

"Yeah, that will solve everything, won't it? I do what you say, and those boys will forget about me," he said sarcastically. "Who knows? Maybe they'll all stop bullying me at school."

Bev noticed that his breath had quickened. She stood up and stepped backward in order to give him some space. "I don't expect that to happen."

"But you do. But you have no . . ." He paused, obviously catching himself before he started cussing up a storm. "Idea."

"Then tell me."

"No."

She almost smiled. "Sorry, but that's not an acceptable answer."

"I don't think I should have to talk about it."

This boy. This poor, damaged, vulnerable boy. Instead of pushing some more, she changed tactics. "How about I talk for a while, and you listen?"

He rolled his eyes and stuffed his hands in his jeans' pockets.

But he didn't move.

"Justin, I know why the gang is targeting you. One way or another, they're going to want you to join them."

"I don't see why."

"I do. You're big for your age. You're confident. You look like you don't have a lot of fear." She paused, then added, "You are also essentially alone in life."

"Just say it. I'm a foster kid."

"All right. You're a foster kid."

His jaw clenched. Yep, she'd hit a nerve. She felt that pinch. Regretted it. But continued, because he was her responsibility and she needed to make sure that he was prepared for whatever obstacles he faced in the upcoming years.

"So, you're all those things, but that's not *all* you are." Stepping closer, she said, "You are confident, but I know that you aren't always that way. And I know you put on a good act, because I also know that you aren't always fearless. That sometimes you're scared."

His jaw worked. "That's not true. I'm not a wimp."

"I didn't say that. I don't think you are. I think you're one of the bravest people I've ever met. Which is yet another reason I think you're being targeted. These guys want you. They want you around for a while. I think they're going to want to train you to work for them. They think you're so alone in the world that they will be your new family. But they're wrong."

"You aren't around all the time, Bev. You're hardly around at all."

He wasn't lying. He wasn't even exaggerating. But what could she do? The child wasn't her only concern. "I know."

Disappointment flashed in his eyes again. "So, whatev. We're done."

She shook her head. "Justin, I wish I was able to visit you more often. I wish you were the only kid I know who's in foster care. But you and I know that's not true." She drew a breath. "Now, the way I see it, you have some choices. You can ignore everyone's warnings, join the Arrows, and then see what happens."

"Or they can make my life miserable."

"Or . . . I could move you."

"No. No way." He looked away. "I know I'm not going to get to stay too much longer, but things are pretty good here. The Hendersons are nice."

"I agree. They want you to stay too."

"So, you only came over to tell me what?"

"That you're going to have to turn the other cheek and try to wait them out. Because these guys are trouble, Justin. One of their new recruits—a former foster kid I worked with—just found out how much trouble they are."

"What happened?"

Bev shook her head slightly. "All you need to know is that it's bad, and it will get worse." Leaning closer, she lowered her voice. "Listen to me, Justin. These Arrows, they're not just older teenagers who are surviving. They're actively hurting innocent people."

Justin studied her face, obviously looking for signs that she was giving him some kind of social worker nonsense.

"Are you telling me the truth?"

"I wouldn't lie about that. Please. Hang in there a little bit longer."

"But the principal—he gave me a warning."

"I know. But he also knows what you're dealing with. So

do the Hendersons. So do I. You might think that you're alone, but you're not." She squeezed his hand before quickly letting go. "You're not."

He blinked, showing that her words affected him more than he wanted to admit. "I've got to go."

"All right. I'll see you in two weeks."

He'd already turned around but looked back to meet her eyes. "So soon?"

"It's our regularly scheduled visit, right?"

For a split second, pure relief shone in his eyes before he hid it again.

But that was enough. The two of them still had a relationship. He'd probably never know it, but she was as relieved as he was. "I'm going to text you, so don't blow me off."

"Yeah, all right."

"Justin, I mean it. Tell me you're going to text me back."

"I'll text you back, Bev."

She grinned at him. "Don't tell anyone, but I've gotten used to you calling me Bev." When he almost smiled, her heart filled. "You have a good day, now."

He waved a hand but continued to walk away.

As she watched, a little bit of her heart went with him.

After saying goodbye to Jean Henderson, Bev got back into her car and finally checked her phone.

And saw that Carter had called.

Before she could talk herself out of it, she called him back as she pulled out of the driveway. He answered on the first ring.

"This is a nice surprise."

"Why? You're the one who called me."

"That's true, but I also texted you last night and . . . crickets."

Put that way, she felt embarrassed. "Sorry about that."

"You're busy. I get it."

"Well, we're talking now. How are you?"

"I've been better. Not only do I have an injured Amish girl hiding out on my ranch, but a friend of mine might be in danger as well."

"Who are you talking about?" Was he worried about Hardy?

"Who do you think, Beverly? You, of course."

His voice was gentle, almost teasing. She couldn't get a read on it, which made her nervous. "There's no need to be worried about me. I'm fine."

"Not from my point of view. Hardy told me that you were seen helping that girl, Beverly. In my book, that also puts you in danger. You need protection."

"I'm used to taking care of myself. And listen, I haven't been doing anything stupid. I've been watching my surroundings and being careful."

"I'm sure you have been, but this isn't an angry parent or domestic dispute you're in the middle of. We're talking about a gang here." His voice deepened. "I know you said you'd come in a couple of days, but I don't want you to put it off any longer. I want you to come to the ranch with me. I'm going back in a couple of days."

Hope rose inside her before she tamped it down. Yes, they'd talked several times in the past, and he'd always acted warm and friendly. More than once over the years, she'd misread a smile or a teasing comment directed her way. She'd think it meant something, only to realize that he said sweet things to women all the time. He was a charmer. That was his way.

Firmly reminding herself of that, she murmured, "I guess I could. Thanks to Hardy, we have known each other awhile."

"That's not what I'm talking about." After a pause, he added, "I'd like to see you soon."

She was glad she was at a red light because she was caught off guard. "Excuse me?"

"I'm asking you out on a date, Beverly. And before you shut me down, let me clarify. My preference would be to pick you up at your house, take you to dinner someplace nice. But if you want me to meet you at some coffee place, I'll do that."

He sounded so grumpy about the idea, she had to giggle.

"Bev, don't break my heart and start laughing at me."

"I was only giggling at your tone of voice. You sounded so grumpy about meeting at a coffee shop."

"So . . . does this mean you'll let me take you out?"

It had been so long since anyone had treated her like she was worth a fancy night out. But it was still tempting to say no.

But what if she did say no? Would she regret it later? Yes. Yes, she would.

"Yes, Carter."

"That makes me very happy. Thank you."

"You're welcome," she teased.

"I'm not going to let you change your mind."

"I'm not planning on it."

"I've gotta get off this phone, but I'll call you tonight with the details."

"That sounds good."

After Carter disconnected, Bev pulled forward through the light and allowed a little shiver of desire to filter through her.

And then she smiled.

16

Timothy was becoming desperate. No, that wasn't exactly right. He'd been feeling desperate for a while now. Desperate and edgy and nervous. None of it was good.

"Think about that sea," he whispered to himself. "That was some powerful stuff."

His thoughts returned to that Bible and all the stories that Mark had told about Jesus. Sure, the guy had performed a bunch of miracles on people. But what had stuck with Timothy the most was when He'd calmed the Sea of Galilee and saved those guys' lives.

"Jesus, how about calming my storm?" he said. "'Cause I could sure use some help right about now."

For a full second, he waited. Half expecting a lightning bolt or something to appear from out of nowhere. But he didn't even feel better.

Nothing had happened, which was a real problem. Considering he had only one option, Timothy felt like crying. What he needed to do was stop thinking and do what he needed to do. Then he could return home and get to stay alive for a while. Maybe even have a life.

How could he, though? If he followed through on his

orders and actually killed the Amish girl, her death was going to be on his shoulders. Like, forever.

He didn't know if he was going to be able to live with that kind of burden. Sure, he'd killed that dealer, but his death wasn't the same.

Not really.

Plus, he'd looked into her eyes and had seen nothing but a pretty, frightened blue. There was nothing mean or evil inside of her.

Staring at the phone in his hand, he contemplated smashing it to pieces. Anything to avoid another call from Kane.

But if he did that, he'd be even worse off. If he didn't answer whenever Kane called, they might hurt Audrey.

Glancing down at the small tablet he found in the motel room, he reread his notes.

Name: Stephanie Miller. Location: a cabin on the east section of the Russell Ranch. One of the men who watched her was vigilant and ex-military. The others? Two of them seemed like they were just as tough. The last? Well, he was a snitch and a liar, since he'd told Timothy a lot about Stephanie for just a hundred bucks.

He'd also promised to be late on his rounds so Timothy could look around a little bit.

Which, ironically, made Timothy want to beat him so badly he wouldn't be able to walk for a couple of days. What kind of guy would knowingly let a stranger onto his boss's land for a hundred bucks?

He was just wondering if he should drive by the guardhouse again when his phone buzzed.

Already feeling the cold pool in the pit of his stomach, he answered.

"Hey, Kane."

"Timothy, long time no contact. You should have checked in by now."

"Um, yeah. Well, I was waiting to get more information for you."

"Yeah? What do you have?"

"I've gotten a lot of information about the girl. She's staying on a big ranch." Timothy paused, hoping that Kane would understand just how difficult taking out the Amish girl was going to be.

After two beats, Kane said, "Is that a problem for you?"

"Yes."

"Why?"

"Well, it's private property."

"And?"

"And there's a lot of security there."

"Even if they have a whole security team, no one can be everywhere at once. You just have to take your shot and then get out of there."

"I understand." When silence met his words, Timothy forced himself to continue. It wasn't like he had another choice. "I think I have a plan."

"Good. When should we expect it done?"

"Soon?"

Kane's voice lowered. "We need more than that, Timothy. We're going to need a lot more than that."

Cussing under his breath, Timothy felt sweat drip down his spine. "I'll have it done within two days. The guy who I talked to is shifty. I don't know if he can be trusted. He might be setting me up."

There was a pause on the other end of the line. "You have two days. If I have to call you again, you aren't just going to be hearing my voice on the other end. You're going to be hearing Audrey's. And she won't just be scared, buddy." His voice deepened. "Do you believe me?"

"I believe you."

"Are you sure? You think I can trust you to do what I say?" He lowered his voice. "Or do you think I need to come down there and supervise? Of course, if I have to drive all the way to Crittenden County, I'm not going to be going there by myself. I'll want to travel with a friend or two, and they're not going to be as understanding of your deficiencies as I am."

Bile surged in his throat before he choked it back down. "You won't need to do that."

"Good. Then stop overthinking everything. No, just stop thinking. No one expects you to do that. Take care of the girl and come back. And don't forget to bring some evidence of her passing."

Evidence? He cringed. What was he going to have to show them? "Okay," he replied.

"Don't sound so sad, buddy. If you do a good job, there's some benefits for you. You'll have proven yourself. You'll be one of us."

"Really?"

"Yeah. Sure. The dealer was supposed to be your initiation, but we can count her as it instead. We'll be all good then."

Timothy wished he could believe that, but by now he knew when Kane was lying through his teeth. His words came a little too fast and the cadence slipped. Even if Timothy killed the Amish girl and brought back proof, it wasn't going to be enough to make them forget. They still wanted that dealer's money, and instead all they'd gotten was the police hanging around, asking questions.

"I'll take care of her."

"That's what I like to hear. Two days. Max."

His mouth went dry. "I might need more time."

"You're not going to get that. Not only have the cops started asking questions, but they found your guy's body. Things aren't looking good for you, buddy. We need to get rid of that witness."

"They found him? I thought you dumped him in a lake or something."

"What we did with him ain't the problem. All of this is on your shoulders. That girl can't testify, Tim. If the DA gets her to testify, we're all going down. I was there, and Stew ordered you to meet with the guy. You understand?"

"Yeah."

"Good." Kane clicked off.

Feeling tainted, Timothy tossed the phone on his bed. Stood up. Paced.

All he had to do was sneak onto the property, break in the door, and kill the girl. The guard told him the cabin wasn't near the big house. No one would hear either her screams or the gunshot.

Then he could drive back home and finally put all this behind him. If they weren't lying and didn't kill him as soon as he got back to Ohio.

But . . . as he remembered those blue eyes, Timothy knew he couldn't do it. There had to be another way.

What he needed was to scare her off. Make her want to run farther. So far that neither he nor anyone in the Arrows could ever find her.

Then maybe he could run too. Call up Audrey and explain everything to her.

Then, yeah. Maybe she'd follow him, and they could start a new life someplace else. Somewhere where they could start over fresh. In Georgia or Seattle or Mexico. Anywhere she wanted. He didn't care.

As long as he had her, everything would be just fine.

He forced himself to pretend that he still believed in fairy tales.

With his new plan in mind, he headed out. He had a package to deliver to Miss Stephanie Miller. It was time to pay a visit to the Russell Ranch.

17

Stephanie had been living in the quiet, pretty, secluded cabin on the Russell Ranch for three days. She was surprised how quickly she got used to wearing jeans and sweatpants.

She'd also become a fan of Fritos, Archway oatmeal cookies, and frozen pizza. And a fan of an old television series she'd found, *The Love Boat*. Three days ago, all those things had been completely foreign to her.

Looking at herself, currently lounging on the couch in the middle of the afternoon in jeans and a pink hoodie and watching cruise ship director Julie avoid the attentions of a passenger from Virginia, she was struck by the fact that she was completely comfortable.

She didn't know how any of this had happened.

She was even more confused by how content she felt, which did make her feel guilty. Of course she was feeling content. Usually, she watched over her cousins and helped with all the cooking and cleaning. In addition, she did most of the laundry. Now, she didn't have to do anything but take care of herself.

Was it selfish to enjoy this new life she'd been thrown into? Or was it something else?

Once again, Stephanie's mind drifted back to her home in southern Ohio. Though things weren't easy at her aunt and uncle's, she fit in with the Amish community. She had a few girlfriends who she visited with during church services or when there was a large gathering. She might not be happy, but she wasn't unhappy either.

Every time Aunt Jo asked if she was ready to be baptized in their faith, she said she wasn't ready. She didn't feel like she could explain it, but she often felt as if God was quietly calling for her to wait. When Stephanie had confided this to their bishop, he said he understood. Her aunt and uncle didn't feel the same way, but they didn't argue their point.

Now she was beginning to wonder if the Lord had been quietly preparing her for this moment. Maybe He really had been wanting her to not get baptized—because He felt she would be better suited to an English life.

She wasn't sure, but it was something to pray about, for sure and for certain.

When a knock came at the door, Stephanie clicked pause on her remote and peeked out the window, wondering if it was one of the ranch hands. Even though Hardy had said that all the ranch hands were reliable and harmless, Stephanie wasn't sure that she believed it. Every time Dan stopped by to either drop something off or to speak to Hardy, she felt uncomfortable. He always seemed to be half smiling, like he was playing a joke at her expense.

She was in luck today, though. Standing on the other side of the window was Hardy. Breathing a sigh of relief, she opened the door. "Hi."

"Hey, you." He smiled slightly. It warmed his eyes and also seemed to warm her heart too. "May I come in?"

"Of course." He asked permission to enter every time,

which she thought was really considerate of him. He acted like she had some control in her life. She desperately needed that.

"How are you doing today?" he asked as he strode forward. Then paused midstep. "Wait. Are you watching *The Love Boat*?"

Hardy sounded so appalled, Stephanie wasn't sure if she should be embarrassed or not. But since he was the one who was making her stay here, she figured it shouldn't matter. Besides, the evidence was frozen on the screen. "Yes. I'm in the middle of an episode. Have you seen this show before?"

"It was popular before my time, but yeah. I've seen it." Rubbing back a chunk of dark hair that had fallen over his forehead, he added, "Pretty much everyone over twenty has seen at least a couple of episodes. The reruns are everywhere."

She couldn't tell if he liked the show or not. She supposed it didn't really matter. She was stuck in hiding and appreciated having something to take her mind off her worries. "I'm enjoying it."

The corners of his mouth lifted. "Are you, now?" He sat down on the couch. "What's going on?"

Noticing that the paused screen showed Julie confiding in Isaac the bartender, she blurted out, "The man who likes Julie lives in Virginia. That's a problem since she's, you know, living on a ship."

He kicked his feet out and crossed his boots. Just like he was settling in. "What do you think's going to happen?"

She thought about it. "I've only seen a couple of these episodes, so I'm no expert, but I'm guessing that it isn't going to end well." Since he looked so interested, she continued. "Last time, Gopher kissed a woman because he thought it was love, but it was only a fling. Love onboard a ship isn't all that easy."

He burst out laughing. "I reckon you might be right, at that." He looked bemused as they watched more of the scene.

When a commercial came on, she studied him. "Did you come over for a specific reason?"

"Yes. To check on you."

"Obviously, I'm fine."

"Good." Looking her over, he added, "I like that sweatshirt you're wearing. Pink suits you."

Why did that make her happy? "Thank you."

"You're welcome." Looking completely comfortable, he folded his arms across his chest.

"Are you planning to stay here awhile?" She wasn't sure if she meant her couch or him staying in the cabin next door.

"Yep."

Starting to worry, she whispered, "Why?" Had something happened and she was in danger again?

"Why do you think, silly? I'm going to watch this show with you."

"Are you sure?"

"Girl, don't leave me hanging. I need to find out how Julie's heart is about to get broken by that loser from Virginia."

"I don't know if he's a loser . . ."

"You let me be the judge of that." He pointed at the television screen. "Commercial is over."

She turned her attention back to the episode. Isaac, who she was now coming to realize was the most knowledgeable when it came to love and romance, was warning Julie not to get too attached.

And then, right after several commercials for drugs and lawyers, there the couple was, standing against the ship's railing. Julie wearing a blue gown and the Virginian wearing a tuxedo, and they were dancing under the stars. It was all very romantic.

Until Hardy started to laugh.

"What's so funny?"

He motioned to the screen. "They are. It's not going to end well, you know."

"I know." She lifted her chin and pretended she was an expert at romance. "They're too different." Just like she and Hardy were very different.

"They are," he agreed. "They also live in two different worlds. Plus, he's talking about himself a lot. That's a big problem right there."

"I thought that too."

After they listened to a conversation, Hardy grunted. "Just for the record, she's a whole lot better off without him."

"Because they're so different and live too far away from each other?"

"No. If they're in love, they'll work those things out. But listen to him, Steph. He's an idiot. And a liar."

"You think so? He seemed sincere."

"He's slick. No one is as successful as he's trying to sound like."

"He could be." Though, the more she listened to the Virginian, the more she wanted to wrinkle her nose. Plus, he had no muscles in his arms. Not even half what Hardy had.

"Nope. No man who's really a multimillionaire is gonna be floating around on the *Love Boat*, Steph. They're going to be sailing on their own yacht. Remember that next time some guy starts trying to sweet-talk you."

It took effort not to roll her eyes. "Hmm."

"I'm right. Just you see."

She folded her arms across her chest and tried to act like she couldn't wait to find out what happened. But her traitorous mind only seemed to care about the fact that Hardy was sitting next to her.

And that he smelled good.

Had he just showered? She closed her eyes. She shouldn't be thinking about things like that. No, she should be thinking about the time. That was what was safe. It was almost four in the afternoon. Didn't he have other things he'd rather be doing instead of watching television with her?

Fifteen minutes later, the credits were rolling and Hardy was gloating. "See, I told you. That man was a liar."

"He really was. Poor Julie's heartbroken."

"Ah, she'll get over it. I have a feeling she'll be flirting with some dude in a couple of episodes."

He sounded so sure, she chuckled. "I fear you might be right."

"I know I am."

"You shouldn't be gloating, though," she said as she clicked off the TV. "It's bad manners."

"I don't disagree, and gloating is nothing to be proud about. But you can't blame me, can you? I'm only human."

"I guess not. He wasn't very nice. I think Julie is going to be sad for a while."

"She'll be right as rain in the next episode. That's the charm of the show. Drama happens, but then everything's all good in sixty minutes."

"Perhaps so."

His gaze lingered on her. Making her feel good. Making her wish that things were different. If only for a little while. Like Julie McCoy, she'd enjoy experiencing love for a little while. Just to know what it felt like.

"What are you going to eat for supper?"

"I'm not sure." Did this mean he wanted to eat with her? If so, why?

"Want me—" His phone buzzed. When he glanced down at the screen he stiffened. "Hold on a sec. I've got to take this."

To her surprise, he walked out of her living room and stepped out of the front door too. Peeking out the window at him, she frowned as he ran his fingers through his hair and became even more agitated.

Then his voice rose. She wished she could hear his words through the door.

When he came in again, he was scowling.

"What's wrong? Did something happen?"

"Yeah. That was Dan. A package was just dropped off for you at the front gate."

Her pulse started racing. "But no one knows I'm here."

"No one is *supposed* to know you're here. I thought whoever followed us had given up. Maybe not."

"What kind of package is it?" Imagining all sort of things, she blurted, "Maybe Bev sent something?"

"Bev wouldn't risk your safety by doing that."

"But—"

"Dan said that the guy who dropped it off was all business. All he said was that he was told to deliver it to the front gate." Looking irritated, Hardy clenched one of his hands. "And Dan didn't think to get the guy's name. He didn't even think to point out that the license plate had been taken off the vehicle. I discovered that on the security camera. Man, I thought I trained him better."

She shook her head. "I don't understand. I didn't do anything. I haven't told anyone where I am."

"No one thinks you did. Because there were two things in the box. A package of .22s . . . and a note."

"What are .22s?"

"That's the size of the bullet. I think it's a calling card from the gang member back in Batavia. He knows you're here." He cleared his throat. "But the note is what is disturbing."

"What did it say?"

Softening his voice, he said, "I don't think you need to know the exact words."

"I think differently." She lifted her chin. "I'm involved and I'm a grown woman. Don't treat me like a child."

"All right. Fine. It says that you should leave, because the next time you're around a .22, it will be lodged in your heart."

Slowly the message sank in. And then it took almost everything she had not to sink onto the floor.

18

Sit down, Stephanie," Hardy said. "You look like you're about to fall over. I'm calling the sheriff."

Gone was the sweet and teasing tone he'd been using with her while watching *The Love Boat*. In its place was the return of the barking he'd done when he'd driven her to the ranch.

At least now she wasn't afraid of him anymore. Now she realized he only got this way when he was on edge or felt like he was losing control of a situation.

Which somehow didn't relieve her mind. If Hardy was worried, then she should be petrified.

And just like that, the moment that had changed her life flashed before her eyes. Once again, she recalled the slight movement around the cars. The low buzz of engines running in the distance. The children's laughter. She felt the sun on her cheeks, and when the wind shifted, she caught a whiff of the dumpster. Just as she spied the shadow of someone lurking behind it.

And then there had been all that blood on the pavement.

Suddenly, a buzz filled her ears, her vision went blurry, and she felt a little faint.

How could she have allowed herself to settle into this new, unfamiliar life? Why had she dared to be happy that her hands weren't cracking and sore from cleaning the floors with vinegar?

She'd been such a fool. She'd honestly been content to lounge on the couch watching silly television dramas in a pink hoodie. Somehow she'd pushed the real reason she was in Crittenden County to the side.

That wasn't right. She should be ashamed of herself.

"Yes, I'm sure. Dan is bringing over the box now," Hardy barked into the phone.

Focusing back on the present, Stephanie turned her attention to him.

Hardy was pacing now. Pacing as he talked to the sheriff. Back and forth he went, his ear to the cell phone. His hand nearly pulling out strands of his hair as he listened to the sheriff.

While she listened to him. She needed to hear what he was saying. Hear what he was thinking she should do.

"Yes, I can be there whenever you need me . . . afternoon works." Pause. He turned his head. Looked directly at her. "Yes, sir. I will."

After he disconnected, he hung up the phone. Stared off into the distance for a moment before walking to her. "You all right?" He crouched by her side.

"I don't know. I don't think so."

"You don't need to be afraid. I'm not going to leave you."

His voice had been gravelly with emotion. It made a lump form in her throat. "I understand. I'll try not to be." She hated saying those words, though. Because that's all they were. Just plain old words that meant nothing. Someone had sent her a box of bullets. How could she not be scared to death about that?

He perched on the edge of the sofa. "I'm not going to let anything happen to you. I promise."

"It really was from him, wasn't it?"

"The sheriff's gonna ask around, and we'll touch base again tomorrow afternoon." He sighed. "But, yeah. It's almost a certainty that the guy who dropped off the box was the man who's after you. I mean, who else would be doing this?"

She was still in danger. "Maybe I should leave."

He scowled. "What? No."

"But I'm not safe here. Anyone could show up . . ."

Hardy shook his head. "One more time. You're not alone. You're not even close to being alone."

But she was. Just like she'd been from the time her parents died and she'd moved in with Jo and Mark and their kinner.

Hardy resituated himself. Scooted a little closer to her, close enough for her to smell his cologne again. Feel the warmth radiating from his body. "Stephanie."

"Yes?"

"What's going on in that pretty little head of yours?" he asked softly.

Unbidden, a tingle skittered across her skin. Making her feel electrified. Just from the thickening of his drawl. "Nothing."

"Come on." He reached out, curled a strand of her hair around a finger.

How come that made her feel breathless?

She took a fortifying breath. "I was just thinking that I've been alone for a long while now."

"Not just here."

"Not just here. And now . . . I'm scared, and I'm so very

far away from everything I've ever known. I don't know how he found me."

"I don't know either, but our security team knows to take extra precautions. And the sheriff's working on it. We'll get some help from one of the deputies if we can. You don't need to worry."

His words were as sweet as the almost-tender expression on his face. But still, she didn't believe him. How could she when that man—that awful, terrifying man—sent her that box?

"I'm going to worry."

He blinked. Softly, he said, "Don't you think that God has your back? Don't you think God is big enough to hold on to your worries for you?"

"He is, but He can't know . . ."

"He can, Stephanie. If you can't trust the sheriff, then trust me. If you can't trust me, then trust Bev, who sent you here. Better yet, trust in the Lord. He put Bev in that parking lot to save you. He gave Bev me, because He knew she would call me if she needed help. And He knew that I would do anything she asked of me. That I would protect you, Stephanie. Finally, the Lord gave me Carter Russell, who gave us a safe place to stay." Leaning closer, he repeated the words, but this time in almost a whisper. "You. Are. Not. Alone."

"All right. Fine."

He looked frustrated but didn't argue anymore. She was grateful for that.

"Come on. Let's watch another episode of *The Love Boat*."

"What? Nee. I don't feel like it."

"Come on. Maybe the Captain will fall in love this time." He waggled his eyebrows. "Or two people will fall in love and actually end up happy together."

That sparked a giggle. "You'll really sit and watch another episode?"

He picked up the remote. "I'm already on it."

When the theme song started playing, Hardy grimaced but then changed his expression. He kicked his feet up on the coffee table, boots and all, and sank into the cushions. "Remember how you have your cell phone now? Remember you have my phone number programed into it?"

"I do."

"Beverly gave it to you for a reason. Text me if you get scared. Call me if you get scared. I'm right next door, re-member?"

"What if it's in the middle of the night?"

"Then you call me in the middle of the night. Steph, if you call me then I'm going to pick it up," he said, all while sounding like if she didn't do that, then he was going to take it personally. "You with me?"

"Yes." She giggled. Who would have ever thought she'd be taking directions from such a bossy Englisher?

Well, maybe she would've thought that.

Because he was better than she imagined. As bad as the situation was, she didn't feel as petrified because she believed him when he said he was going to protect her. That maybe, just maybe she didn't want to be anywhere else, because if she was, then she would be alone again. And she wasn't ready for that.

"Here, Stephanie." He tossed one of the throw pillows that had been sitting on the easy chair.

"What's this for?"

"Get comfortable. You're still looking like you're waiting for bad news."

"It could still happen."

"Of course it could. But not tonight. We're going to watch this show, then we're going to raid your fridge and find something to eat. And then, if we really feel adventurous, maybe we'll play a game of cards. I'm going to be here for hours."

That seemed to be all her body needed to finally relax. As she slowly became engrossed in the newest love stories on the ship, her eyes became heavy. She shifted. Puffed up the pillow a bit under her head. Stretched out her legs.

And eventually succumbed to slumber.

When she woke up, she was lying on top of her bed. Still in her sweatshirt and sweatpants, but the elastic band had been taken out of her hair and it was in tangles around her arm like the tentacles of an octopus.

It took her a minute to figure out what had happened. To remember that she'd fallen asleep on the couch watching *The Love Boat*. That Hardy had been sitting next to her when they'd watched the show. And . . . a box holding bullets had been delivered to her in Kentucky.

Jerking to a sitting position, she pressed her hands to her face and tried to breathe deep.

And then she noticed that on the bedside table was a note. And her cell phone.

Don't be mad that I put you to bed. You would've had a crick in your neck if you'd slept on the couch all night long. I locked the door so don't worry. You're safe. If you get scared, you call. I promise I'll answer.

She stared at the cell. Reread the note. Then, to her amazement, she felt her eyelids get heavy.

It might be wrong, but she felt secure.

Hardy's note and promise were enough.

19

Sheriff Johnson was usually a good listener and bent over backwards to help out someone in need. Unfortunately, that was not how he was acting now.

"Hardy, when I visited with Stephanie, my heart went out to her. It's obvious that she's been through a lot."

Hardy felt his muscles ease. "So we're on the same page."

"I wouldn't say that. Not exactly," he added after a short pause. "I spoke with an officer in Batavia." Looking down at his notes, he continued. "Officer Will Monnon seems like he's on the ball, but things are moving slowly on his end too."

"Why? He has a body."

"Yes. And he's even sure it has to do with one of the Broken Arrows. But he doesn't have the weapon, and the kid Stephanie described is nowhere to be found."

"That's because he's around here, Billy," Hardy said impatiently.

"I hear you, Hardy, but I have to follow the law. Technically, nothing illegal has happened in my jurisdiction."

"I know I was being followed. That was him. I didn't make it up. That's why I didn't put Stephanie in Carter's apartment in Marion."

"I remember, but even if I could use your story to make a case for getting more involved, the chase was in a different county." Looking uncomfortable but also determined, he added, "I'm sorry to point out the obvious, but you've got to think about what will stand up in court. If Stephanie refuses to do anything, then we have no witness. You have to remember that you think you were being followed in the middle of a torrential downpour. The defense could find a dozen witnesses who said that cars were hydroplaning and it was hard to see four feet ahead, let alone a vehicle behind you."

Hardy gritted his teeth but couldn't deny the sheriff's words. "I hear you."

"Just to be sure, you haven't seen the vehicle since, have you?"

"No, sir."

"If this guy is on the run for murder, he's likely desperate enough to have changed vehicles by now. I want to help, but I've got a big county and a small department."

Man, but he hated that the sheriff was right. "I understand."

Right then, the sheriff's computer dinged, and his phone lit up. The sheriff had a lot of other things to do, and Hardy needed to respect his time. "Thanks for seeing me, Billy." He made a move to stand up.

"No. Listen. If something else happens, call me and I'll get someone out to the property."

"Something besides dropping off a box of bullets?"

"You know as well as I do that dropping off some ammunition isn't against the law."

"Yeah, I can only imagine how many people a defense attorney could drum up to say they've done the same thing."

Sheriff Johnson looked impatient. "I'm not trying to be uncaring, man. I feel your pain and I agree that this Amish girl really might be in trouble. But if I start getting involved in things without due cause or get involved in affairs out of my jurisdiction, not only will I get in a heap of trouble, but any case they might eventually come up with may get thrown out."

"I hear you."

"I hope so."

Standing up, Hardy offered his hand. "Sorry I've been acting like an impatient jerk. It's just that I was used to handling insurgents for the Army. I knew what to do. All of this surrounding an Amish girl? Well, it's out of my comfort zone."

"For what it's worth, this would be out of most folks' zone too," Billy replied as they shook hands. "Don't give up, though. If the guy is dropping off bullets, he's getting desperate, and desperate people make mistakes."

Those words rang in Hardy's ears as he drove back onto the ranch's property. When he approached the gate, Crenshaw pushed a button to let him in.

"Afternoon," he said when Hardy rolled his window down.

"How's it going?"

"It's been quiet. We've had a fair share of vehicles pass by, but no one slowed down." Stuffing his hands in his pockets, he added, "I've also been trying to see if anyone is driving by more than once."

"Any luck?"

"Nope. The only cars that have done that are the usual vehicles I always see. You know. Mrs. Peabody getting groceries and such."

Crenshaw was good. Very good. But he couldn't see everything that happened every second of the day. "Do you need another set of eyes? I can call in a couple of guys who used to work here."

"Dan is at the other gate right now, and Foster's home but is heading in soon. He'll take Dan's place. Dan will come here, and then I'll go off for a spell. We've got a rotation going on."

"Fair enough, but I'll see if Sully can come in."

Crenshaw raised his eyebrows. "Sully? You sure? He's almost sixty."

"He's not that old and he can handle a firearm better than either Dan or Foster."

"Understood, Boss."

"Good. Pass the word. If someone sees anything suspicious or out of the ordinary, let everyone know."

"Yes, sir."

Rolling back up his window, he drove down the gravel road, taking a moment to look left and right. Scanning the fields.

Ahead was a paved road leading up to the big house. It reminded him that he still needed to touch base with Carter about the package that had showed up. Busy as he'd been connecting with the sheriff and checking the perimeter all day, he'd only made one attempt to call his boss, but it'd gone straight to voicemail. Might as well start prepping the big house in case Carter decided to return. More than likely, he'd want to come down once he heard about the latest developments. He knew the housekeeper had visited there yesterday, but he wanted someone to turn on lights for Carter.

Wanting to check on Stephanie, he realized that he didn't trust Dan or Foster to wander through the big house unescorted. He trusted them for security on the grounds, but the Russell house was filled with expensive things. And it was his friend's home.

He stopped in the truck and dialed Sully's number.

"Hardy, long time no hear."

"How you doing?"

"Good, but I hear something in your voice that says this call ain't about fishing."

"I wish it was, but you're right." He paused. "You got a minute?"

"Always."

"I need you here for a couple of weeks. Probably part time, but it might be more than that."

"Hardy, if you need me, I'm there."

"I can't tell you how glad I am to hear that. Let me fill you in." As succinctly as possible, he laid out everything that had happened and why Sully was needed.

"Understood. You need me now?"

"Yeah."

"I'll get dressed, pull out my weapon and harness, and be over within thirty."

"Go in the main gate. Crenshaw's there."

Sully chuckled. "That man's demeanor alone will scare off half the population. He any friendlier?"

"I'm not sure. You tell me. Anyway, I'm also going to send you the codes to the big house. I want you to come straight over, do a walk-through, and turn on lights."

"Mr. Russell on the way?"

"Not sure yet, but it'd be good to have the house ready just in case."

"Gotcha. And then?"

"Talk to Crenshaw about getting on some of the shifts. If I need something more, I'll let you know."

"Roger that."

"Thanks, Sully."

"Glad to be needed," he said before hanging up.

Feeling better, Hardy took the gravel road off to the left and headed toward the cabins. He tried Carter's cell again while he drove, but hung up as soon as he heard voicemail kick in. He'd have to try again later. Maybe it was time to hang out with Stephanie for a spell. Just to make sure she was okay.

Maybe she'd be watching *The Love Boat* again. He could tease her about that and watch an episode or two by her side. He'd enjoy that.

He was starting to enjoy anything that would put a smile on her face.

20

The restaurant that Carter took her to was everything that Beverly had imagined it would be. No, it surpassed her expectations, which was pretty hard to do, since she'd always wanted to dine here.

The Board Room was situated on the main floor of an old mansion in downtown Cincinnati. The home had been built at the turn of the century, when the area had been a popular spot due to its proximity to both the Ohio River and the train station. Over time, like the rest of the area, it had gone through a variety of owners and remodels.

As she looked around the cozy dining room with its fireplace, soft music, and candlelit tables, Bev sighed. This place was gorgeous, expensive, and romantic.

Beverly had tried for maybe a second to pretend she wasn't dazzled by the place. After that, she knew she was wearing the same giddy expression small children wore when they went to Disneyland for the first time.

She wasn't ashamed either. The place was special, and she was not likely to visit again. She was so glad she'd given in to impulse and bought a new dress and heels. She couldn't remember the last time she'd worn a pair of high heels. They didn't feel comfortable, but whatever. At least she hadn't tripped walking up the mansion's front steps.

Sitting across from her, wearing a pair of dark slacks, a gray shirt, and a navy blazer was Carter Russell. He looked handsome, natty, and perfectly at ease. He was also smiling at her in open amusement.

She might have been embarrassed if she'd been with some-one other than Carter. Or, if she wasn't so darn excited to be sitting in the place. But she'd known the man for years and had heard stories about him from her brother for lon-ger than that. He might be her secret crush, but he didn't intimidate her.

At least, not too much.

"You doing okay there, Beverly?" he asked. "I'm sorry we had to push this dinner back so late."

Carter had an emergency to take care of and had asked to push their date back two hours. Now it was close to nine o'clock. Far later than she ever ate, but she wasn't complain-ing. At least she had his complete attention now. "I am. Better than okay, actually."

His lips twitched. "Good."

"I bet you're thinking that you've taken a hick out to din-ner. If you were, you'd be right."

His eyes flashed as he leaned back in his chair. "I didn't think that at all. As a matter of fact, I was sitting here feel-ing pretty proud of myself. Not only did I get you to agree to come out with me for dinner, but you seem pleased with my choice."

"This restaurant is one of the most gorgeous places I've ever seen. It's even better than the pictures I saw of it in the magazines."

"Magazines?"

"Don't ask. Anyway, I should probably be telling you that you didn't need to take me here. A burger place would be just fine with me. But I just can't bring myself to do that."

"Good."

Though it was a tad awkward, she forced herself to continue. "I was also thinking that I was really glad I said yes to you. I . . . well, I'm beginning to realize that you're a lot more than I thought, Carter."

All traces of amusement fled his expression. "I'm hoping that's a good thing."

His voice sounded strained, as if he was weighing his words. Like he wanted to be careful not to misspeak. All of it surprised her. First, because he knew she was a social worker and had to have guessed that practically no one at work ever worried about offending or upsetting her.

But also because he was Carter Russell. Her brother's boss. He was rich and powerful and well-known. She was none of those things.

"It is." She was tempted to say more but was pretty sure any explanation she gave would either sound rude or condescending. The truth of it was that he'd always been so handsome, charming, and polished, she'd never given too much thought to the person he was inside. Of the man he was at his core.

"Now you've got me curious. Does Hardy never talk about me?" He smirked. "Or was he so full of stories about his green, hapless lieutenant that you pictured me to be completely ineffectual in real life?"

She felt a blush heat her cheeks. Hardy had told her stories about the green lieutenant that he'd had to look out for. But he'd also stated that Carter ended up being a fine officer—

which said a lot because Hardy hadn't held too many officers in high esteem.

But most importantly, Hardy had stated that Carter might not have been cut out for Army life, but he sure did well in the business world. He was shrewd, successful, and a little feared. Mr. Russell was a man that few people took advantage of—and especially not twice.

Carter laughed. "He did talk about me, didn't he?"

"He shared a few stories about his deployment, but not a lot."

"Uh-huh."

"Okay, he shared more than a few stories, but not too many stories involved you." Practically feeling skepticism rolling off of him, she added, "And the stories that did mention you weren't bad."

"It's okay if they were." Carefully aligning the silverware in front of him, he continued. "When your brother and I first met, I really was as green as a cucumber. Even in ROTC in college I'd been coddled a bit. I hadn't believed that was possible, but when I landed in Afghanistan, I discovered that to be true."

Her heart went out to him. "I'm glad you survived."

"Me too. But more importantly, I'm glad that my ignorance didn't inadvertently hurt any of the soldiers in my command. I mean, more than they were hurt."

She knew he was talking about the angry scar on Hardy's face. "I don't think you should be so hard on yourself. I wasn't there, but you did serve honorably. You must have been better than you think."

Meeting her eyes, he added, "If I was, I have Hardy to thank for that. He was everything I wasn't. A good leader. Never got ruffled. Focused." He chuckled. "It's a wonder the two of us got along as well as we did. There were moments when he was probably wondering what he'd done wrong to have to put up with me."

"Do you regret serving? Hardy says his life in the Army was hard, but he's never regretted it."

"I've never regretted it either. I'm proud of serving my country and met a lot of men and women who were pretty special. Hardy, especially."

They were interrupted by their first course. Each had ordered a green salad. Hers was supplemented with blue cheese, toasted pecans, dried fruit, and pepitas. His was simply a bed of lettuce with a vinaigrette on the side.

"May I get you anything else, Mr. Russell?" the server asked.

He turned to her. "Beverly, do you need anything?"

"No. I'm fine."

"We're good for now. Thank you, Alaina."

She smiled prettily. "Of course, sir."

When they were alone again, Beverly murmured, "I guess you come here often."

"I used to. Back when I spent more time here. Now I spend as much time at the ranch as I can."

Unwarranted, jealousy stabbed her. She was just one of many dates to be by his side. Glancing at her dress, she noticed that the silky material was in fact a polyester blend, and the bold flower pattern probably looked like she was on her way to a luau instead of an elegant restaurant.

"I should've asked you about your favorites on the menu," she said in a light tone.

He set down his fork. "It doesn't matter what my favorites are. I want you to get whatever you want."

"Hmm."

"Beverly, what's going on? You seem uncomfortable all of a sudden."

"It's nothing. I, uh, just feel like I don't fit in here."

"I think you fit in just fine. I'm glad you're here."

"Is that something you tell all your dates?"

A line formed between his brows. "No. I'd be lying if I told you that I didn't date much. Or, if I said that I've never taken a woman here. I have. But you're mistaken if you think that any of those dates meant as much as this one does to me."

"You sound so sure."

"That's because I am. You're important to me, Beverly. If you're nervous, then I'm glad, because I'm nervous too. I don't want to mess this up."

Glad she didn't have her mouth full of food, she carefully set her fork down. "Carter, you don't have to say—"

"Truth is that I've heard a lot about you from Hardy, Bev. When we deployed, he emailed you as often as he could. He shared stories about how smart you were. About your scholarship to college. About how your reputation in your high school made his teachers give him a second look, even though it was apparent that he was never the student you were."

He took a deep breath. "More recently, he's told me about your work with foster kids, especially the teens. He's proud of you. Very proud of you." He lowered his voice. "I knew I wanted to meet his sister in person long before our paths crossed. And ever since we first exchanged a few words, I wanted to see you again. Talk to you more. And now, here you are, looking so gorgeous and sitting across from me."

Who said things like that? Her mouth suddenly dry, she tried to come up with the right response. Not surprisingly, nothing came to mind. "I don't know what to say."

"You can let me know that you need more time to eat your salad."

She looked up to her left. Alaina was standing there.

"Was the salad not to your liking?" she asked.

What had she been doing? Carter's plate was half empty. She'd barely taken two bites. "I'm sorry, I seem to be taking my time."

"Give us a bit longer, please," Carter said. After Alaina walked away, he said, "I want you to take your time."

"Thanks." She forked a piece of romaine and popped it in her mouth.

Leaning back, he took a sip of his drink, swirled the brown liquid around the giant ice cube for a second before replacing it.

"The truth is that I haven't dated much in the past couple of years."

"Why not?" She frowned. "I'm sorry. That's none of my business."

"I don't mind. I got out of a longer relationship a few years ago. Diane . . ." He paused. "Diane and I had our share of ups and downs."

"I'm sorry it didn't work out."

"I was too, for a time." He shrugged. "She found a guy and married him a year after we broke up. What about you?"

"I used to date a lot more than I do now." She winked. "Which is hardly ever. Can you tell how rusty I am?"

"What are you talking about?"

Why had she opened her mouth? "Nothing. Forget I said anything." She focused on her salad.

A few moments later, after Alaina had returned to pick up their plates, Carter said, "Beverly, your brother adores you. You take care of people all day long but never act as if it's a problem or get overwhelmed. Every time I've had the chance to see you, you've been smiling. Positive." He lowered his voice. "You also happen to be beautiful."

Beautiful? No. No, she was not. She was a lot of things. Smart. A hard worker. Feminine. A poor conversationalist at cocktail parties.

But she'd never been all that pretty. Hardy had gotten the looks. Even with the wicked scar running across his face, there was something about him that was striking. Something compelling about him. Almost an aura that made a person want to be in his circle, just because he would be there.

"Beverly, what did I say that upset you?"

There was that dark, sexy drawl that somehow sounded high-class and dangerous all at the same time.

Feeling like the wind had just gotten knocked out of her, she froze. Studied his expression. Just to make sure that he hadn't been teasing. But all she saw in his face was sincerity. "Nothing."

"It was something."

"Fine. I don't like false compliments."

"I don't either." When she raised an eyebrow, he said, "I wasn't lying. I think you're beautiful. Gorgeous."

"I don't know how to respond to that."

"Sure you do. Say thank you."

She gaped. Wanted to tell him that he was being far too full of himself. But that would just be surly. So she dutifully said the words. "Thank you."

"There you go." His eyes warmed. Obviously pleased. "That wasn't so hard, was it?"

She felt like rolling her eyes. "Mr. Russell, you are almost as bossy as Hardy."

He grinned. "That's doubtful. You forget, I've seen your brother in action. I can't compare."

"I beg to differ."

"Fine. How about this then? I'm not going to boss you around. But I'm also not going to let you put yourself down."

"I'm not."

"Then believe me when I tell you that I think you're beautiful."

Tears pricked her eyes. She never thought a compliment like that could make her cry, but it seemed she was wrong. Luckily, Alaina had returned with their meals. She smiled as she placed Beverly's salmon in front of her.

"Thank you."

"Does the fish look like it's prepared to your liking?" she asked.

"I think so. Thank you."

After placing another piece of fish—this one sole—in front of Carter, Alaina smiled a tad more brightly. "Does everything look to your liking, Mr. Russell?"

Carter didn't spare her a glance. "Everything looks good. Thank you."

Just as Alaina walked away, Carter's phone rang. He froze, then reached for it out of the inside of his jacket. "Sorry about this. Most people know to leave me alone . . . but this is your brother," he explained as he connected and held it up to his ear. "Hardy? What's happened?"

Beverly figured the right thing to do would be to take a bite of her meal. It would be rude to stare and listen. But how could she not? He was speaking to her brother.

After a few more seconds passed, he said, "What do you think? Do you think the sheriff's advice has merit?" He swallowed. "I see." Carter's voice turned clipped as his expression grew more concerned.

Bev gave up trying to eat. She even gave up her best intentions to look anywhere but directly at him.

After meeting Bev's gaze, Carter averted his eyes. "Are you sure?" His lips pursed. "No. No, you did the right thing. I'll be there soon. Tell Stephanie to try not to worry. We'll take care of it." He shook his head. "Of her."

She couldn't take it anymore. "What happened?" she whispered.

He held up a finger. "I'm not sure," he said to Hardy as he raised his chin and met her gaze again. "No. There's no need. I'm with her now. I'll ask and let you know."

He frowned. "I'm not going to answer that. You already know the answer, Hardy," he said before hanging up.

The moment he disconnected, Bev leaned closer. "What happened?"

"A package arrived at the ranch for Stephanie," he said. "It was from Timothy."

She shook her head. "I don't understand. I mean, she was supposed to be safe there."

"I agree."

"How could Timothy know where she is? How could he have found her so easily?"

"I'm not sure. Maybe he's connected to someone bigger—or there are more people from his gang interested in Stephanie talking." A dark look filled his gaze. "Or not talking."

"What was in the box? Did Hardy tell you?"

"Yeah." His expression hardened. "Inside was a box of bullets—.22s."

She was horrified. "He's taunting her."

"He is."

"I can't believe it. He . . . he wasn't like this a couple of years ago. There was a sweetness to him." She sighed. "I really failed him."

"You can't put his actions on your shoulders. You know that, Bev."

She nodded. "How's Stephanie?"

"She's asleep. Hardy's already contacted the local sheriff. Between the ranch's security and the county stepping in, Stephanie will be safe."

Safe felt like such a relative word. No one might be bruising Stephanie, but the psychological effects had to be worse. She'd seen a murder, been injured, forced to leave home, and then put into the company of Bev's nice but scary-looking brother.

And now everything she endured was for nothing. The murderer still found her. "I bet she's scared to death, though."

Looking grim, Carter nodded. "Hardy said he stayed with her most of last night. They watched TV until she fell asleep."

"What?" She wasn't sure if she was more shocked about Hardy doing that or that Stephanie had watched TV in the first place.

"Stephanie didn't want to be alone, and Hardy said he didn't want her to be scared." He waved a hand. "Something about how he wasn't going to be able to sleep anyway so he might as well make sure she wasn't in danger."

"Hardy's a good man."

Carter's expression didn't ease. "He is a good man, but he's worried, Bev. Hardy can't help with security if he's trying to keep her calm and happy. And he needs her calm. If she gets too rattled . . ."

"Stephanie's going to do something rash."

"Exactly." Looking resigned, he continued. "I'm sorry, but I'm afraid I'm going to have to cut our meal short. I'm going to head down tonight. I've got a lot of men on the property, but I need to be there too." Looking pained. "I knew that too. When I called you the other day, I was determined to stay awhile. But after being there twenty-four hours, I figured I was just in the way. I should have stayed."

"I understand." It was his ranch, after all.

"I'm still hoping you'll come with me, Bev. I don't want you to put it off any longer. I know you've got those kids . . . but I think she's really going to need you. Stay with Stephanie in the cabin. Give her support until she feels more comfortable or until these guys are taken care of. This girl needs you."

"I know she does." Just then, Justin's face appeared in her mind. How he was so alone and trying not to care. Worse, he wasn't the only one who was depending on her. "I . . . I want to be there. But Carter, some of my kids? Well, they really need me too."

But, her conscience reminded her, the only reason Stephanie was there was because she'd asked Hardy to look out for her in Kentucky. And now she was living on Carter's ranch and had turned the whole place upside down.

"I understand." Carter continued to stare at her, though. Telling her without words that he was hoping she would still come.

"I don't have a choice, do I?" she asked, speaking out loud as much to him as herself. "I'm the one who set everything in motion. She's my responsibility."

"You did not start this, Bev. Stephanie witnessed a murder. She was grazed by a bullet. When you first tried to get her to go to the police, she refused. When she wanted to go home, you convinced her to go to Crittenden County so she—and her family—would be safe. You've done the best you could."

"Maybe. I don't know anymore." Was Stephanie in a better place than if she was back at home? Should she have ignored the girl's wishes and forced her to talk to Will?

"You tried to help her, and you did. If not for you stepping in, Stephanie would probably already be dead."

"So what are you saying? That I've done enough?"

He grinned. "I guess I'm not. I mean, here I am, saying that I recognize your other responsibilities but still asking you to head south with me."

Unsure what to say, Bev was still staring at him when the server returned to their table.

"Mr. Russell, is everything to your liking?"

Carter turned to Bev. "What matters is the lady's opinion. Beverly, is there anything you don't like?"

She almost felt as if it was a trick question. She was in a five-star restaurant with her longtime crush. Hiding her amusement, she nodded. "Everything is perfect."

Something flickered in his eyes as he met her gaze. Without looking away, he said, "Thank you, Alaina."

After the server walked away, Beverly chuckled. "Goodness, Carter."

"What?"

"You . . . you're making me feel like someone out of an old Doris Day movie."

"I don't understand." He looked perplexed, which she belatedly realized was an understandable reaction. He did not look like the type of man to watch old 1960s romances on late-night TV.

She waved a hand. "You know, completely catered to."

He visibly relaxed. "If that's how I'm making you feel, I'm glad. You deserve someone to spoil you a little."

"That's sweet."

He lifted a brow. "But?"

"But you make me feel off-kilter."

"I feel the same way."

She stared into his eyes. Knew that he was being completely sincere. And that sincerity seemed to erase all her doubts and slip all her intentions into place. "Okay, I'll go with you. I need to help Stephanie. And Hardy. And you. If I don't, I'll regret it. I just hope . . ."

"Yes?"

"I just hope I won't let Stephanie down. Or somehow get in your way."

"You won't."

"We'll see."

Reaching out, he took her hand and pressed it between his palms. "It would be impossible for you to get in my way. I'm glad you're going."

She liked how her hand looked in his. Liked the way his voice had softened again when he spoke to her. "Me too."

"I'll let Hardy know that we'll be on our way soon. Now, we better finish this meal."

"This gorgeous, perfect meal."

"That is probably half cold by now." Still holding her hand, he ran one finger along the top. So lightly, she should've barely felt it. Instead, it was as if his every touch went straight to her nervous system. She felt goose bumps rise on her arm.

"I'll make this up to you."

That sounded promising, but she wasn't going to count on that happening. So much could happen in the next few days. Someone could get hurt, or his patience could run out with both her and Stephanie.

Or once he got to know her better, he might realize that she really wasn't beautiful and she really wasn't special.

She was just Hardy's older sister.

The idea that one day she'd become something more to him was tempting, though.

So tempting she was willing to see this through. For herself, her brother, Carter, and most of all for one Amish girl who was afraid and all alone.

And wondering what in the world she had done to deserve what happened.

At least Beverly knew she could tell her that. She'd done nothing at all. That was undeniable.

21

Though it was midmorning and she'd been awake for hours, Stephanie was still having a hard time believing that Beverly had arrived. Late last night, long after she'd fallen asleep, her phone had started ringing.

Frightened to death, she'd answered it quickly, certain that it would be Hardy telling her that more danger was on the way. Instead, Bev had been on the line.

"Stephanie, I'm so glad you answered right away," she said in a chatty tone. "Any chance you were awake?"

"I'm awake now."

She sighed. "Sorry about that. I didn't want you to get scared when I walked in your door."

"Hold on, what did you say?"

"I'm with Carter Russell. We decided that we couldn't let you and my brother have all the fun," she joked. "He's going to drop me off at your cabin in about an hour. See you soon."

After they disconnected, Stephanie had practically jumped out of bed, she'd been so happy. Later, when Carter came in the cabin with Beverly, Stephanie had felt nervous and awkward. Yes, she was pleased to see Beverly, but they were strangers.

And Carter was movie-star handsome and had a way about him that oozed confidence and power. Stephanie hadn't known what to say.

She should have expected Beverly to take care of things. She'd lightly hugged Carter, said that he could visit with them in the morning, and then ushered him out the door.

Then, while Stephanie was wondering about sleeping arrangements, Beverly announced that Hardy had told her that the couch folded out and there were extra linens, blankets, and pillows in the tiny hall closet. Fifteen minutes later, she told Stephanie that she was exhausted, and they could talk in the morning.

Which was why Stephanie was tiptoeing around the kitchen now. Beverly was still sound asleep.

Now that she was a pro at her coffee machine, Stephanie made herself a cup of coffee and sat at the small table to wait. If she felt more comfortable, she would've gone outside on the porch, but that wasn't an option.

"Sorry," Bev said, startling her thoughts. "I didn't mean to sleep in."

"You're fine."

"Give me a minute and I'll join you. Would you mind making me a cup too?"

"Of course not." She was delighted to have something to occupy her hands.

When Beverly emerged again, she was dressed in faded jeans and a long-sleeved T-shirt, and her hair was brushed and shiny. "Thanks for the coffee," she said as she sat down in the chair across from Stephanie. "Now, tell me how you are."

"I don't know."

"You don't?"

"It's a mixture of a lot of things, I guess. Sometimes I'm okay. Sometimes I'm bored. Other times I feel angry and out of sorts. I don't like that this happened to me."

"Of course you don't. I'm sure all those emotions are common in a situation like this." After taking another sip, she added, "Even though Will told me that the cops in Batavia are still on the case, I'm sorry you've been here alone."

"It's all right. Hardy's been spending a lot of time with me."

"He has?"

Beverly looked shocked. Stephanie felt her cheeks heat. "He's been nice. We've become friends."

"That's good." She smiled. "I'm sorry. It's just that my brother's always had a reputation for being rather gruff. I knew he would protect you and be kind. I . . ." She laughed softly. "I guess I've never thought about him being good company."

"He's been easy to hang out with," she said, electing not to mention all the hours he'd spent by her side watching *The Love Boat*.

"Well, that's good." Looking a little scattered, Bev rubbed her arms. "Are you chilly?"

"A bit."

"Do you ever light the fire?"

"No."

"You know what? I think a cozy fire is just what we need." She walked around the unfolded couch and crouched down in front of the fireplace. "Do you know if the flue is open?"

"I have no idea."

Bev peered in and jiggled a lever. "I got it!" After putting a couple of pieces of wood in the grate, she lit a match. Then another one. "Uh-oh. This might take me a minute. What do you think?"

A knock at the door saved Stephanie from replying.

"Steph, it's me!" Hardy called out. "Carter's here too. You ladies decent?"

"We are!" She hurried to unlock the door.

And then promptly felt self-conscious again. Hardy's eyes went directly to her, searching her face. "You all right?"

"Yes." She nodded to Carter. "Gut matin."

"Good morning to you, Stephanie," he murmured. "Okay if we come in? Hardy and I have been up for hours."

"Hours?" Beverly said as the men walked in and Hardy closed the door behind them. "Did you not sleep at all, Carter?"

"I slept enough." Looking sheepish, he added, "Sometimes it takes me a while to get settled back into the big house. It's a lot of space for one man."

"You going to give me a hug, Bev?" Hardy asked.

"Of course."

Stephanie felt a lump form in her throat as she watched Hardy wrap his sister into a warm hug. It was obvious that their bond was strong—even though they didn't see each other very much.

"Would you like some coffee?" Stephanie asked.

"I'll take some, if it's no trouble," Carter said.

"It isn't. I'm good at making coffee now."

Walking into the kitchenette, she pulled out another cup while Beverly and her brother folded up the couch and put the pillows back in the closet.

In no time, the four of them were gathered in the living room. She and Bev sitting side by side on the couch, while Hardy was sitting in the lone chair and Carter was leaning against a wall and staring at the fireplace. "What have you gals been doing?"

"I was just attempting to light the fireplace."

Hardy chuckled. "Attempting?"

"I couldn't get the wood to start."

"I'll take care of it," Carter said. Kneeling on the hearth, he added, "You should've texted me or your brother. One of us could've helped you."

Bev folded her arms over her chest. "I'm not about to start calling my little brother to do something so basic. And certainly not you."

"Why not?"

Stephanie tried not to smile as Bev blushed.

"Because I can do it, Carter." She got to her feet.

When Stephanie looked at Hardy, he met her gaze and winked. And did nothing.

"Bev, go sit down," Carter said.

When it looked like she was going to argue, Stephanie couldn't help but speak. "Danke, Carter. We would appreciate your help."

Bev stilled, then finally moved to one side. "Fine."

Looking at the pile of logs, Carter rearranged them. Opening up a small wooden box situated to the right of the hearth, he pulled out three pieces of treated kindling and added the kindling on top. Finally, he opened up the container of matches, scraped the end of one along the fireplace, and lit the wood.

Two minutes later, after a few forceful puffs of air, the wood caught and a fire began to blaze.

"You got it!" Stephanie said. "Gut job."

"Thanks." He grinned at her. "Things should warm up in no time."

Instead of looking grateful, Bev looked impressed. "You did that so fast."

"I wouldn't be much of a rancher if I couldn't even start a fire, Bev."

"I know." She looked away. "I just thought . . . well, I don't know what I thought."

"Maybe you thought I only knew how to make reservations at fancy restaurants?"

"Of course not," she said quickly.

But even Stephanie caught the look of guilt in Beverly's eyes. Hardy grunted. "Bev."

Carter found his cup, drained half of it, and then placed it on the coffee table. "Stephanie, I'm going to take my leave and let you and Hardy fill Bev in about everything."

"Please be careful," Stephanie said.

He patted the holster that she now realized was hidden in the small of his back. "I'll be all right, and I'll be only a call away. I know you already know the drill, but we have a lot of people here seeing to your safety. If anything seems off or odd at all, you need to let us know. Someone will come running."

"Danke—for everything."

"Of course." He smiled at her before slipping out the door.

When it was just the three of them, Bev pressed her palms to her face. "Boy, I sure messed that up, didn't I?"

"By insinuating that my boss—who grew up on this ranch—wouldn't know how to light a fire in the fireplace?" Hardy asked in a sarcastic tone. "Yeah, sissy. I'd say you messed up real good."

22

The jarring ringtone pulled him from a restless sleep. Timothy grabbed the burner on the second ring. "Yeah?"

"Timothy?"

He sat up with a jerk as every one of his nerve endings seemed to catch on fire. "Audrey, is that you?" He couldn't believe it. The woman who'd long held his heart had existed in only his dreams for so long, it was hard to comprehend that she'd reached out to him. Maybe . . .

Then reality hit him hard. He was holding a burner phone. Only one other person had that number, and it wasn't anyone Audrey should ever know. "Where are you?" he asked in a rush. "Are you okay?"

"I'm on campus. I was walking back to my dorm when, uh, I met one of your friends."

Her voice was trembling. She was scared and confused. The thought that she'd ever think that he'd allowed someone from the Arrows near her brought him to his knees.

Though, wasn't that what he'd done? He'd needed to feel like he belonged so badly that he'd chosen a gang over her. Deep regret lodged in his throat, making it hard to speak. "What's going on? Talk to me."

But all he heard was a cry as the phone shifted hands.

"I'd forgotten your girl was such a pretty thing. So sweet too."

Timothy ached to lash out. To tell Kane that he should have left her alone. That Audrey had nothing to do with his life anymore. It was by choice too. By her choice. And, as always, she was right. He was not only not good for her, he was so bad.

"You not going to say anything, buddy?"

At last, Timothy found his voice. But did he have anything of worth to say? He didn't know. "Audrey has nothing to do with me. We broke up when I chose the Arrows over her. She's a college student now. She doesn't know anything."

"I don't doubt that's true. Right now, I don't want anything to do with you either. You've made a mess around here and owe us money. Stew ain't pleased. That's why I decided to take a walk and just happened to run into Miss Audrey. After we got to talking, she agreed that you might need a reminder about being responsible. No one's forgotten about what you owe us, Timothy." Kane's voice sounded almost playful, like he was enjoying the game he was playing with them.

"I haven't forgotten."

"That may be true, but the problem I'm having, at least at the moment, is that two full days have passed."

"There's been nothing to report."

"You need to change that, Timothy."

Sure, he'd delivered that package to the Russell Ranch, but he wasn't going to tell Kane that. Timothy was trying to get Stephanie to run away and hide, not die.

"Look, I've been all over Crittenden County. I've talked to people. Asked questions. No one's seen the girl." Technically, that was the truth.

"That's where you're wrong, Tim. Someone has."

"But what if she's moved on? I'm no detective."

Kane sighed. It was a long, drawn-out affair. Timothy was familiar with it. He knew it was meant to convey irritation and a whole lot of sarcasm in one fell swoop.

"Timothy, Timothy, Timothy. It's like you hear the words but don't understand what I'm saying. Let me try to be clearer. If you want Miss Audrey to stay alive, kill the witness—and give me proof." His voice took on a new, almost teasing tone. "And give us the money we're owed. That's it."

Panic was setting in. Kane was giving him two almost impossible tasks. "You know it's going to take time to do both. If I give you the money, will it be enough for you to leave Audrey alone?"

"It might buy you some time, but not much. If you really want Miss Audrey to never see me again, then you need to learn to follow directions, Tim."

A sinking feeling settled deep inside his soul as he processed every word that Kane hadn't said. He wasn't going to live much longer. His only problem now was how he was going to be able to accomplish both tasks in order to make sure Audrey remained alive.

"Audrey is innocent. Don't harm her."

"No one's hurt her. I'm not hurting her now. Like I said, our paths crossed when I just happened to be taking a walk on the campus. Isn't that so?" he murmured to her. "Of course, there's a whole lot of other guys who wouldn't mind paying her a visit before we hand her over to Stew."

Timothy listened for Audrey, but he didn't hear her say a word. She was probably so scared she was incapable of speaking. "How long do I have?"

"We've already played this game, son. You're way past the time limit we gave you."

"For Audrey. What's the timeline for you to leave her alone?"

"I'm glad you understand the seriousness of the situation. And because you've finally gotten smarter, I'm willing to be generous. You have three days."

That surprised him. "Three days. Are you sure?"

"Positive. We've got some other things going on. Believe it or not, we can't be sitting around, waiting for you to do what we ask you to do."

"Can I speak to her?"

"Audrey, do you want to speak to the man who's the root of all your problems? No? Well, that don't surprise me none. I would have broken things off with him too. You can do better, doll. A whole lot."

"Kane—"

"She don't want to talk to you, boy, and all I'm doing is feeling frustrated because you're making me do things I don't want to do. I really don't like bothering nice girls like Audrey. I'd rather her never know that people like me exist."

Softening his voice, he added, "Wouldn't that be something, if a person could live their life with blinders on? Purposely oblivious to the evil surrounding them? It's a shame that she won't be like that no more." He lowered his voice. "You've ruined her, Timothy. And you've got three days to determine whether or not a man like me becomes just a bad memory . . . or her new best friend. Because I promise you, Stew won't be kind."

"I understand."

"You'd best be either wiring or delivering the money as soon as possible, Timothy. And don't you start thinking that I don't mean what I say. If you run off, I will find you. And then I'm gonna make you sit bleeding while I play you videos of Audrey's last, very difficult days."

When he heard Audrey whimper, tears filled his eyes. She'd been the best thing to ever happen to him, and he'd not only broken her heart, he was on the verge of ruining her. "I'll call. I'll call before the deadline. I promise."

The phone disconnected.

Then he started to cry. He cried like he hadn't in years. In over a decade. Since the day—

No. He wasn't going to go there. He wasn't going to remember. There was only so much trauma and pain a heart could take, and he'd already reached his limit for the day.

With shaking hands, he rolled out of bed. Lit a cigarette and inhaled. Felt the burn in his lungs and appreciated it. This, he knew. He now had $631 in his pocket. The guy he'd killed had owed the gang two grand.

Knowing Kane, he was going to expect more. He'd call it interest or whatever else he could make up to make sure that Timothy came up short.

So, three grand would be better.

Either three grand or find a way onto that ranch and kill the girl. Take a picture and get out of there before he got shot too.

He never thought he'd play roulette with women's lives, but he had no choice. If he had to choose between Audrey's life and the girl's, there was only one option.

If he failed, Audrey would pay the price. And she'd already lost too much because of him.

Extinguishing the cigarette by tossing it in an old soda can, he headed to the shower. The clock was ticking. He had to go find a couple of people to rob.

The more, the better.

23

Time was going far too slow for Stephanie. The problem was that she didn't know how to do *nothing*.

After the excitement—and yes, the confusion—about lighting a fire, the cabin was toasty warm. That was a good thing too, since the wind had picked up and rain was starting to fall. Yet again.

Hours passed. After she and Bev talked for a while, Bev pulled out a book and started reading, while periodically looking out the window. She hadn't said a word about Carter, but Stephanie suspected the man was on her new friend's mind.

Or perhaps Bev was also looking for Hardy. After visiting with them a few more minutes, he'd left the cabin too. Stephanie imagined he was probably driving around the perimeter of the property, meeting with the other hands and guards, checking the horses, and whatever other things he seemed to have on his plate.

What didn't escape Stephanie's notice, however, was that Bev hadn't seemed too worried about him. When Stephanie had shared that she would feel terrible if Hardy got hurt because of her, Bev had merely said that he was fine.

But to Stephanie's mind, Hardy was neither bulletproof nor inexhaustible. Sure, he was big and strong and possessed a self-assuredness about him that few people could carry so well.

But that didn't mean he didn't also need a gentle touch or a look of concern.

Which she had no business thinking about.

Bothered by the direction of her thoughts, Stephanie walked into the kitchen, pulled out a soup pot, and filled it with water.

Beverly looked up from her book. "What are you up to?"

"I'm going to make soup."

"You've got enough ingredients for that?"

"There's always ingredients for soup, Bev. At least, that's what mei mommi used to say."

Walking closer, she leaned on one of the counters. "You call your mother Mommy?"

"No. Mommi." She repeated the word, this time with more of an accent. A slight addition of a guttural sound. "That means grandmother. It's an endearing way of saying it. Like Grandma."

"Ah. Well, that makes sense what she said about soup, then. Grandmothers have that way about them, don't you think?"

"I suppose." Pulling open the refrigerator, she got out the carrots and celery and started chopping them on the counter. There were no cutting boards, but she didn't need that. She'd chopped plenty of vegetables on top of plates and countertops.

"Would you like some help?"

Stephanie glanced up in surprise. She didn't know why, but she hadn't imagined that Bev was the type to enjoy working in the kitchen. "Would you like to help?"

"I wouldn't ask if I didn't."

She pointed to a cupboard. "There's an onion inside. Chop it up. If you wouldn't mind?"

"Of course not." Picking up another knife, she was soon dicing the onion into uniform cuts on a plate.

"You've done this before."

"I have." Bev flashed her a smile before returning her attention to the project. "My mother wasn't around much growing up. She worked a lot—one of the places was a grocery store. She was always bringing home old produce."

"Then she would cook it for you?"

"No. Our mom did her best for us, but she was always trying to fall in love." Looking a little pained, Bev said, "Being alone was hard for her." After dicing more of the onion, she added, "In any case, sometimes I'd check out a cookbook from the library and try a couple of things. Or Hardy and I would simply experiment. Then Mom would eat whatever we made when she got home."

"You and your brother raised yourselves."

"We had a lot of responsibility, that is true. But I wouldn't say we never got any help. Mom taught us a lot. When she actually was around, she was with us, you know?"

"Kind of." Their situation sounded confusing.

"See, when Mom was home, she wasn't trying to clean or watch TV or whatever. She wanted to be with us. Every once in a while, we'd go to the park or something else that was free." Her voice drifted off. "Once a year we'd go on a vacation. Sometimes it was just a motel with a pool with our meals at fast-food places, but that was special."

Stephanie was mesmerized by Bev's sweet tone. She'd accepted her mother's imperfections, and somehow she'd done the same with others in her life. Like her foster kids. Like her. "You made the best of your situation."

"Yes, we did. There was no other choice." Looking a little melancholy, she added, "In that house was where I learned to make the best of my reality instead of spending all my time wishing things were different."

Remembering Bev's tough talk when they first met, Stephanie nodded. "I didn't like hearing your advice, but I can't say that it wasn't helpful."

"You may not believe this, but it was the only thing I could think of to get you to accept my help." Bev shrugged. "Anyway, I guess I'm trying to say that there was a silver lining to the way Hardy and I grew up. All our chores and activities and time alone taught us to work hard and take care of ourselves. We did our homework because we had no choice. There was no way I was going to goof off or make up an excuse not to do something that needed to be done. I couldn't count on my mom to help. She was too tired or too in love." She smiled wryly. "Hardy and I have often said that our childhood served us well."

While she'd been talking, Stephanie had been sautéing the vegetables in a little bit of oil. After adding a can of broth and some water, she inspected the pantry more closely. "You went to college, yes?"

"Yes, the University of Cincinnati."

"And Hardy went into the Army and met Carter."

"Yes. And now Hardy lives here full time."

"He seems to like it."

"I think so. Where we grew up, it was crowded and noisy. I think Hardy likes the openness here. You can see for miles. Plus, it's quiet. After the Army and two deployments, he's told me that he needs the quiet."

"I like the quiet too. But it's what I'm used to," she said as she put in some dried peas.

Bev looked into the soup pot. "Looks like we're having pea soup?"

She chuckled. "Jah. Maybe I'll add some rice or noodles next. I haven't decided."

"I'm impressed."

"I'd believe that if you couldn't boil an egg, but now I know you're just being kind. You could probably have made a better meal, Bev."

"I don't think so."

"Hey, Bev. Open up!" Hardy called out.

Stephanie stayed where she was while Bev unlocked the door and let Hardy inside.

"Man, it's miserable outside," he said as he toed off his boots and slicker.

"Let me go get you a towel," Bev said.

While she disappeared into the bathroom, Hardy joined Stephanie in the kitchen. "Please tell me that's soup."

"It's soup," she said with a smile.

Looking pleased and very boyish with damp hair, he leaned over and peered in. "It smells good."

"Thank you. Your sister helped."

"I reckon she did. She's a good cook."

"I heard you both are."

"I can make a few things, but I wouldn't say that. Not like you."

She glanced at him in surprise. There was something in his voice that was new. Turning away from the soup pot, she searched his face. Realized Hardy was staring at her with something that looked . . . well, she wasn't exactly sure what expression was on his face.

Or, maybe the truth was that she didn't want to acknowledge it.

Feeling self-conscious, she picked up the wooden spoon and stirred the ingredients again. Glanced down the hall. Bev had closed the bathroom door. They were still alone.

"Stephanie, do you have a boyfriend?"

She almost dropped the spoon. "Why do you ask?"

"I was just curious. Is that too personal?"

"I don't know if it is or isn't." She shrugged. "But, nee. I do not."

"Why not? Are all the boys in your hometown blind?"

"As far as I know, they can see quite well." She fought off a smile.

"Then what's the problem? Do none of them interest you?"

Not wanting to admit how little she'd been allowed to leave the house, she asked, "What about you? Do you have a girlfriend?" She hadn't thought to ask, but she knew she was a job to him.

"No."

"I guess it's my turn to ask why not."

"The easy answer is that I don't have time. I live on this ranch, handle security, and supervise the hands. If someone's in a bind, I give them a hand, whether it's in the fields or repairing something in the barn. It's more than a full-time job."

"You said 'easy.' Is that not the only answer?"

"Nope." Averting his eyes, Hardy continued. "The better answer is that I've been a little gun-shy. I had a girl in high school for a while. I thought we were close, but she didn't like me enlisting and moving away. I asked her to wait for me."

"But she didn't want to."

"She didn't want to." Picking up a rag, he wiped down the counters. "Later, I dated a bit when I was in the military, but I couldn't give the women what they wanted."

"What did they want?"

"My time and attention."

"Because you were working so much."

"Yeah, but also because it didn't feel right." He stopped, looked out the window over the sink. "I never asked Bev about it, but sometimes I think growing up with a single parent gave Bev and me a different view than most grow up with. We didn't see a relationship in action so in some ways sharing one's life with a sweetheart seems foreign." As if he was embarrassed about his words, he grimaced. "Of course, I was in the military too. It's hard to form a serious attachment with someone when you're out of the country for months at a time."

"I wouldn't have thought about those things, but I can see your point." After making sure that they were still alone, she confided, "I once liked a boy very much, but I didn't have much time to devote to him. My aunt and uncle are kind enough, but I am needed. I have to help take care of my young cousins. That didn't leave me much extra time."

He frowned. "And that boy didn't like that?"

"He didn't. And I didn't realize it at the time, but my aunt and uncle didn't encourage me being courted."

"Maybe because they'd lose your help?"

"I think that might have been one of the reasons."

"We're a pair, aren't we? Two people who are so different but are now forced to spend time together and get to know them, without the usual distractions in life."

"We're also discovering that maybe we're not as different as we thought."

"What do you think that means? That God has a sense of humor?"

She didn't think that. She thought that perhaps the Lord had a plan and that was for the two of them to spend time together. But she didn't want to admit that to Hardy. He was faithful but would probably not agree that her witnessing a murder had anything to do with God's plan.

The bathroom door opened.

"Sorry, Hardy. I decided to brush my hair and put on a little bit of makeup. I was looking kind of rough," Bev said as she joined them. "Here's the towel."

He grabbed it and moved into the living room.

Unable to help herself, Stephanie watched him rub the towel across his face. Dry his hair.

Realized Bev had noticed her staring at Hardy.

And so she redirected the conversation yet again. "What do you two think about adding a can of green beans?"

"Hmm. Let's see," Bev said as she gave the soup a stir before taking an experimental sip from the spoon.

"Well?" Hardy asked.

She grimaced. "Instead of beans, I think we need some seasonings and maybe some bacon or something."

"So, no green beans?"

"No green beans. Not yet, Stephanie."

"Understood." She smiled at Bev. "I guess it's time to fry some bacon."

"I'll do that," Hardy volunteered as he opened up the refrigerator.

Then there they were. Three of them working together.

Even though the danger was still out there, Stephanie felt at peace.

Until she started to wonder what she was going to do when her adventure was all over and she was back with her aunt and uncle.

She'd be alone again—and it would be so hard. In so many ways.

24

Satisfied that all the men on duty were doing a good job, Hardy had decided to stay with the women. He could tell himself that it was because it had been ages since he'd spent so much time around his sister, but it wasn't the truth.

The fact was that the more time he was in Stephanie's company, the more he wanted to stay near her. She was calm and quiet and sweet. But she was also good company. And when they'd done things like watch *The Love Boat*, she'd had a very cute sense of humor that he delighted in.

She seemed to have the same effect on his sister. Little by little, some of the nervous energy that always seemed to surround Bev dissipated. She'd even opened the puzzle and had encouraged them to work on it.

Much to his amusement.

Later, Carter came and offered to take Beverly to town for a couple of necessities. Hardy had then taken Bev's place at the table and pretended to work on the puzzle though he was really only observing Stephanie.

But then, after Beverly and Carter returned from their errands, Carter asked Stephanie if she'd like to visit the horse barn. "With the rain and such, a couple of them get a bit antsy, especially my palomino Jet. Would you like to pay him a visit with me?"

"Truly?" Stephanie asked.

"I wouldn't lie about Jet," Carter teased. "Besides, your company would be welcome. You've likely been around as many horses as I have, right?"

"I don't know if that is true, but I would enjoy meeting Jet."

"He'd like meeting you. Like I said, he's not a big fan of bad weather." He winked.

It took everything Hardy had to keep his mouth shut. Carter shouldn't be flirting with Stephanie, not even a little bit. But then he noticed that Steph thought Carter's teasing was amusing. And, more than that, it was obvious that she was eager to visit the horses.

That's when he realized that Carter had come up with that little errand just for her. An Amish girl would be comfortable around horses. Petting and fussing over Carter's palomino would give her something to do besides worry.

When Steph went to put on her shoes, Hardy was tempted to remind his boss that the gang member knew Stephanie was on the premises. As if reading his mind, Carter cast him a look that conveyed that he might not have been the soldier Hardy was, but he was far from a fool.

In that moment, he remembered Carter was carrying, and Hardy was reminded that he did have a tendency to underestimate the man. He might have been a trust fund baby, but he was nobody's fool. He wouldn't allow Stephanie to either go far or be in danger.

But even though all of those things were true, it was the way Stephanie looked that made Hardy keep his mouth shut.

She needed to leave the cabin. She needed an opportunity to forget about everything, at least for a little while. All their problems would still be there an hour from now.

So he kept his mouth shut, but his heart leaped a bit when she walked out the door. Somehow he'd decided that he needed to be her protector. Only him.

Which was as ludicrous as it was untrue. Anyone who had a decent aim and experience with a pistol could do that job too.

But the most obvious reason he should back away was the hardest to swallow. That she was not his girl. Not anywhere close to that. And furthermore, there wasn't a chance of that happening.

Which pinched. He wasn't going to lie about that.

"Hardy, what is going through your head?" Beverly asked when he finally turned away from the door.

"Nothing."

"I hope it's not what I think it is."

"Which is what?"

"That you're developing feelings for Stephanie."

"Why would that be so terrible?"

"You know why. There are about five reasons I could list off the top of my head, beginning with the fact that she's Amish and ending with the fact that she is too young for you."

"I'm aware of both of those things."

"Are you also remembering that she's not here by choice? That she's in danger of being killed or hurt by a gang member?"

"I haven't forgotten, Bev." He was also pleased with himself for not reminding his sister that *she* was the reason he was around Stephanie in the first place.

"Then?" Her voice rose an octave.

"Then if all that's so bad, you should know that I'd never do anything to hurt her."

"Hmm."

"Hmm?" Her skepticism grated on him. While he wasn't perfect, she was acting like he was every woman's last resort when it came to looking at a future.

"Hardy, I know you think I'm being harsh, but I'm only trying to save you—and Stephanie—heartache in the long run. Her place is not here. Even if she was English—which she is not—the girl has a whole life back in Ohio."

She kind of didn't, though. Honestly, the more she described her life, the more it sounded fairly Cinderella-esque. "People can move." He inwardly grimaced. He wasn't making sense, and he knew it.

But he was too old to be listening to a lecture from his sister. Especially since she seemed to be happily oblivious to her own issues. So, because he was hurting and he was tired and because she probably needed to hear it too, he lowered his voice. "Maybe you need to think about the fact that I'm not the only one around here flirting with trouble, relationship-wise."

Dismay, followed by hurt, entered her eyes. "What is that supposed to mean, Hardy?"

She knew. "If you want to play innocent, I'll play that game too. But I don't think you're going to like it, sister."

"I'm not playing a game."

"You're not guilty of imagining that you have a chance with a very rich man who happens to be in the sights of pretty much every eligible woman in two states? If not more."

She looked away. "What a way to make me feel good, Hardy."

"You feeling good isn't going to get you very far when your heart is crushed."

Hurt flashed in her eyes. "You really don't think Carter Russell could ever feel anything for me?"

"I think if he did, and he was smart enough to act on it and put a ring on your finger, that would be the smartest thing I've ever seen him do. But the chances are slim. And not because you're you, Beverly. You know I think you're an amazing person and any man would be lucky to have you."

"But . . ."

"But Carter Russell doesn't just live a different life, he lives in a different universe. Don't get me wrong—he's a good man. A decent one too. He's also done a lot of things for me. I owe him a lot. But that doesn't mean that I think he's the right match for my sister."

She bumped him against his shoulder. Just the way they used to do to each other when they were walking to the bus stop all those years ago. "What do you think is wrong with us, Hardy?"

"Nothing."

"Do you think we haven't had good luck with relationships because we didn't grow up around one?"

Their father had never married their mom and then landed in prison. Later, he'd died in a fight or something. Their mother had hated to talk about him.

"I don't know," he said at last. "Mom seemed to think Dad was pretty worthless and no good. Maybe he was? All I know is that she always acted like she needed a man but could never seem to settle."

"I wish she was still around."

"Me too." He chuckled. "But if she was, she'd probably be giving us all sorts of advice."

"You're right. No doubt, she'd be telling us to get married and give her some grandchildren. Which is never going to happen."

"It might." Tossing an arm around her shoulder, he added, "Just not today."

"True. What do you think? Have we talked enough?"

"Probably. There's no telling what Stephanie and Carter are doing."

"Hopefully he's turned them around and is walking her back. She shouldn't be out too long."

"Do you think they'll have anything to talk about?" Carter could be charming, but Hardy didn't think that would make Stephanie happy. He knew his boss would keep her safe, but he didn't want her feeling uneasy.

"I don't know," Bev said.

He glanced out the window. They needed to return soon. It would be better for all of them if they did.

25

It was a lot harder to keep someone alive than to kill them. Night after night, Timothy had been besieged by nightmares. They were disturbing and too-real, constantly replaying the moment he drew his gun and pulled the trigger.

Just the way he'd practiced in a vacant field.

There hadn't been a victim in the field, though. In the midst of those disturbing dreams, Timothy almost wished there had been. Maybe it could have been a bird. Rabbit? He didn't know. Something alive to hit home just how violent killing a living being could be. The blood. The sound of the bullet hitting flesh. The cry. The gasp. The look of surprise followed by nothing.

Maybe if he'd witnessed that firsthand, he wouldn't have drawn that gun so fast. Or he wouldn't have let the guy's derisive comments about him bother him so much.

But then again, maybe the opposite could've happened. He might have discovered that he could commit murder. That he did have a conscience that could go walking at will.

All Timothy knew, as he parked on the edge of a parking lot in front of a no-name convenience store in rural Missouri, was that if he hadn't shot that guy, he wouldn't be doing what he was doing now—which was robbing stores for dollars.

Doing whatever he could to scrape up enough money to be able to pay for Audrey's life.

So far, his new career of robbery and breaking and entering had garnered uneven results. The most he'd been able to get was four hundred and five. The least had been two.

It turned out that a lot of people didn't have much cash on them. They didn't keep it in their vehicles either.

On a positive note, so far he hadn't been caught and he hadn't been killed. He also had close to eighteen hundred dollars. If this store had over two hundred, he was going to give up his dream of bringing Kane almost three grand and settle for the two he'd asked for.

Anything for the nightmare he was now living to end. He couldn't survive much longer when he was struggling so much both awake and asleep.

After the older lady who'd walked in when he'd arrived glanced his way and then hurried to her older model Nissan and drove off, Timothy knew it was time to head in. He hadn't showered in two days, and he knew he looked like it. No doubt he smelled like it too. The nervous sweat he'd begun to wear like his old favorite hoodie was his constant companion.

After checking his gun and pulling his ball cap low, he exited his vehicle and strode in.

He had a system now. Walk in, turn to the right toward the beverage cases. Use that time to check for cameras and customers. Open a refrigerated section. Hold the glass door open while he stared at bottles of water or soda. Finally pick one out, like it mattered.

Only then turn to gauge the clerk's age and manner.

Then he'd begin making plans.

Sometimes, he bought the soda and left, because there were too many people or the clerk looked like he'd shoot Timothy before he'd give up a dollar. Other times he left because it was obvious that the cameras weren't just for show. They were no doubt recording him, and the store had a direct line to the cops.

But if that didn't look to be the case and the store was vacant, he knew it was his chance.

"Can I help you find something?" the clerk called out.

Timothy, still with his hand on the open glass door and staring at the soda, jerked.

Then noticed that the clerk had moved away from the counter and was halfway down one of the aisles. He'd upset his routine.

"Yeah," he said after realizing that the store clerk was studying him. Like it was his job to memorize faces. Timothy knew then that the guy would be able to identify him in a heartbeat.

So he pulled out his gun. "I'm going to follow you to the cash register and you're going to open it. Hand me what's inside."

"I don't think that's a good idea, son."

Son? "I'm not your son, your buddy, or your friend."

"What are you then?"

What was with this guy? "I'm either going to be the last person you ever see or just a bad memory. Take your pick."

Finally, finally the thirtysomething clerk looked like he was taking him seriously. "Settle down. I'll get it. Follow me."

Maybe it was his paranoia, but Timothy was sure he was walking into a trap. "I don't want to hurt you, but I will."

"Yeah. I get that," the man said, edging away. "Easy, now."

When he turned and started for the counter, Timothy watched. Felt the sweat pouring off of him as he stared at the guy's every move.

Inhaled when the man turned a key and the drawer opened.

And then the guy smiled. "Hope this will get you what you need," he said. Just as he lifted a stack of money with one hand and his gun with the other.

Instincts clicked in. At last. Timothy fired. Not to kill. Aimed for the guy's shoulder.

Of course he missed. He wasn't a killer, and he wasn't well trained. He'd hardly been trained at all.

Which meant he hit the guy's midsection.

The man groaned as he fell to his knees. Hate and shame filled Timothy's soul as he strode to the counter, grabbed the wad of cash that had fallen out of the clerk's hand, and pocketed the rest that he could find.

Just as another vehicle pulled up.

He grabbed some chips from the counter, ducked his head as the couple inside the other car continued arguing about whatever they were arguing about. He hurried out to his car, started the engine, reversed, and drove out. Maintaining the speed limit. Focusing only on the cash stuffed in his pockets as he headed toward the state line. He needed to get out of Missouri before the couple called the cops and the guy got to the hospital and then eventually identified him.

Before the young arguing couple remembered the guy holding an armful of chips and a sandwich and a pop.

Before Kane called again and wondered what was happening.

Before he had a chance to count the money and pray it was enough to take him north.

Hours later, sitting in his vehicle at a busy rest stop on

the outskirts of Crittenden County, Timothy finally took the time to count his spoils.

And realized that he'd shot a man for eighty-seven dollars, a turkey sandwich wrapped in plastic wrap, two bags of chips, and a Mountain Dew.

His total was still far too short. There was no way he was going to hit another store either. Instead of getting easier, it was only getting harder. Far too hard to make less than a hundred bucks.

With a sinking feeling, Timothy came to terms with his life.

He had no choice.

He was going to have to go back to his original plan and kill the Amish girl.

Because if there was anything he'd learned since he'd been in Crittenden County, it was that it was much easier to kill someone than keep them alive.

26

After two days of waiting for something to happen, everyone's nerves were beginning to fray. Even though Carter had been spending the evenings in his house and Hardy had been in cabin two, the four of them spent the majority of each day at Stephanie's place. And while she was used to not having much privacy, she wasn't used to talking very much.

In addition, since her cabin had only one living space and a very small kitchen, they all seemed to get in each other's way an awful lot. Last night, Bev had declared that it was a bit ironic that all four of them were loners.

On the second day, it was obvious that each was reaching the end of his or her patience. It turned out that they all had something in common, and that was that none was good at sitting around and doing nothing.

Or jumping every time a strong wind blew something outside or there was a knock at the door.

When Carter suggested that they relocate to his house, Stephanie breathed a sigh of relief. Hardy had told her that the house was huge, that each of them would have their own bedroom and bathroom, and that there were so many living areas, they could sit and read a book without feeling like three people were watching.

After they'd moved, Stephanie had been pleased to discover that Hardy hadn't exaggerated. There really was space for each of them. It was comfortable and plush, and Carter had made it clear that they should feel at home.

But the fact of the matter was that no matter how nice the surroundings were, all of them were on pins and needles. Waiting for something to happen. All of their nerves were beginning to fray.

Or maybe hers already were frayed and she was simply hanging on. Barely.

After reading the same paragraph in her book for the fourth time, she closed the novel and stared out the window instead. It was hardly fair that she was in such gorgeous surroundings but had yet to spend more than a few minutes outside.

"Stephanie, how about you get a sweatshirt and put on your shoes?" Hardy said. "I think it's time we got out of here and went for a walk."

Even though her body wanted to jump to her feet, she couldn't completely disregard the situation. "Do you think we'll be safe?"

"I'll keep you safe. I promise."

"You're sure."

"Very. I wouldn't lie about your safety. Hurry now, darlin'."

"I'll be right back." She was barely out of the room when Stephanie heard Bev speak in a low voice. "Don't speak to Stephanie like that. She doesn't know what you mean by it."

"I agree," Carter added, somehow sounding even more

forceful than Bev. "You need to watch yourself with her, Hardy."

"You've got to be kidding me."

"Do I look like I'm laughing?"

"No sir. But you do look confused."

Listening to the exchange, Stephanie felt like rolling her eyes. What kind of woman did Bev and Carter think she was? She still had a sense of humor. She wasn't going to be offended by Hardy calling her darlin'. She knew he hadn't meant a thing by it.

Just as Stephanie was about to march back in the room, Hardy's voice turned clipped. "I kept her safe for quite some time before either of you decided to play chaperone. Not once did I overstep. I'm offended that either of you think I would now."

"What is that supposed to mean?" Bev's voice seemed to raise a notch.

"Exactly what you think it does. I'm in no hurry to start watching my mouth around all three of you. Not when there is another reason we're all here. I haven't forgotten."

"I haven't either, Hardy. No offense meant," Carter murmured.

"Understood." Hardy nodded as she rejoined them. "Go get on your shoes, Steph. Let's go before the blasted rain starts up again."

Just as she was about to walk away, Bev touched her arm. "Stephanie, maybe you should rethink going outside with—"

She was not going to let Bev finish that sentence. "Nee. I'm going out for a walk with Hardy."

"I could go too. Maybe all four of us could go."

"We will be fine." Standing to her full height, Stephanie continued. "Yes, I am Amish. I have also been scared. But I am not a child, and I certainly am not near as sheltered as you seem to believe I am. I'm twenty-three, not sixteen."

"Of course," Bev replied. "I was out of line and I'm sorry."

After she put on her shoes and her pink hoodie, Stephanie returned to Hardy's side.

Carter was now sitting on a chair and perusing a magazine while Beverly looked embarrassed and was playing on her phone.

Relieved, Stephanie turned to Hardy. "I'm ready now. Shall we go?"

"Absolutely." Glancing at the clock on the wall, Hardy said, "We'll be back in thirty. If we aren't here in forty minutes, something's wrong."

"You got your phone?" Carter asked.

"Always."

"Understood."

Opening the door, Hardy gestured for her to wait for a moment while he stepped outside first. After a minute, he nodded to her.

Stephanie couldn't get out of there fast enough. When the door closed behind them, she looked at Hardy warily. Was he now wondering what in the world he'd gotten himself into? Her stomach knotted as she waited for him to say something about his sister.

Instead, he pointed to a faint trail nearby. "I think the best path is to our right. Some of Carter's fancy gardeners planted about a hundred daffodil and tulip bulbs in the fall. Last time I checked, they'd started to come up."

"All right. But if you are regretting—"

"I'm not regretting anything, Stephanie." His mouth twisted. "Except, perhaps, the fact that both my boss and my sister have decided that I can't be trusted." He moved to the side so she could walk on his left. Then, together, they took the worn bridle trail that veered right.

After a few minutes passed, he grinned. "It's been a minute since I've gone walking with a woman who walks as fast as I do."

"I have long legs, and I'm used to walking a lot."

"I reckon you're right about both." The path meandered next to a copse of trees, then began to go up at a steady incline. Stephanie had no problem keeping up with Hardy though she was breathing heavier than he was.

"Stephanie," he said in a far softer tone. "Come look at this." Hardy stopped and pointed to a creek about thirty feet away. From their position they could look down on it. "Do you see it? Just off to the side?"

Stephanie gasped when she saw what he was pointing to. "It's a beaver dam."

He grinned. "It is. It's quite a fortress, don't you think?"

"It almost puts Carter's house to shame."

Hardy chuckled. "If Carter were standing here, I'd venture that he'd say it was better."

"You think?"

"For sure. Those beavers built theirs by hand."

Unable to resist, she quipped, "Or paw, ain't so?"

He chuckled. "Good point."

"The beavers cut down a lot of wood and might even be disrupting the flow of the creek. Aren't you worried?"

"I was worried, but we went down and looked around. The creek is still flowing. And as for the trees, well, there's a lot of them."

"Have you ever seen them? I mean, the beavers?"

"Sure. Have you ever seen a beaver?"

"Nee."

"Well, if you do, give them a wide berth. They're bigger than you would think. And on those furry paws are sizable claws. They could do some real damage if they felt threatened."

"You enjoy them, don't you?"

"I do." Looking sheepish, he added, "Now, I don't sit around and watch beavers do their thing all day, but whenever I've spied one, I've never been too busy to stop for a spell. Just to see what they were up to."

"I hope I'll get to see one while I'm here."

"Me too. I should've been taking you out more. We'll walk over here again if you'd like."

They shared a smile. "I would like that." She took a deep breath and said, "And Hardy, I don't think Carter and Bev meant to hurt your feelings."

"I don't think they did either. But I did think they were out of line. It's been my experience that every opinion doesn't always need to be shared. Especially not at the very moment one thinks of it."

"My aunt and uncle would say the same thing."

As they started walking again, Hardy glanced her way. "Honestly, I was more worried about how you took their interference than my ego."

"May I be honest?"

"I'd love to hear your honest opinion."

"I thought it was funny."

"What was? Their caution, or the way I was talking to you?"

"Their caution. Some people look at me and think, oh, she's a sweet and meek Amish girl. I better treat her like spun glass. But I'm far tougher than that. I've had to be."

"Because you lost your parents?"

"Jah. When I lost them, I was only sixteen. I had to move in with my aunt and uncle." She paused, not wanting to misrepresent them but still make her feelings heard. "It was a difficult adjustment, but I am grateful for their charity."

"You're family, though."

"I am, but not close. Anyway, as much as I love them all, it's never felt like I belong there. Their haus, and my life there, helping to take care of my young cousins, it doesn't feel like home."

"Home is a tricky place, isn't it?"

"Indeed."

Looking down at her, his eyes warmed. "I enjoyed this, Stephanie. And I just realized that I never took you out to see the flowers."

"I'd forgotten about them too."

"Maybe we could go again tomorrow?"

"I'd like that very much."

"It's a date," he said just as the door opened.

Carter stepped out, his expression dark.

Immediately Hardy's entire demeanor tensed. "What happened?"

"Crenshaw called. He spied on one of the cameras someone attempting to not only cut the barbed wire but dismantle the electric line."

"Did he catch them?"

"No. He sent Dan over, but he didn't get there in time."

"We need to check that."

"I already thought about that too. Unfortunately, a couple of the cameras along the fencing are no longer working." Carter's eyes were cold, mirroring the tension that was emanating off Hardy.

When Hardy turned to her, there was regret in his eyes.

"Looks like it might be a minute before we get to check out that dam again or those flowers."

"I understand." Glancing at Carter, she noticed that he was staring at her intently.

"You need to get on inside, Stephanie," he said.

She nodded. And then, because she wasn't sure what she was feeling at the moment, she walked past Bev without saying a word.

It was rude, but she needed a minute to herself.

Maybe even two.

27

After the phone call and a brusque conversation with Carter, Hardy stepped outside. The home's front and back lawns had been professionally landscaped. Lush foliage and a variety of native trees were counterparts to the blooming perennials and a trickling man-made fountain.

Unlike the outside of the cabins, there were no logs in need of splitting or stacks of firewood waiting to be carried inside.

There were a dozen things he needed to focus on. First and foremost was the attempted breach of the fence. Not only did he need to think of more than one way to monitor the perimeter, but he also needed to acknowledge that the person after Stephanie had not given up and likely wouldn't anytime soon.

He also needed to remind Carter that there was a chance that he could also be at risk. Carter wasn't just rich. He was close to being a billionaire. And it didn't matter if a lot of his assets were in land and stocks. The man was worth a lot and therefore could be a target for kidnapping. That was, after all, the reason they had such tight security protocols in place.

Bev was also at risk, since the person who'd tracked

Stephanie probably figured out that Bev was the reason the Amish girl had been able to get English clothes and on a bus so quickly. And maybe they now knew—she was a witness herself. That was all important. Vitally important.

Finally, there were things like groceries and the farm animals and the hands who worked with the horses and cattle and the fifty other things that were usually at the top of his to-do list but now had been woefully neglected.

All that was why it made no sense at all for him to be focused on Stephanie right now. And not even on her safety.

Nope, all he currently cared about was her feelings. And, perhaps, his jealousy. Every time Carter spoke to Stephanie in a soft way or encouraged her to open up a bit, he felt a twinge of jealousy.

It was obvious that Carter felt nothing for Stephanie beyond the fact that she was a young woman under his care. But that was beside the point. Hardy knew he had no business feeling jealous. Beverly had been right to point out that there were numerous reasons why he should be keeping his distance.

Not be calling her darlin' even on accident.

Why, God? Why are You encouraging these feelings for someone who I shouldn't be feeling that way about? I've had too violent a life to be around someone as peace-loving as her.

As he rejoined them in the house, Stephanie rose to meet him. "Hardy, are you all right?"

That was all it took. Just a few words from her made his body ease and his worries fade.

She reached out. Curved her fingers around his arm. "Hardy?"

He shook his head as if he was clearing it. "Sorry." Hoping

he now appeared a lot calmer, he flashed her a small smile. "Of course. I'm worried about you, though."

"I know you're worried about me. I wish you didn't have to be."

"If the reason I'm worried didn't exist, I wouldn't have met you in the first place. I guess I should focus on that."

She blinked. Seemed to take a moment to follow his train of thought. And then laughed. "So you're saying our friendship is the silver lining in me witnessing a murder?"

"It's not the only hidden blessing, but yes. I'm glad I've had the chance to know you. I promise I'll do my best to ensure that you stay safe so you can go back home as soon as possible."

"That's good."

She'd averted her eyes, though. What did that mean? Just as he was about to delve into that can of worms, he pulled himself together and noticed Carter and Bev having a heated conversation in the corner of the living room. "What's going on with them? Do you know?"

"Maybe." Lowering her voice, Stephanie added, "I have a feeling that Bev might be the most frustrated member of our little group."

"Why is that?"

"She revealed to me last night that she wants to carry a weapon, but she doesn't know how to shoot."

"What?"

"Lower your voice, Hardy."

"Sorry," he said in a lower tone. "But . . . what?"

Sneaking another look Bev's way, Stephanie added, "Your sister said she doesn't want to be a victim. She wants to be able to defend me if the two of us are cornered, and she knows she's not strong enough to hold her own in a fight."

"Of course she isn't. That's why she has me and Carter. And a whole security team."

She paused then added, "And then there's everything about her job. I think she's really worried about work. Maybe she wants to go home."

Hardy realized he was guilty of taking her work for granted. Sure, he knew she was a social worker and took her job and the relationships she had with her kids seriously. But did he often stop and think about what that actually meant for his sister? When she missed work, she didn't just miss a day of pay, but she felt like she was letting her kids down.

Nope. Those things had rarely crossed his mind over the last few days.

But was he willing to let her drive back to Cincinnati alone?

No. No, he was not.

Especially not now. He knew things were about to come to a head. He could feel it.

"Do you think you should teach her to shoot?" Stephanie asked hesitantly.

"No."

"Are you sure?"

"Very sure. It's not that I don't trust her. It's more of the fact that she might know how to shoot but she sure doesn't have any skill with it. Someone untrained with a firearm is more at risk than if they didn't have a weapon at all. And no one has time to practice with her right now."

"I understand. And now I don't have to worry that you'd ask me to handle a gun."

"Of course I wouldn't do that. Not only is it not safe, I don't want to go against your beliefs."

"My beliefs?"

"Well, yeah. I mean, even I know that Amish don't hold with violence of any kind."

"This is true. But it's more than that. I . . . well, I just don't think I could ever handle a gun. I would be too frightened."

"I'll do my best to make sure that never happens."

A smile played on her lips. "Danke."

Her use of Pennsylvania Dutch made him realize that he'd taken something else for granted too. "Are you uncomfortable dressing English and living in a modern house?"

"Sometimes." She waved a hand. "Part of me misses my life. I mean, of course I don't like feeling like a murderer is after me and all."

"Of course."

"But, that aside . . . I have been thinking a lot about how I miss the quiet and the peace. At times, I've missed feeling useful too. But . . . there was so much that I should and shouldn't do, and my uncle likes to imagine that very bad things will happen if anyone strays beyond those perimeters."

"They used fear tactics to keep you home."

"Maybe so." She inhaled. "I never agreed with that. Mei eldras didn't either. They were also Old Order, but from a more progressive community. The definition of 'Plain' was far more broad. I kept putting off my baptism."

"So, are you actually Amish?"

"Nope. Right now, I'm just Stephanie." Turning to face him, she added, "Maybe that's why I haven't hated being here. I've needed time to figure out who I am. Plus, it's been nice not to have every move I make scrutinized."

"But you've been alone a lot."

"Jah. But before Carter and Bev joined us, I thought it was kind of fun when you stopped by and we watched television for an hour or two."

"I can't believe you got sucked into *The Love Boat*. You really liked it."

"How could I not? Everyone is warm, relaxed, sailing on the ocean, and falling in love. All of their problems are done within an hour."

He leaned close. "Put that way, I think I should be watching it more often."

Her giggle was adorable. And it soothed him in the best way possible. It didn't make any of their problems go away, but it sure made them seem like they were problems, not life-changing obstacles that were going to ruin everyone's lives if he didn't do the right thing. "Danke," he said.

"Thank you for what?"

"Reminding me to take a moment and breathe. To remember to not only thank my sister for her help but to ask how she's doing and if there is a way I can help her." He grinned. "And for reminding me that even though we're in the middle of a very sticky situation, that every minute of the day doesn't need to be high stress and giving 100 percent."

"Since we're talking about thinking about each other, I don't believe I've asked you how you're doing. Are you all right?"

"Of course."

"I don't think the conversation will go so well if you're not honest. Is there something I may help you with?" She tilted her head and smiled. "Would you like to learn Deutch, perhaps? Maybe how to milk a cow or churn butter?"

"As much as those sound like fun activities . . . what I would love is more conversations like that one we just had. I need them. Can we do that?"

"We can. I would be happy to converse with you as often as you'd like."

"If you can promise me that, then you'll be helping me a lot."

"I promise," she said softly.

His heart clenched. He had to fist his hand because he wanted to reach out and run a finger along her perfect cheekbone. Then run his lips along that same path. Hold her close and feel her curves and softness and let that femininity remind him that while the world was hard, there was goodness in it too.

It came in the sunrise, the stars at night, the baby bunnies and lambs in the spring.

Or maybe in brief, precious moments of peace when the only thing to do was share something special.

Giving in for just one short second, he leaned down, brushed his lips against hers.

When he lifted his head, he murmured, "I bet there's a dozen reasons why I should apologize to you right now, but I just can't."

Stephanie didn't say a word, but her expression warmed.

The soft expression of a beautiful woman. Gazing at him. Just for a second.

Yes, for just one second, their situation was bad, but the rest of their world was very, very good. Perfect.

28

A phone buzzing at two in the morning was never good news. Out of habit, Hardy reached for his phone, but his head felt as if he was a couple of steps behind. He'd only been asleep for an hour.

"Yeah?"

"Hardy, we got a problem."

Immediately, all traces of grogginess left him as he stood up from his bed. His heart started beating double time. If someone sent Stephanie another weird package, Hardy knew he was going to freak out on someone. "Talk to me, Dan," he said as he bent down for his jeans.

Knowing it was Dan at the front gate, all his senses went on alert. He'd been the one to tell them about the box of bullets delivered and he'd been the one who couldn't find anyone when Crenshaw had discovered someone had tried to cut the electric line.

Hardy didn't want to think that Dan could have something to do with someone discovering Stephanie's whereabouts, but someone had to have given Timothy information. "What's up?" he asked in a clipped tone.

"You've got a visitor."

He stilled. A visitor wasn't a break-in. But it made no sense. "Who is it?" he asked as he buckled his belt.

"It's Timothy Jones."

"You have got to be kidding me."

"I wouldn't lie about this, Hardy. And for the record, he doesn't look good."

"Give me a sec." Tossing the phone on the bed, he reached for his henley and pulled it over his head.

"What's wrong with him? He strung out?" he asked as he started looking for a pair of socks.

"He could be, but I don't think so," Dan said slowly, like he was sizing the man up right in front of him. "I mean, if he is, it ain't from drugs. It's more like he's wearing an expression that I've only ever seen on inmates, back when I worked at the state pen. Sometimes guys would get cornered or join with a group that was deadly. Those guys would walk around either looking like they were scared to death or on a doomed mission."

"Okay. Where is he? And do you have your gun out?"

"He walked here, Hardy. He's on the other side of the gate. He doesn't look like he's fixin' to go guns blazing or anything."

Slightly calmer, Hardy shook his head. Only Dan could sound both intense and like they were shooting the breeze at the same time. "What does he want?"

"Well, he wants to talk to you."

"To me or Stephanie?" Timothy wasn't going to get within a hundred yards of her, but that didn't mean he wouldn't try.

"He only said you. I mean, he said he wanted to talk to the dude who was watching the Amish girl and works for the rich guy." A hint of humor entered his voice. "I figured that wouldn't be anyone but you."

"It sounds like it," he said as he walked to the bathroom and splashed some water over his face.

"So . . . he's watching me through the window. What should I do?"

"Keep an eye on him. I'm heading your way right now. You sure he didn't drive in? You check the cameras yet?"

Opening a cabinet, he pulled on a pair of socks then padded back to the bed and stuffed his feet in his boots.

"I checked them and it's all clear. Honest to God, the kid just walked on up to the gate."

"Hopefully you saw him before he got that close."

"Sorry, but I didn't notice him at first," he replied after a brief pause. "It's pitch-black out here tonight. Guy scared me half to death when I noticed him."

"Let me get Carter and we'll be there in five. You checked for a gun, right?"

"Yes, sir. He was armed, but he handed over his weapon. He said that was all he had on him."

Hardy felt like rolling his eyes. Timothy could have easily lied about having another gun or a knife on him. But, at the end of the day, Dan didn't have the experience that Hardy did. He'd done what he'd been taught to do. Be the first line of defense and then call for help. "Hang tight. I'm on my way." He grabbed his wallet, a ball cap, and his keys.

"All right. But um, I don't think he's going to be good with Carter showing up too."

"He'll have to deal because he doesn't have a choice."

"Yes, sir."

He walked down the hall and knocked twice on Carter's door.

Carter answered immediately. "Yeah?"

Still standing in front of the closed door, he said as loudly as he dared, "Carter, it's me. We got trouble."

"Come on in."

When Hardy walked in the plush, huge room, he had to scan the area to find Carter. He was already throwing on his jeans and a flannel. "Dan called from the guard shack. Our guy Timothy showed up. He's outside the gate and waiting for me to come on out to talk to him."

He froze. "Are you serious?"

"I pretty much asked the same thing. It doesn't make sense, does it?"

"Not unless it's a trap."

"If it is, it's a pretty poor one."

"I agree."

Hardy stood next to the door as he watched Carter take down a picture, enter in a combination to the safe behind it, and finally pull out a handgun and a round of ammunition.

There was more than one gun in the safe.

"You need anything in here, Hardy?"

"I'm good."

"All right then. Let's go see what this guy wants."

Hardy followed Carter down the stairs and shrugged on his jacket as Carter pulled out a leather coat. Just as they were leaving, Stephanie found them.

She was dressed in a robe and slippers. Her hair was hanging in sheets around her shoulders. Against his will, he couldn't help but notice that she looked as beautiful as ever.

And completely scared to death. He hated that—and vowed to do whatever was in his power to make sure this would be one of the last times she'd ever feel that way.

"Hardy? Is everything okay?"

"Everything's fine," he assured her. There was no reason for her to know what was going on. Not yet, anyway.

"Are you sure?"

She'd come up to his side. She was so close that he could smell the faint scent of lavender on her skin. "Of course. I'm sorry I woke you, Stephanie."

"I couldn't sleep anyway. Why are you up?"

He'd give a lot to tell her it was nothing she needed to worry about. No. He would give a lot for her to still be sleeping and getting a break from the constant stress she'd been living under.

But perhaps it was just as well that she was aware of what was going on. Well, some of it, at least. She was the one with a target on her back. Giving in to the urge, he curved a hand around her cheek. Allowed himself a moment to caress her skin. When she leaned into his touch, he knew that she needed the connection as much as he did. "Someone's at the front gate," he said, trying his best to keep his tone light. "He wants to speak to me. I thought I'd better get Carter too."

"At this time of night? Why?"

"I don't know. That's why we need to go see him." He ran a hand down her hair, liking the way the strands tangled in his fingers. Giving him a reason to keep touching her a little bit longer. "Now, it would be wrong of us to keep him waiting much longer. It's pretty miserable out, yeah?" When she nodded, he moved his hand away. "We've got to go."

"Hardy." Carter's voice was firm.

"Don't worry," he whispered.

"Wait. Is it about the ranch?"

"I'm not sure." Not really the truth but not a complete lie either.

"When we leave, I'm going to put on the alarm. Don't

open a thing, Stephanie," Carter said. "Not even a window. You hear me?"

"Jah." She swallowed. "Should I wake Bev?"

After a pause, Carter nodded. "It might be a good idea."

She continued to stare at him. "This man, this visitor. It's about me, isn't it?"

Man, he didn't want to answer. But he couldn't lie. "Yeah." When she paled, Hardy stepped forward. "Stephanie, I'm sorry. I know you're scared and I know you have questions. But I don't know anything else yet. I need to go."

She swallowed. "All right." She clutched part of her robe in her right fist, wrinkling the section as she held it in a death grip. "I guess you might be gone awhile?"

"No telling," Carter said. "But we'll be gone as long as it takes to put a stop to this."

She visibly relaxed. "All right."

"All right then," Carter echoed as he went to the door.

Hardy couldn't leave her without adding another batch of warnings. "Listen. You keep your phone nearby, you hear me?"

"Yes."

"And turn the dead bolt as soon as the door closes. We'll call soon."

"All right."

He hesitated, telling himself not to do what he wanted, which was to pull Stephanie into his arms and hold her close. Tell her all sorts of sweet things but most of all reassure her that she didn't have anything to worry about because he would make sure she was fine.

But they didn't have time, and those words would be lies. He honestly had no idea what was going to happen. All he knew for certain was that it was unlikely that this situation was going to end happily.

With that littering his mind, he turned to follow Carter out the door.

He didn't look back at her. Instead, he slammed the door shut behind him. As soon as he heard the dead bolt click into place, he punched in the security code.

She was as safe as he could hope for her to be. Hopefully it would be safe enough.

While he drove the five minutes to the front entrance, frowning at the rain splashing against the windshield, he filled Carter in on what Dan had reported.

"What's your gut feeling?" Carter asked.

"No idea. I have a feeling that we're going to learn a lot when we see Timothy."

"I concur."

When he stopped beside the guard shack, it was easy to spy Timothy lurking just beyond the gate. He was leaned up against an arrangement of boulders, part of the design of the grand entrance to the Russell Ranch.

Carter got out first. He didn't have his gun in his hand, but it was clearly visible on the side holster that was strapped to his chest and peeking out of the leather coat.

When Hardy alighted, he kept his weapon in his hand. He'd long since gotten over pretending that he and Timothy were ever going to have a reasonable conversation.

Dan popped his head out. "He's been over against that rock the entire time."

"You see him on his phone?"

"No, sir. He's hardly moved. It's like he's worn out or something."

"Did you call the sheriff yet?"

Looking unsure, Dan shook his head. "I didn't want to do anything without your instructions."

"Good thinking," Carter said.

"Do you want me to call now, sir?"

Carter shook his head. "Let's wait a sec. I want to know what's going on first. What do you say, Hardy?"

"Same." They could have just walked into a trap, but it didn't feel like that. Instead, he was getting the feeling that Timothy was relieved to see them. Like they were the answer to one of his prayers.

Of course, that made no sense at all.

But there was only one way to find out.

Walking a few steps forward, he called out, "Timothy Jones, is that you?"

The man stood up straight. "Yeah. You the man who's been looking after the Amish girl?"

"I am. My name is Hardy. Now how about you tell me how you know about her."

"I just do. And now I need your help."

Carter laughed softly. "That's a pretty big request, boy, seeing as you've had a pair of women scared to death for over a week now."

Timothy opened his mouth. Shut it again. Seemed to half look like he was going to pass out. "Everything I've done has gone wrong. I . . . I just got in with the Broken Arrows, but I'm in over my head."

"Why do you want to talk to us?"

"Because I can testify against them, and you can get the law involved and put them away."

"Word around here is that you deserve to serve time."

"Yeah, well, it doesn't matter to me one way or the other. If I go behind bars, they're going to send someone to kill me. But if we don't stop them, they're not only going to go after the Amish girl, they're going to take Audrey."

"Who's Audrey?" Carter asked.

"My ex-girlfriend."

"His ex-girlfriend," Carter mumbled. "Now ain't that a new spin on this fork?"

"How come she's your ex?" Hardy asked.

"She broke up with me when I joined the Broken Arrows."

"She's a smart girl."

Instead of looking the least bit relieved, Timothy seemed to get more agitated by the second. "So, will you help me? This is important. Like, there's no time to spare."

The rain had just started coming down harder. Timothy was soaked to the skin.

"I'll let you come in, but you're going to be cuffed," Carter said. "I'll shoot you if you try anything."

"Yeah. All right. Please."

Hardy exchanged looks with Carter. Something wasn't right. Not even close to being right. "Why are you so freaked out?"

Dan popped his head out. "Mr. Russell, we got us another problem. The south fence was just breached. Whoever's there cut the wire."

"That's them," Timothy said.

Carter turned to him. "That's who?"

"Kane. And I don't know. Whoever he has with him."

Carter's voice rose. "You had the gall to ask us for help when you knew you were being followed? You brought them onto my land?"

"I didn't know I was being followed," he protested, looking more pained by the second. "I'm begging you—help me help Audrey."

He wasn't lying. The kid—who was likely not even twenty years old yet—might be a lowlife and not even all that smart.

But he was desperate.

He was also telling the truth about one thing. There was an Audrey in his life and he was scared to death about her getting hurt or abused. Hardy motioned to Dan to open the gate.

"Come on."

"What?"

- "Get in my truck. And Lord help you if you mess up those leather seats. Those are the King Ranch edition. I'm going to secure you, all right?"

"Yeah, sure."

As Hardy pulled out some zip ties from a side compartment in the truck, Carter said, "I've got Sheriff Johnson on the line. He's trying to get here, but the storm's knocked out most of the power in town and uprooted a tree. It's blocking most of an intersection. Plus, the creek is rising on account that everything's already been saturated."

Of course it was.

"Understood."

They were on their own.

Luckily for everyone involved, he liked it that way. He could have some control. "I'll take care of Timothy."

"I'll be with the women."

Carter stared hard at him before turning away, leaving a trail of unspoken words and warnings in his wake. There was a very good chance that even with the best security money could buy, they were about to be in a fight for survival.

Things had gotten worse, but he was ready.

He was ready enough.

29

The house was secure. The alarm was on, and the men had driven out to see whoever had just arrived. Common sense told Stephanie that there was nothing she could do at two in the morning. She should go to bed. If the men had been really worried, they would've acted like it.

Instead, they'd seemed pretty calm.

Sure, there was a storm raging outside and the wind had picked up. Rain was pelting the windows. It might have even turned to sleet by now. Sleep would be difficult, but she'd feel better for it.

That was the last thing in the world that Stephanie was going to be able to do. Every nerve was on fire and every single worry that had almost eased during her time at the ranch had reared its ugly head.

Or maybe it was the feeling inside of her that she'd tried so hard to forget. The sense that something bad was about to happen.

The last time it had been so prevalent was the night her parents had died.

It had been another dark and stormy night like this one.

Decision made at last, she walked back upstairs and

tapped on Beverly's door. When there was no answer, she tapped again. "Bev? Bev, I'm sorry, but you need to wake up."

"Come in, Steph."

Bev's voice was husky. She'd been sound asleep.

When she entered the room, Stephanie spied a night-light. It cast a bluish white light across the room, enabling her to see Bev fairly clearly.

Bev was wearing a sleepy, sheepish expression. "I know. I've always slept with a night-light. I don't travel anywhere without it."

"I was surprised, not judging."

"Sorry. What's going on?"

"Someone arrived at the gate, and Hardy and Carter went out to meet him."

Bev frowned. "Who was it?"

"They wouldn't tell me, but I'm pretty sure it was someone dangerous." She swallowed, then added the complete truth. "That it is someone related to the shooting."

Bev's eyes widened. "Hand me that robe, would you?" She pointed to a hook behind Stephanie.

Sure enough, there was a sturdy-looking white terry-cloth robe that she'd seen Bev wear whenever she went downstairs to get a cup of coffee. "Here you go."

"Thanks." Standing up to pull on the robe, she startled as thunder clapped outside. "Man, this is a bad one."

"It's strong. I fear it's starting to sleet."

"It's like God decided we needed this night to be both dark and stormy, huh?" she joked. "Like we didn't have enough scary things to worry about."

"The Lord doesn't do things like that."

"I hope not. But it sure seems that way, doesn't it?" She padded to one of the windows that faced the back of the house and looked out. "I'm sorry to report that I can't see a thing." Turning back to her, she smiled. "I'm officially no help."

She was also officially far too relaxed. "You seem so calm. I don't think you understood what I said. You see, a stranger—"

"I heard. And I'm not calm. To be honest, I hate the idea that the two of us are alone in this big house." After a second, she added, "And I hate the idea that I've gotten so dependent on those guys that I'm thinking we're lost without them."

"I locked the door, and Hardy set the alarm."

"Okay. That's good. It's a fancy, state-of-the-art security system, Stephanie. If someone breathes on a window from the outside, those sensors are going to know."

"I think we should get dressed and wait."

"Me too. Meet you out in the hall in five minutes?"

"Jah. I'll be right back." She hurried out of Bev's room, walked down the hall, and then turned on the light in her room. With efficient movements, she put on her jeans and a sweater. Neatly folded on a chair was a pair of tights and a long, loose skirt. Both were items that Bev had brought with her. They weren't Amish clothes, of course, but they were more along the lines of what she usually wore.

But instead of looking reassuringly familiar, they looked too confining. She was no longer the person she'd been a week ago.

After she brushed her teeth and ran a warm washcloth on her face, she pulled back her hair in a ponytail. Just as she was walking back out to the hall, her phone buzzed.

Reminding her that she hadn't taken her phone with her like Hardy had asked her to. All this time her phone had been resting on the side table next to her bed.

Irritated with herself, she rushed over to pick it up, just as it began to ring.

She didn't recognize the number. "Yes?"

"Where have you been?" Carter barked in her ear.

"I . . . I was waking up Beverly and then we got to talking."

"Stephanie, listen to me good. Hardy has the guy who shot you in his truck. Get Beverly and go down to the basement. There's a room there. It's a gun room."

She shook her head. "I don't want a gun."

"No—listen. All my rifles and such for hunting are inside. It's a good place for you to wait. It's secure and it has reinforced walls. I was going to use it as a safe room eventually. When I had time to fix it up. Go there right this minute."

"Is Hardy in danger?"

"Don't worry about Hardy."

"Carter, please."

He sighed. "He can take care of himself. He could take care of half the county if someone needed him to. However, he is not going to be able to take care of anything if he's worrying about you. Do you understand?"

"Yes." Her hand was shaking. "But—"

"Oh, for heaven's sakes. Where's Bev? Go get her now."

Shaking—and trying to connect the kind and charming man she'd come to know with the mean one on the line—Stephanie hurried out in the hall. Bev was standing in the hallway. She frowned at Stephanie when she approached. Thrusting the phone at Bev, she said, "Talk to Carter."

"Carter, what's going on?" She paused. "What?" After another pause, she nodded. "Yes. I mean, yes, I understand. No, I don't need to write it down. I can remember a code, Carter. Yes. Yes, we will. Well, we would be doing it if you'd get off the phone."

As she clicked off, she said, "We've got to get inside that gun room. You take this phone, the charger Hardy gave you, and one or two things that you want."

"Like what?"

"I don't know," Bev muttered impatiently. "Get something that will help you get through this. Like your robe or a book. It doesn't matter. Just go get them."

"But—"

"Stephanie, now! We have to hurry."

Finally, finally her legs and brain seemed to start working together. Stephanie rushed into her room, unplugged the charger from the wall, and drew a blank. And then she saw the Bible.

If there was ever a time when they needed it, it would be now. "I'm ready."

"Me too." Beverly was also carrying her phone, the charger, and her night-light. "Ah, good thinking about the Bible. Okay, let's hurry before Carter calls and starts chewing us out again."

They hurried down one flight of stairs, unlocked a door with a code, and then entered another flight leading down to the basement. Bev stopped and reset the code. "Come on."

Down more stairs they went, then through the fancy game room and a storage room.

"Help me, Stephanie. It's behind this rack of clothes."

She shoved the clothes rack to one side as Bev punched in another set of numbers. A small buzz unlocked the door, and it clicked open.

"Pull the rack back so we can try to hide the door as much as we can."

With an umph, she did just that. When Beverly closed the door behind them, it buzzed again.

"We're locked in," Beverly said, looking around in the small room. On one wall was a case holding at least eight rifles.

Stephanie hated that there was even one on the wall. "Do you know how to get out?"

"I think we just punch in the code, but I don't want to risk it." Looking around, she covered her arms with her hands. "Boy, it's chilly in here. Let's grab those two blankets."

Stephanie got up on the bench across from them and pulled down a pair of thick, brown blankets from a top shelf. "They are rather scratchy," she murmured as she got down and handed Bev one.

Running a hand along hers, Bev said, "They are scratchy, but not terrible. They look like something people might use in the military. You know, like a regulation-type blanket."

Stephanie had no idea if the blankets looked like that or not. But as she unfolded hers and wrapped it around herself, she couldn't deny that it was warm and plenty big. "I'm thankful for them."

"Me too." Sitting down on the bench, Bev arranged the blanket around herself. "This isn't too bad, is it?"

"Not at all," she said as she sat down next to her.

"Still, let's hope and pray that we don't have to stay here too long."

Stephanie was happy to pray for that. The space was cramped and cool, making her feel as if they were in a giant refrigerator. Its walls were so thick that all sounds outside of the room would likely be muffled.

Bev might find that comforting, but since Stephanie wasn't able to hear anything outside of the space, she found it frightening.

The only thing worse than being locked in a safe room in a strange house was not knowing when Hardy or Carter would show up to get them out.

Or if they would return.

Or if someone else was already there, combing the rooms, looking for them.

That was the worst part, Stephanie decided. She didn't like not knowing if someone was standing right outside their door or if they were lying in wait in one of the many vacant rooms filled with nooks and crannies.

Lord, please be with Beverly and me. Give us patience and strength while we wait. Please be with Hardy and Carter too. I know You're already watching over them and guiding their moves, but if You could try to keep them safe too, that would be so nice.

"Stephanie?"

"Jah?"

"I know your faith is strong. Do you think God is listening right now?"

She had no idea, but she sure hoped so. She wasn't going to tell Bev that, however. Someone needed to sound confident, so it might as well be her.

After all, she was the reason all of them were in this mess.

And so, Stephanie answered as confidently as she could, even with a dash of bravado thrown in for good measure. "Yes," she said.

Next to her, Beverly released a big sigh. "I'm so glad you said that."

"Me too." Because she, too, needed to hear it—and believe it. Stephanie decided to concentrate on that while they waited. She'd learned a long time ago that dwelling on things she couldn't change never made one's life easier.

All it did was remind her that some things could never be changed.

30

Hardy didn't know where to take Timothy. His original plan had been to take him to Carter's. The house was enormous and there was a section near the kitchen that could be secured.

Between him and Carter, Timothy wouldn't be able to cause any trouble. Plus, if needed, they would be able to take advantage of Beverly's relationship with the kid. He might not remember her, but Bev sure remembered him, and also knew a few other guys that had joined the gang. And his sister was great with those kids. At the very least she could advise Hardy about what to say to Timothy.

On the other hand, he didn't want Stephanie to see or hear him at all. He still wanted to protect her. Protect her body, protect her heart. He wanted to do whatever he could to make this awful situation more bearable for her.

If that was even possible.

Even if Stephanie did end up seeing Timothy again, at least Hardy would be close by.

But now that he and Carter had separated and at least two gang members had followed Timothy to the ranch, there was no way Hardy was going to do anything to put the women in danger.

Therefore, he elected to take Timothy to the cabin where Stephanie had first stayed on the ranch. It was out of the way, which would keep Timothy isolated on the off chance that everything went wrong and somehow Timothy got the best of him. That was unlikely, but Hardy had seen lots of the best-laid plans go sideways when he was in the military and on patrol.

One of his guys used to say that the best plan was Plan D, because that meant that there were three other plans to go through first.

At the last minute, he decided to park behind a different cabin. It was a risk to take. If he needed to get to the main house or meet Carter somewhere, he was going to have to run fifty yards to get back to the truck.

On the other hand, he wanted the area to look vacant in case the gang members on foot spied his truck.

Now all he had to do was get Timothy inside without screaming for help or putting up a fight.

The zip ties would likely keep him from being too difficult, but he wasn't gagged. Yet, he mentally added. He wasn't gagged *yet*. He could absolutely take care of that if it was needed.

When he parked the vehicle, he turned off the lights. The darkness enveloped them. That, with the rain and wind continually pelting the vehicle, made it feel like they were completely isolated.

When he turned around, Hardy could barely make out Timothy's face. However, he did see enough to meet the kid's eyes. They were filled with stress and dread and exhaustion. The kid had been through the wringer and was out of both hope and faith. It was very obvious that he didn't expect to be alive in the morning.

All of his will seemed to have faded from him as well. Timothy simply stared. Not daring to say a word.

It was time to get going.

"Here's what we're going to do, Timothy. I'm going to get out, go get you, and then together we're going to walk to that cabin over there."

Timothy nodded.

"I'm carrying my favorite gun. As far as I'm concerned, you don't deserve much. You've already taken a man's life and shot at an innocent woman." He barely refrained from mentioning how perfect Stephanie was and how wrong it would have been if Timothy had snuffed out her life.

He took a breath and continued. "In addition, your continual need to focus on only yourself has caused everything that's happened. Your ex is in danger. So is Stephanie. So are you. And that's just the tip of the iceberg of the people who were affected by your actions."

"Then what?" Timothy scoffed, suddenly throwing attitude. "What are you going to do to me when we get out of this truck?"

"We're going to talk."

A grimace passed over Timothy's face.

Hardy reckoned Timothy was imagining a whole world of possible scenarios, none of them good. But, if he had to bet, he reckoned Timothy believed he was about to be interrogated. If their positions were switched, that's what he would have been thinking.

"Do you understand?"

"Yeah."

"I'm going to gag you."

"Whatever, though it ain't necessary. I came to you, re-member? If I wanted the other guys to find me, I wouldn't be here."

"All right then. We'll go without the gag."

The kid's eyes widened. "You believe me?"

"I have so far, right?" When Timothy turned silent again, Hardy figured there was nothing left to say. After yet another burst of lightning flashed overhead, he opened his door and got out, opened Timothy's door, and then guided him out of the truck.

And then they started walking.

No fifty yards had ever felt so long or foreboding. The land underfoot was soggy and slick.

Beside him, Timothy kept pace, though his steps were a little wobblier, on account of his hands being tied and being unable to balance himself.

He had to stop when a fierce burst of wind tore through the field, pelting them with cold raindrops and debris. If the temperature had been a little warmer, Hardy knew he'd be watching the sky for funnel clouds.

Only when they reached the cabin did something occur to Hardy. Timothy never said how he found Stephanie. Only those on the ranch and the sheriff knew she was here.

And just like that, everything he'd believed that was true was tossed on its side again. Timothy got his information from someone. And that someone was still out there, work-ing against him.

That idea stuck in his throat like a piece of meat that he hadn't chewed enough. Threatening to choke him.

Only with years of training did he refrain from mention-ing it while he unlocked the door and ushered them both inside. "Stay here," he ordered.

Timothy's eyes widened at the new tone, but he didn't say a word.

Instead, he barely moved. Dripping on the little rug that Stephanie had placed next to the door when she'd told Hardy that his boots were bringing in mud and grass onto her cleanly swept floors.

Practically hearing her chide him for not taking off his boots, he walked farther into the tidy, compact cabin and then quickly pulled down the shades. Needing at least a little bit of light, he lit a candle before returning to stand in front of Timothy.

To his surprise, the kid had been leaning against the wall and his eyes were closed. Was he so comfortable that he was able to fall asleep?

Or was he so weak and exhausted that his body was taking any opportunity to recharge?

Or had Dan been right, and the kid was jacked up on something?

"What is going on with you?" he bit out.

"You know."

"No. All I know is that you never told me how you knew the Amish girl was here. Who told you?"

"No one."

"I want the truth, Timothy."

"Fine. Bev once told me about this ranch. She'd joked that it was so big that someone could hide on the property for weeks. I started thinking that maybe she'd told the girl about it too."

"And you knew what ranch she was talking about?"

"No. I mean, not at first." Fresh agitation entered Timothy's eyes. "I started asking around. Turns out everyone knows about this ranch and all the people who work here. I left my car on the road and then walked to the guard gate."

"You expect me to believe that?"

Timothy shrugged. "It don't really matter what you believe. It's the truth. My car's out there for anyone to see."

Hardy doubted it. "I'm thinking that maybe you got your information from someone on the ranch's payroll. And maybe you're thinking that Carter Russell was an easy target. That he had a ton of money and not enough people to keep trespassers off the property. Maybe you decided to take advantage of that fact." He lowered his voice. "Or that maybe we wouldn't turn you over to the sheriff after we learn what you plan to do with the Amish girl." He didn't bother to hide his contempt for the kid. "What are you planning to do, Timothy?"

"Nothing!" he screamed. "I'm not planning anything! I never meant to shoot her in the first place. The gun went off." He shuddered. "Then everything went sideways and I was in trouble."

"Well, yeah."

"No. It was because a group of the Arrows were there, hiding." Glaring at him, Timothy raised his voice. "They were there to watch me get money owed to Stew from some drug dealer. It was my initiation." He released a ragged sigh. "But I messed it up. I killed him when I wasn't supposed to. And I didn't get the money. I messed everything up and I've been in trouble ever since."

"You should've gone to the police."

"Yeah, right. Like they would have believed anything I said."

Hardy was getting tired of listening to Timothy's excuses. "You were a prospect. They would've listened to a lot of things you had to say about the Arrows."

"It doesn't matter now anyway. I didn't go to the cops, and Kane gave me my orders. I had to find that Amish girl and make sure she didn't talk."

"So. Why do you want to go into police custody now?"

"Because if the police are involved now, they can help Audrey. I love her. I don't know what the Arrows will do to her, I don't want to think what they'll do! No matter what happens to me, I need her safe."

Against his will, Hardy felt sorry for the guy. Not much, but he knew enough about growing up around a bunch of bad kids with no future that he could sympathize. "Maybe it's an empty threat."

"It's not. They've done stuff to other girls." Tears filled Timothy's eyes. "Kane made her talk to me on his phone. He said she's being watched too. Audrey can't get away. It's all on me."

"If you need my help, why did you set us up tonight?"

"I didn't."

"Come on. You didn't distract me and Carter just to get those other guys on the property?"

"No. They . . . they got there on their own."

Something wasn't ringing true. "Timothy. I can't help you stay out of prison, but I can help you stay alive."

"Don't you understand what I'm saying? My life is already ruined. It was bad before I joined the gang and it's a whole lot worse now. Someone from the Arrows is going to make sure I die. If not tonight, then in prison. And if there's some reason that I'm not either tied up in this cabin or in a jail cell, someone else from the gang will track me down before the sun comes up."

"And you believe them? You think they're that powerful?"

Timothy looked at Hardy directly in the eyes. "I believe them enough to be standing here talking to you."

31

Time seemed to stand still when one was in a gun room in the middle of the night. No matter how hard she tried not to look at the clock on her phone, Bev still glanced at it regularly. Each time, only a minute or two had passed.

What if they were locked inside for eight hours? How was she going to handle that?

As much as Bev wanted to be brave and act as if their current situation wasn't the most frightening thing that had ever happened to her, she was pretty sure that she was failing miserably.

Stephanie was seated next to her on the bench. Unlike her, the girl sat almost motionless. If she hadn't moved every so often, Bev would have thought she was asleep.

She didn't know how that was possible, though. It was chilly in the safe room. Even though they were both completely dressed and wrapped up in the brown, scratchy blankets, the cool, damp air seemed to sink under her skin.

She knew Carter had intended to one day use the space for more than just hunting rifles. Presumably that was why he'd filled it with the kind of things you'd find in an Army surplus store. Everything was serviceable, but the rather spartan environment seemed to make their situation even worse.

Bev decided that if they ever made it out of here alive, she was going to buy Carter a set of new, plush, soft blankets. Lots of them.

Unable to help herself, she chuckled. That would be the perfect gift for the man who had everything, she decided. New blankets for his safe room.

"What are you laughing about?" Stephanie asked.

"Nothing worthwhile. I . . . well, I was just thinking that I'm going to give Carter new blankets for his birthday. These could use an upgrade."

"If you give him blankets, I'll give him some better lamps," she said. "The only one we have doesn't work, and I hate that we could find only one flashlight and we have no idea where the extra batteries are."

"You and me both."

Glad that Stephanie seemed happy to chat, Bev said, "Seriously, whenever we get out of here, I'm going to give Carter the biggest hug."

"That's it?" Stephanie teased.

"Well, sure. I mean, what else would I do?"

"Kiss him? I mean, that's what you should do if you like him as much as I think you do."

"Have you kissed Hardy?" Bev knew they were on a touchy subject. After all, Hardy was her brother. But discussing hugs and kisses was a lot more enjoyable than stewing on possible worst-case scenarios.

"Yes."

"Oh. Really?" She wasn't sure if she was shocked or not. She now realized that her feelings didn't matter. Hardy and Stephanie were grown adults. And, well, God was obviously reminding her that life was short and to live life to the fullest. She'd been wrong to try to steer Hardy away from Stephanie.

"Yes. Really," Stephanie said, bringing her back to the present.

Beverly wished she could see her face. "I guess you have feelings for Hardy too."

After a pause, she answered. "I do, which is too bad, don't you think?"

"Why would you say that?"

"Well, because nothing can happen between us."

Hating that Stephanie sounded so sad but certain, Bev knew she needed to tread lightly. They were in a tough enough situation without making each other cry. "Because you're Amish and he's not?"

"I'm not actually Amish yet. But there are other reasons too."

Stephanie sounded so subdued. Beverly reached out for her hand. "What are those? Because I promise you that Hardy—"

Two hard raps on the door shattered the moment and the last of her composure. Bev screamed.

Beside her, she sensed Stephanie's shoulders moving, as though she were crying silent tears.

"Bev, come on. Open up!"

Stephanie, whose hand was still nestled in hers, squeezed. "That's Carter."

Jumping to her feet, Bev called out, "Carter, we're in here!"

"I know. Now, will one of you please punch in the code and come on out? Once someone's locked in the room, it can only be opened from the inside."

To Beverly's shame, Stephanie was the one who acted first.

Before Beverly could recall the code, Stephanie had typed it in the keypad.

Instantaneously, a beep sounded, followed by a click.

When the door opened, the brighter light streaming through was near blinding. She ducked her head as her eyes attempted to adjust to the light.

"Carter, I'm so glad to see you," Stephanie said. "Beverly and I were getting tired of sitting in here."

"I bet," he said as he gave her a gentle hug. "You okay?"

"I'm fine."

"I'm glad." Carter released Stephanie.

Bev watched her walk away, obviously happy to move around and stretch her legs. She knew she needed to get up as well, but somehow her body refused to budge.

After standing outside the room for a few seconds, Carter entered.

"Bev," he whispered as he crouched down in front of her. "What's wrong? Are you hurt?"

"No. Of course not." And yes, most every word that was coming out of her mouth was a mixture of staccato words and blubbering. "I was worried about you."

"Me? I'm fine."

"I see that. I'm sorry, I don't know why I'm crying. I'll be okay in a moment."

He moved to the bench beside her. "Come here, Bev."

Next thing she knew, she was sitting on Carter's lap. His arms were holding her close and he was whispering sweet things. Sweet words mixed with light kisses to her cheek, her brow, her neck, wherever he found bare skin. Each touch and brush brought comfort and peace.

And a nestling of hope threaded with desire. When she lifted her head, it was to meet his lips. To share something life-affirming and passionate. Within seconds, it was heated.

So perfect.

"Uh, Carter? Bev?" Stephanie said from the doorway.

Something was wrong. Breaking apart, they stood up.

"Stephanie?" Carter said. "What's going on?"

"We . . . we have company." With tentative steps, Stephanie came into view. Making Beverly's heart constrict. Dan the guard was holding a knife to her side.

"Hey, Boss," he said.

32

We've got company.

Carter's text might have sounded cryptic, but Hardy knew him well enough to understand every underlying meaning. The other gang members had arrived.

Who's there?

It's Kane and Company. Dan too.

On my way.

Call Johnson.

Already done.

Timothy, who was still tied up beside him, was staring at Hardy's phone screen. Obviously, he'd been able to read the texts. To his surprise, the guy wasn't reacting much at all. His body had tensed, but he remained silent.

Was he waiting for Hardy to tell him what was happening? Or fill him in about what they were going to do next?

Or was it something different entirely?

Maybe Timothy Jones had given up.

Though he could understand why the kid was probably thinking that he had nothing left to live for, Hardy hoped that wasn't the case.

Again and again, he'd been reminded that he couldn't take care of everything by himself. He knew that he and Carter were going to need Timothy's help for Stephanie and Bev to remain unharmed.

"Did you read my texts?" he asked.

Timothy shrugged.

"If you didn't, it looks like your friends broke into the main house. Carter needs help."

"It's gonna go bad."

That was the last thing Hardy needed to hear. He jerked Timothy's elbow, pulling him up to his feet. "Don't say that. Just come on. We've gotta go."

After a momentary hesitation, the kid stepped forward. Waiting for instructions.

Hardy was surprised. He'd half expected Timothy to let out a string of curses. Maybe even fight him a bit.

Hardy wouldn't have blamed Timothy if he did. The kid was desperate, and the gang members were on a mission to avenge the imagined wrongs against them. He was starting to believe that they thought Timothy was the root of all their troubles.

"You still armed?" Timothy asked.

"Yeah."

"Good."

He didn't put up a fight when Hardy loaded him in the truck and remained silent as Hardy sped down the road to the main house.

He was glad of that. Hardy's head felt like it was going a

million miles an hour, making plans about how to keep the women safe, support Carter, and not get either himself or Carter killed while doing so.

He came to the conclusion that the only way to have any semblance of a chance was to free Timothy's hands. If he was telling the truth, his former friends would use Timothy any way they could in order to silence Stephanie. The kid needed a fighting chance.

And if for some reason Timothy had been telling Hardy a heap of lies and it was all a convoluted plot to get the best of him and Carter, then he would have to deal with that when the time came. He and Carter had dealt with more than one untrustworthy person when they'd been deployed overseas.

Pulling into the drive, he cut the motor, then pulled a knife from out of his boot. "Turn sideways," he said.

Timothy tensed but once again did as he was bid. The moment his wrists were free, he slowly moved his arms, no doubt attempting to ease the cramped muscles.

Hardy paused for a second, half expecting the kid to turn on him in anger. Instead, he faced front again.

"What did you do that for?" he asked in a low tone.

"You need a fighting chance."

"You serious?"

"Obviously. Timothy, I want the men who came after you caught. When the sheriff arrives, I want him or one of the deputies to take you into custody. You need to pay for your crimes. But I don't want you to be killed while tied up. I don't want that on my shoulders."

"You really think that matters?"

"To me, it does." Not wanting to waste another second, he opened the driver's side door. "Come on."

He heard Timothy exit his side of the vehicle and his

footsteps follow him through an open carport, and finally to a set of stairs that led to a mudroom of sorts.

The hair on the back of Hardy's neck tickled, whether it was because he was half waiting for Timothy to attack him or because he was scared about what he'd find. He wasn't sure.

Then, he remembered all the times in his past when trusting others had been the right thing to do. Trusting the other men and women in his unit. Trusting the soldiers they'd flown overseas to protect.

Even trusting his officers enough to follow their directives without hesitating.

Finally, he remembered that moment on the bus. When he'd been seven and scared and alone . . . and Edward had stepped out of nowhere to help him. For no reason other than that it was the right thing to do.

Just like the Lord had done for him on many an occasion.

And a sense of calm filled him. Eased his muscles. Gave him hope.

He opened the door to Carter's house and walked inside. And felt his life come full circle when Timothy followed.

The mudroom was dark, but the hallway and rooms beyond were bright. He pulled out his gun. The comforting weight of the piece settled in, and muscle memory took over.

"We were wondering when you were going to show up," a man said as he stepped out of the shadows. "Timothy, look at you. Hiding behind more coattails?"

Hardy pulled back the safety. "I don't know who you boys are, but you're trespassing on private property."

The guy raised his hands. "Don't worry. We're not here to rob you. We only came for our friend, here."

"Where's Audrey?" Timothy said as he walked forward.

"Last I checked, she's still all right. One of the guys is watching her. And waiting." The man winked. "They're waiting to see what happens here."

"You need to set her free, Kane."

"We can't do that until you come with us—and we take care of the Amish girl."

"I don't know where she is."

"That's okay. She's right here with Dancer."

Hardy sucked in a breath as Dancer entered the room. The gang member had his arm around Stephanie's throat. In his hand was a blade. There was already a trickle of blood dripping down.

Rage filled him. The guy had been playing with them. "No," he bit out.

"Put the knife down!" Carter said as he appeared from a dark hallway. Everyone turned.

Hardy couldn't believe his eyes. "Where is Dan?" Dan should've seen the men on the security cameras.

"He's injured, I'm afraid," Carter said in a cold voice. Turning to Kane, he added, "When I realized that he not only turned off the electric fence but had been the one to tell Timothy about Stephanie, I told him that I was going to make sure he rotted in prison a long time. When he ignored my warning, I shot his kneecap. He's not going anywhere anytime soon." His gaze hardened as he focused on Dancer. "You'd best put the knife down before I do worse to you."

Hardy could barely hold himself together when Stephanie looked his way. Tears were in her eyes. Silently, he attempted to reassure her.

Then, as if she was in slow motion, she glanced at Timothy.

After meeting her gaze, Timothy charged forward and

jumped Dancer. The knife clattered to the ground as Dancer fell. A gun went off.

Seconds later, Hardy subdued Kane, Stephanie was free, and Timothy Jones lay on the ground, dead.

After several minutes had passed, the door burst open and Sheriff Johnson entered the foyer. He took in the gang members tied up, Timothy's dead body, and Stephanie's bleeding neck. His expression hardened. "Sitrep."

Hardy shared a look with Carter before walking to Stephanie's side. Since she looked like she was about to collapse, he gently pulled her into his embrace and held her tight.

"Hardy." She grabbed hold of his shirt with her fists, as if she was afraid he'd step away. There wasn't a chance of that.

Pressing kisses to her face, he gently rubbed her back while holding her securely with his other arm. "I've got you, Stephanie," he whispered. "I've got you."

He didn't know if he was ever going to be able to let her go.

33

She didn't like to admit it, but dressing Plain didn't feel comfortable any longer. Maybe it was because the dress, apron, and prayer covering she was wearing were made by a woman in the Amish community outside of Marion. Though the style of dress and kapp were the same, the light, almost vibrant blue of her dress felt foreign. The women in her community in Adams County often wore more somber clothing.

Or perhaps it was just her aunt and uncle who did?

Whatever the reason, she couldn't seem to get comfortable in the passenger seat of Hardy's truck.

"Girl, you've been shifting and fidgeting for the last seventy miles. What can I do to make you more comfortable?" Hardy asked as he continued to drive on the highway toward Bowling Green, then eventually Louisville and the Ohio state line.

Embarrassment made her neck and face heat.

"I just can't seem to sit still. I'll do better."

Hardy sighed. "See, this is why I was reluctant to say anything. I didn't want to hurt your feelings."

"You haven't."

His hands tightened on the steering wheel, just like the skin around his mouth pinched. "I wish I wasn't driving seventy miles an hour right now. I'd give a lot to be able to study your expression when we talk."

It was on the tip of her tongue to suggest that they pull over at the next rest stop. She was in no hurry to go home—which was difficult to admit to herself. But she also knew that Hardy had put his whole life on hold these last two weeks. He'd also put his life—and his sister's life—in danger. She needed to let him be.

"See, like now," he said.

"What are you talking about? I haven't said a word."

"Exactly. I feel like you've got a whole novel of thoughts floating around in your head that you aren't sharing."

"If I do, it's because those thoughts aren't important."

"That's where you're wrong. They are to me."

Unbidden, her eyes filled with tears. She blinked, hoping to slow their descent down her cheeks. But of course, it was inevitable. One tear escaped, then two.

She swiped one with the side of a palm.

"Stephanie?"

"Don't worry about it."

"This. I can't take this. Hold on." Looking angry, he clicked on his turn signal and moved to the right lane. Then did it again. Two minutes later, he was exiting the highway.

"Where are you going?"

"Somewhere we can talk."

"But where are we?"

"Same answer. Someplace where the two of us can talk and I can look at you."

What did one say to that? Nothing, she reckoned. One said nothing. Especially that's what she should do, since her eyes had decided to become waterworks and didn't seem of the mind to stop. So, she bit her lip and clasped her hands together tightly as Hardy slowed to the town's speed limit, turned, turned again, and then ended up at the town's rather rundown city square. On one end was a courthouse. On the other was a Baptist church. In between was a large field, a copse of trees which probably looked very pretty in the spring and summer months, and several groupings of retail shops. Half of them were empty.

When he parked, he unlocked the doors, then was out and at her passenger door before she'd gathered herself together.

"Come on," he said as he held out his hand for her to take.

In the past, she would have frozen from fright. Today, she placed her hand in his without hardly thinking about it.

Because she was used to him.

Yet another wave of sadness rolled through her, dampening her spirits even further. She shivered, trying to get a grip on herself.

He noticed. Because Hardy always noticed. "Here," he said, pulling off his old green Army jacket and placing it over her shoulders.

"Thank you." It was warm from his body and infused with his scent. And her body responded, like it had from almost the very beginning. Emotion and desire linked and knotted together, pulling at her heart with a yearning so fierce that she ached to both pull the jacket around her more tightly . . . and throw it off in order to feel his arms around her instead.

He stopped. "Stephanie, I wanted to speak with you, and not while the two of us were strapped in my truck. But it's colder than I thought and so open. I feel like if we sit down on one of these benches, we'll be on view for the entire population."

She looked around and noticed something that looked like a cross between a diner and a coffee shop. It had an old sign on the top that said MANN'S, but there were a few people inside. "How about there?" she said. "We could get something to eat and maybe use the bathroom before we get back on the road."

"Sounds good." He stepped to her side and even pressed his hand on the small of her back as they walked.

Stephanie wondered if he was aware of it, then called herself a fool. Of course Hardy was aware of what he was doing. If she'd learned anything about him, it was that he didn't do anything without forethought.

When they entered Mann's, the two of them received more than a few second glances, but she supposed that shouldn't be a surprise. Not only was it probably a rarity to see an Amish woman, but for one to arrive in a pickup truck and walk into a diner wearing a man's jacket was likely even more noteworthy.

"You two sit anywhere you'd like," an older man called out. "Menus are on the table. I'll be by in a few."

"Thanks," Hardy said in his low voice. "What do you think? A booth over on the side?"

"Yes." She smiled softly before leading the way. She scooted in on one side, the red vinyl squeaking as she did. Hardy did the same on his side.

They each took a menu and scanned it. To her surprise,

she realized she was hungry. "I didn't know it was so late. It's already midafternoon."

"The time's gone fast for me too."

"Hey there," the man who'd greeted them said. "I'll bring you some water. Y'all want anything else to drink? Coffee, soda? A shake?"

"Coffee please."

"Two," Hardy said.

"We've got soup today. Two kinds. Vegetable beef and fish chowder. The chowder's better. You think on that and I'll be back."

She shared a smile with Hardy. "I wonder if he's Mann."

"I wouldn't be surprised. He's got that air about him," he said as he continued to look at his menu.

"Do you two know what you'd like?" the man asked when he returned.

"I'd like a BLT, please," Stephanie said.

"I'll take one of those too. And a bowl of chowder."

Looking from one to the other, the server said, "Want it coming right up or should I take my time?"

"Take your time," she said before Hardy had a chance to speak.

When they were alone, Hardy leaned back. "You feel the same way that I do."

"You aren't anxious to return home either?" she teased.

"I'm not anxious to drop you off." A wrinkle formed in between his eyes. "How were your aunt and uncle when you spoke to them?"

She shrugged. "About the same."

"That doesn't tell me much."

"They were thankful that I'm safe and glad that our ordeal was over."

"And . . . ?"

"And, I got the feeling that they, too, had mixed emotions about me returning."

"Why is that?"

She didn't want to sound ungrateful so she chose her words with care. "I was a great help to them. But I also stirred things up, I fear. I haven't been baptized. They don't like that."

"So they're anxious for you to help them with their children but not for you to be Stephanie."

"They're my cousins and I love them. Being with Charity, Evan, and Hope isn't a chore. But, yes. You described it well." She searched her brain. Tried to think of something else to say about them. Something more meaningful. Something honest but perhaps more kind than she'd been sounding.

But once again, her head felt cloudy and vacant. Frustrated with herself, she picked up her coffee and took a sip. It was very hot and very flavorful.

"What about you?" He lowered his voice. "What are your mixed emotions?"

No. No way was she going to open herself up like that. It was just an invitation for him to stomp on her heart, and she was doing a good enough job of that on her own. "Nothing worth mentioning."

"Don't do that." When she stared, he added, "Don't hide from me."

"I'm not."

"You know what I mean."

"It's hard to be so honest," she retorted. "You must know that because you're making me admit things first."

"You're right. I'm not real eager to tell you what I'm thinking, because it's not right."

"Maybe you should let me be the judge of that."

"All right. Here we go. But if I make you embarrassed or mad, you have to promise that you aren't going to do anything foolish. No matter what, you're still going to get in that truck with me."

"Of course I'm going to do that."

"You better."

She rolled her eyes. "Hardy, where else would I go?"

Hardy cleared his throat and looked at her with a mix of tenderness and fear. "I've fallen in love with you. That's what's on my mind. I want you, Stephanie. I want you to be mine. I want your heart. I want your attention. I want you to be English so I can marry you. I want you to live on the ranch, because I want to build us a house to live in there. I want us to have babies. I want to grow old with you. But every bit of that sounds pushy and almost crazy. We've known each other only a few weeks."

He lowered his voice. "If that isn't something you want, if it isn't something you think you'll *ever* want, I'll settle for not dropping you off at your uncle and aunt's house if it seems like they won't appreciate you."

Every word Hardy said sounded as if it came from somewhere deep in his heart. Or maybe her heart was where his words hit her? All she did know was that she couldn't help but replay each word he said in her mind. He loved her. He wanted her. He wanted to marry her.

What was the right way to respond? She took a deep breath. "Hardy . . ."

"Hold on. Let me finish. What I'm trying to say is that I want you to be happy. Your happiness is what matters the most. You don't need to change for them, Stephanie. You don't need to change for me. Or for anyone, for that matter.

Because I can promise you this: You are just fine exactly the way you are."

Somehow tears were forming in her eyes even as her mouth had gone dry. Hardy was staring at her, obviously waiting for her to respond. To say something. Anything coherent.

But her mind had gone blank.

No, that wasn't true. She could still hear his words, each one both fantastical and heartfelt. She wanted to believe them. Wanted to imagine that his words could be true. Or, at the very least, that she could one day be accepted for just being her. Stephanie.

The woman born Amish but orphaned too soon. Who appreciated and loved her aunt and uncle and their family but also resented that they didn't ever put her needs first.

Who'd been shot. Who'd been forced to trust a series of strangers in order to keep both her family and herself safe.

A woman who had survived, but because she had, she was also changed. No one could expect her to act as if she hadn't gone through that. Could they?

Wait. Was that what she'd been doing? She clenched her hands together. "Hardy, I want to believe you."

"You should, because it's the truth."

His certainty made her doubts and insecurities feel even worse. "I want to be able to tell you how I feel, how I really feel," she whispered, "but I'm afraid."

He frowned. "Of what?"

"Of how you might feel when you know the real me." Hating each word but believing them to be true, her voice hitched. If only the Lord had made her different. How could facing a bunch of gang members feel easier than admitting what was in her heart? "I . . . I'm sorry." Her voice hitched as tears formed in her eyes.

He noticed. Because he noticed everything when it came to her. "Stephanie, hey. Don't get yourself worked up. I don't expect—"

"Here you go, kids," their server interrupted as he carried a tray to the table. "Two BLTs and one bowl of fish chowder." As he placed everything in front of them, he said, "There's ketchup on the side and more coffee if you need it. Look good?"

"Yeah. Thanks," Hardy said.

Stephanie smiled at the man but couldn't speak if her life depended on it.

"All righty, then." Picking up the tray, he turned around but then did an about-face seconds later. "This ain't none of my business, so feel free to ignore the good intentions of an old man. But for what it's worth, my wife used to tell me that when all is said and done, the only thing that really matters is if you make each other happy."

Hardy glowered. "Pardon me?"

If the man was bothered by Hardy's scowl and impatience, he didn't show it.

Instead, he just kept talking, one word sliding into the next. "When she lay in bed at the end of her days, she told me that her life became clear as she was dying. You see, doing what everyone expects doesn't feel as good as one might think. But doing what your heart wants? Well, that fills you up and makes all the other garbage in life seem like it don't mean a thing." He shrugged. "Just saying."

When he finally walked away, Stephanie automatically bowed her head, but could only give the Lord and the hands that made their food the most cursory of thanks.

The two speeches were ringing in her ears and making her thoughts run together. But even stronger was the voice ringing in her head. The one that was reminding her that it was finally time to stop putting everyone else first. That it was okay to care about others but also care about herself.

It was time to listen to the words her heart and head were speaking to her. At long last.

34

Hardy had imagined a lot of things about Stephanie's aunt and uncle. It had been hard not to. When he'd first learned that Stephanie's parents had died and Jo and Mark Miller had taken her in, he imagined they'd be a nice couple with a deep propensity for giving.

Later, after hearing more about her life in their house—the way she'd been told to cook, clean, and care for their children—Hardy had adjusted his thoughts. He'd grown concerned. He'd hated to think of her being treated like a servant in her own home.

Almost on the heels of that had been his reminders that just because someone helped run a household didn't mean that they were being taken advantage of.

But after spending so much time with both Bev and Stephanie while they were at Carter's ranch, Hardy had learned a lot more information. Little of it had been good. Eventually, Hardy believed he had a pretty good impression of what they might be like. He'd even gone so far as to guess how they might greet Stephanie's return and how they might treat him.

He wasn't too worried about himself. He'd spent too

many years in the military not to have the ability to speak reasonably with just about anyone from any background.

After sitting in their living room for an hour, however, Hardy realized he'd been naïve. Jo and Mark Miller were like nothing he'd imagined.

They were dour and rigid and, strangely, didn't seem to react to all they'd been told. They didn't seem to realize their niece had narrowly escaped death.

And Stephanie? It was as if the walls of the house were pulling all the life out of her. With each passing minute she became more and more withdrawn and quiet.

He hated it.

He also hated the fact that her aunt and uncle were now actively attempting to get him to leave. Even though he knew he should respect their wishes, Hardy didn't know if he was going to be able to do that.

Especially because Stephanie continued to glance his way. Whether she was doing it on purpose or unconsciously, Hardy didn't care. All that mattered to him was that she was needing him.

Which meant that he wasn't going anywhere until she didn't need him anymore.

After he drank a second cup of coffee, Mark stood up. "Mr. Anderson, we are grateful you brought Stephanie back to us. It was a long drive, yes?"

"It was."

"Will you be driving back today?"

"I will."

Mark's eyes warmed. "Then I'm sure you realize that we are anxious for Stephanie to get settled. She has things she must attend to."

Hardy stood up as well. "I'm sure she does."

"Then you understand that it's time for you to be on your way."

Stephanie bent her head. Said nothing.

She looked cowed. Like she'd given up all hope. Hardy could hardly stand that. Where was the brave girl who'd faced a bunch of gang members? "Stephanie, you haven't showed me your room," he said mildly. "How about we go do that?"

Her eyebrows rose, but she stood up. "All right."

Jo's pinched expression turned even more sour. "Hardy, you forget that we are not living as Englishers. It is unseemly for you to see her room."

"I haven't forgotten. However, I've been looking after her for two weeks, around the clock. Her comfort and happiness mean something to me."

Stephanie's cheeks flushed, but she didn't argue. If anything, it looked a little like she was attempting to not start laughing.

"Come show me your room, Steph."

"You two cannot go by yourselves."

"You do remember that we've been together all day?"

While Mark looked like he was actively holding his tongue, Stephanie said, "It's this way, Hardy."

He followed her down a narrow hall and then down a steep flight of stairs to the basement. Because he'd spent so much time near Marion and the Amish community there, Hardy had been in a few Amish homes. Once, he'd helped an elderly Amish couple build some new shelves along a living room wall.

So he knew that many lived in their basements in the summer. It was far cooler down there.

But this was not a part-time living area. It was essentially an unfinished space with concrete floors, walls, and exposed pipes. Looking around, he spied a large laundry area. There was a washing machine, a makeshift table, and a web of lines hanging on which to pin laundry.

There was a large compilation of boxes and baskets and who knew what else. The family's storage area.

None of that was surprising.

What was surprising was the small room off to the side. It was essentially a curtained area, maybe eight feet by seven. That was where they went.

"Here it is," she said.

It was a struggle to keep his expression blank. In the space was a twin bed, a small, braided rug, and a three-shelf bookcase. The table beside the bed was a wooden crate on its side. On top of it lay a flashlight. On the floor on the other side of the small bed was a basket with some clothes and what looked to be a library book on top.

He couldn't find much else.

"This is your bedroom." He didn't bother to phrase it as a question. It was obvious. More importantly, it was a struggle for him to rein in his temper.

"Yes." Looking around, Stephanie reached out and smoothed the edge of the curtain that was open. "It doesn't look like much, does it?"

He couldn't lie. Not even for her. "No." Turning to face her, he said, "Have you lived here the whole time?"

"Pretty much. The first week or two I shared a room with Hope, but she was very young. We both needed our own space."

"So they moved you here."

Looking away from him again, she said, "I don't know what you want me to say, Hardy. It's a far cry from the rooms we had in Carter's house or the sweet little cabin I stayed in when I first arrived."

"I don't expect you to say anything." No, that was a lie. He wanted Stephanie to ask him to take her away. To find her someplace better. To take her to the courthouse and beg a judge to marry them quickly so he could make her his wife so no one would ever again treat her like a glorified servant.

"Are you sure?"

He could hear walking over their heads. They'd been downstairs ten minutes, but her aunt and uncle were probably not okay with the two of them being alone for even that long. "I was honest with you in that diner. I told you that I love you and I told you that I want you to be mine. If you want me to be honest again, I could say that I hate this room."

"Hardy."

"Sorry, but it's the truth. It's cold down here. I can't imagine that it's much better in the summer. You only have a quilt. I'm already thinking about you shivering in the middle of the night."

"It's not that bad."

"Stephanie, it's close to that, though. This surpasses my worst imaginings of your living situation. Everything inside of me is violently against leaving you here. But I will. If you want to stay, then I will go."

"Hardy, it's not that easy."

"I'm sure making that choice isn't easy at all."

"I owe them a lot."

"They owe you too. You lost your parents, girl. They're your kin. They should've done more than stick you in this spot when you aren't helping to cook, clean, and care for your cousins."

Hurt shone in her eyes. "You don't understand."

"You're right. And I know I'm being brutally honest. But we're out of time."

"Stephanie!" Jo called out. "It is time you came upstairs!"

"I will!" Looking at him intently, she said, "You meant it, didn't you?"

"What? Taking you with me? Marrying you?"

"Yes. And that you love me?"

"I meant every word. I love you so much that I'd leave you here, if that is what you wanted. Is that what you want? Do you want me to leave?"

"Stephanie, now," Mark said. His first footsteps started on the wooden stairs, echoing in the vacant, bare space.

Panic filled Stephanie's eyes. She stared at her bed. At the walls. Finally at him.

"No."

Mark called out to them again. "Hardy, you are overstepping our kindness and patience. It's time you came with me. Stephanie, you may stay down there until we tell you to come up."

Hardy ignored every word. There was only one word he cared about, and that was the one she'd just whispered. "You're gonna have to give me more than that, Steph."

"No, I don't want you to leave me here. I love you too. I'll leave with you now." She took a deep breath, then added, "And yes, Hardy. If you were truly asking, then my answer is yes. I will marry you."

"Stephanie, no!" Mark said.

Hardy ignored him again. Pulling her into his arms, he held her close and kissed her cheek. "I'll make this up to you," he whispered in her ear. "One day soon, I'll propose on one knee and give you flowers. I'll give you a ring, because that's my way. I'll give you sweet words. I'll make this right. I promise you this. I'll make it a memory worth having."

She shook her head slowly. "There's no need. This one is a pretty good memory right here. I'll keep it."

And then, of course, it was impossible to do anything but kiss her. Right there in the middle of a makeshift bedroom in a cold, concrete basement. With her glowering uncle looking on.

And as she melted into him, showing him that nothing mattered but the two of them, Hardy realized that once again, Stephanie was right.

Nothing could top this moment.

Nothing.

It was perfect as it was.

Lifting his head, he pressed his lips to her brow. "Get whatever you want, sweetheart, and hand it to me. It's time we moved on."

EPILOGUE

Stephanie reckoned that there would come a day when she might want to live someplace other than the little cabin near a pond on the edge of the Russell Ranch, but today wasn't that day. Not when the May air was perfectly breezy, the flowers in her garden were starting to bloom, the cabin smelled of freshly made bread, and her husband was pulling into his parking spot on the side of their home.

Sitting on one of the chairs on the front porch, she heard the engine shut off, then a dog bark, and finally the telltale excited chatter of their two-year-old, Bridget. Bridget Anderson was her daddy's girl.

Her family was home.

Well, the rest of her family. Five-year-old Aden Carter Anderson was sitting beside her, his nose in a book as always.

"Dad's home, Aden," she said. "Bridget and Stormy too."

As expected, their boy's head popped up and looked to his right, obviously checking for Hardy's truck. Tossing the book on the table, he trotted out to greet them.

Content to simply observe, Stephanie crossed her ankles and put down the quilt square she'd been working on.

"Dad! Hey!" Aden called out.

"Right here, bud," Hardy said in his low, always scratchy voice. "How's everything?"

"Good." He held still for his father to run a hand through his hair, but just barely. The moment he was free he reached for Bridget, who'd decided to sit down on the ground to look at the pansies Stephanie had planted a few days ago. "Bridget, don't eat the pansies."

"A," she said, which was as far as Bridget had gotten on Aden's name. Stephanie secretly hoped that their little girl would call him that for a while. The way she called out that letter was adorable.

When Stormy clambered up the steps to greet her, Stephanie rubbed the Australian Shepherd's scruff. "Hiya, hund," she whispered. "I missed ya."

After licking her hand, the dog walked to the sunny patch on the porch and lay on his side. He was no doubt ready for a break after spending the morning with Bridget.

"Watch your sister now," Hardy told Aden before walking to the porch. "How are you feeling?" he asked. "Have you been resting like you're supposed to?"

"As much as I can." She looked down at her belly, almost stretched to capacity. Just like she'd been with Aden and Bridget. "This one seems to believe that it's time to do somersaults the minute I sit still."

"Not too much longer now."

She reached out to him. She didn't need his help to stand up, but she had become spoiled by his attentions. As she'd expected, after glancing at their children one more time, he pulled her up and then enfolded her in his arms. "Better?" he murmured, kissing her neck.

She had her arms around him, smelling his familiar scent,

and had two healthy children, plus one on the way, and a very good dog. "Jah. It's gut. How were things at the big house?"

"Almost the same as here."

"Truly?"

He laughed. "Of course not. It's barely controlled chaos over there." Eyes sparkling, he said, "Bridget fit right in."

"She loves playing with the older kinner." Carter and Bev had married a year after she and Hardy but had wasted no time in starting their family. Beverly had gotten pregnant on their honeymoon. They'd also started adoption proceedings with James, a twelve-year-old boy she'd worked with. Now, all these years later, they had a family of seven, with three children they'd adopted and two that Bev had given birth to.

Hardy had once confided that he was glad Carter still allowed him to run the sprawling ranch. Between Carter's work in Cincinnati and all their children, the man had little time for horses or sheep.

After depositing Stephanie back in her chair, Hardy took the one beside her. "I also drove out to see Seth Zimmerman," he said. "I gave him the deposit on the house."

She glanced at him in surprise. Seth Zimmerman was former Amish and a master carpenter. After working for a builder for years, he started out on his own. He was known for building custom homes. Hardy had been wanting to build them a bigger house ever since she'd gotten pregnant with Bridget, but Stephanie had been dragging her heels. This little cabin meant so much to her. It was here that she'd fallen in love with Hardy.

"You don't want to wait a little longer?"

His gaze softened. "Stephanie. Honey. This new baby is going to take up room. More room than we have."

"We could do another addition."

"We're going to need something more than that. Honey, it's time to have our own place."

She slumped. "I suppose."

"We've got to build the whole house, Steph. That ain't going to happen overnight. It might even take close to a year."

"I bet by then I'll be agreeing with you."

"I feel fairly certain you will. Plus, Aden's going to want some space. Everyone needs their own space, don't you think?"

Those words brought back one of the best moments of her life. The moment she knew that she would be willing to leave everything she knew for a future where nothing was certain. She'd walked out of her aunt and uncle's house with tears in her eyes and a full heart.

So much was uncertain in life. She'd learned the hard way that nothing lasted forever. Not even one's childhood. But when she'd kept her hope and held tightly to the belief that God would not let her down, amazing things had happened.

Life had happened.

And while every day wasn't easy, she'd also learned the value of pushing herself and doing what she thought was right.

Her life with Hardy was testament to that.

"Do you ever think about that day?" she whispered.

"Which day is that?"

"The day that Timothy risked everything for Audrey. The day that he made a decision to be different than the moment before. Do you ever think about that?"

"Every day."

"Me too," she whispered right before Aden started guiding Bridget toward them. Her hands were dirty and there was a smudge of dirt on her cheek.

"Sorry, Momma," Aden said. "I tried to get her to not stick her hand in her mouth."

Pushing herself out of her chair, she walked down the steps to meet her children. She leaned down to kiss Aden's brow then picked up Bridget.

"Stephanie," Hardy called out. "You shouldn't—"

"I know, but I'm okay." Turning around, she faced Hardy standing on the front porch of the cabin.

"What matters is that I still can do this today. That's all that matters to me." Only the Lord knew what tomorrow was going to be like.

But today? Well, today was a very good day. She gave thanks to God.

Read on
for a sneak peek at

Shelley's next Amish romance.

<small>AVAILABLE SUMMER OF 2026.</small>

She was so tired of being nice. No, that wasn't true, Leanna Mast decided. She liked being nice. She was a nice person. She was just tired of being nice to the men who had started calling on her on Sunday afternoons. Most of them she'd known all her life. Some were old enough to be her father. None of them were husband material—if she were looking for one. She'd already been married once and had no desire to be married again. Ever.

But, if she *did* decide to get married again, it would not be to the man currently sitting on her couch. Mervin Detweiler was too brash and too bossy. Plus, he stared at her chest too much . . . and he'd been her husband Willis's boss. Leanna hadn't liked him when her husband was alive. She liked Mervin even less now that Willis had gone to heaven.

Unfortunately, that didn't mean she could ask him to leave before his hour was up.

Since she still had eighteen minutes to go, she gestured to his coffee cup. "Would you care for some more kaffi, Mervin?"

"I would." He leaned back so she could reach down to pick up his cup and saucer.

Gritting her teeth, Leanna leaned over and picked them up, then stood up straight. "I'll be right back."

Only when she reached the privacy of her kitchen did she press her hands to her eyes. Tears were threatening. She needed to fight them back before Mervin noticed. She'd learned that all her later-in-life suitors looked for weaknesses. Her weaknesses were something they could focus on. Make her feel bad about. Make her feel like she shouldn't be alone anymore.

Taking a deep breath, she poured Mervin another cup of coffee and hurried back to the living room. The spring day was warm and pleasant. If she'd been alone, she would've walked barefoot on the smooth wood floor. Instead, she was still in her gray dress and black tennis shoes.

Mervin was leaning against the back of the couch and surveying her wall of books when she returned. He was also frowning. So much so, he didn't even bother to acknowledge that she'd refilled his cup.

"Are all of those yours, Leanna?"

Though she knew what he was referring to, she turned around. "Do you mean my books?"

"Of course."

Facing him again, she nodded. "Yes, they're my books. I like to read."

"Willis allowed you to do that?"

"He did." She lifted her chin. "Why do you ask?"

Mervin's expression tightened. "I don't believe in women reading."

"Why not?"

"It keeps them away from more important things, don't you think?"

"What things?" Though Mervin was being rude, Leanna was starting to get curious. Her house was spotless, her coffee fresh, she'd gone to church that morning, and he'd eaten two cookies that she'd baked only yesterday. What else was she supposed to be doing?

"Taking care of one's husband and children."

The proper and right thing would be to nod politely. Maybe smile in a self-deprecating way. But sometime in the last year, her tongue had gotten a little looser.

"Since I have neither a husband nor children, I believe I have time to read books."

Mervin frowned. Finished his coffee. And then stood up. "Leanna, I don't think we would suit."

She knew they would not. But instead of stating it, she demurred and inclined her head. "Thank you for coming by this afternoon."

"Harumph." He picked up his hat and strode across the wood to her door. "I'd like to give you some advice, Leanna. Men don't like women who speak their minds." He looked her over. "Even women as attractive as you. Looks fade, sweetness does not. You would do well to remember that."

She knew he was looking for an apology. That wasn't going to happen. Instead, she opened the door. "Good day, Mervin."

After delivering one more scathing look, he turned and walked down her front porch steps. And almost ran into the rather short woman in a crisp white kapp who was approaching.

The woman stopped and gave him a pointed look.

Mervin quickly moved to the side. "Pardon me," he said.

"It's quite all right, sir. No harm done at all." She smiled at him before walking up Leanna's steps. "I see I came here just in time," she said.

It took Leanna a minute to place her new visitor's name. "Hello. It's Doreen, right?"

"Yes, dear. We've talked a few times at Brenneman's. I sometimes come in with your mother-in-law, Edna."

A couple of times a week, Leanna was a hostess at the cozy Amish restaurant. She remembered Doreen well because the woman was always smiling. But that didn't explain why Doreen had shown up at her house. "Were you visiting Edna today?"

"Nee. I had church this morning too. But I did happen to see Edna the other day, and she told me that all the eligible men in the area had descended upon you like flies to honey. I thought I'd come over to see how you were faring." She smiled again. "May I come in?"

The last thing in the world she wanted was another caller. She also wasn't eager to talk to anyone about all her suitors—especially not someone who would likely report everything she said to Edna.

She really was so tired of being nice. "Of course. May I get you a cup of coffee?"

"I'd love one. That is, if it's not too much trouble."

Leanna was just about to offer Doreen a seat when she noticed that not only was Mervin's cup and saucer and cookie plate still on the coffee table, he'd left crumbs on the seat cushion.

"Um, would you like to join me in the kitchen?"

Understanding filled the older woman's eyes. "Of course, dear. You get your cup, I'll get your caller's."

As they walked into the kitchen, Leanna could practically feel Doreen taking stock of the surroundings. The worn couch, her shelves of books, the clean baseboards. Her small but tidy kitchen. Boy, she hoped the woman wouldn't stay too long.

"Please have a seat at the table. I have peanut butter cookies too. Would you care for some?"

"I would. I've heard stories about these cookies. Edna's a fan."

Leanna chuckled as she prepared Doreen's coffee. "She's easy to please."

When she sat down after handing Doreen her cup and a plate of cookies, Leanna added, "I'm not sure what Edna told you about my suitors."

"Not much." She chomped down on a cookie, chewed, and swallowed. "These cookies are incredible, dear. Not too sweet and not too chewy. Just right."

"Thank you."

Doreen took another bite, washed it down with a sip of coffee, and then daintily wiped her lips. "Leanna, may I be blunt?"

"Yes."

"From the moment we first met, I couldn't help but think what a lovely woman you are. So proper and ladylike. My husband would've said you were a catch."

"Ah, thank you?"

"However, I happened to notice that you never flirt with any of the men at Brenneman's. Never seem to give any man more than a cursory look. Now, I know you've only been widowed for a year, so forgive me if I'm overstepping. But something tells me that maybe you aren't in as quite a big of a hurry to remarry as some of the men around here might be imagining." Folding her hands neatly in her lap, she asked, "Am I right?"

Doreen was being rude and intrusive.

She was also right.

Before Leanna could stop herself, she nodded.

Doreen smiled. "I thought so."

"How did you know?"

"Because, my dear, I am a lot like you. I'm a widow too, you see. Not a recent one, I'm afraid. My Mike died thirteen years ago." When she smiled again, her bottom lip quivered. "He was a wonderful man. The best of men. I adored him." Regaining her composure, she winked. "Better yet, he adored me."

Leanna smiled. "You were blessed."

"Yes, dear, I was." She took a deep breath, then added, "When my Mike died, I knew I lost the love of my life. I knew it."

"I'm sorry." Something inside of Leanna twisted painfully. She had loved Willis too. But they'd been childhood friends, and their marriage had been essentially arranged by their parents. They'd been happy together but not passionate. She'd been content. She missed Willis very much. But had she ever felt about Willis the way Doreen seemed to feel about Mike?

She didn't think she had.

"I'm sorry too," Doreen said. She shook her head. "But that isn't why I came over here." After staring at Leanna for a long moment, she pulled out a card. "I came over to give you this, dear."

Leanna turned the small white business card over to see the front. The words AMISH WIDOWS CLUB in bright black letters blazed across the front of it.

Shocked, she dropped it on the table.

"What is this?"

"It's an invitation, dear." Reaching out, Doreen enfolded Leanna's hands in her own. "I came over to let you know that there are quite a few widows in the area who don't necessarily want to marry again. They're tired of being set up with friends of friends and tired of being courted by desperate men in need of homecooked meals." Taking a breath, her voice gentled. "Now, some are like me, who had a wonderful marriage with the love of their lives and don't want to marry again. Other women weren't so blessed. Still others have their own private reasons for wanting to remain single. However, we all have something in common."

"What's that?"

"We yearn for friendships with like-minded ladies. We meet together about once a month in private. At each other's houses. People think we're doing sewing bees or making food for charity auctions or a host of other things. While we actually do all of that, we mainly just sit and chat and laugh and support each other. I think you would fit in just fine."

After squeezing Leanna's hands one more time, Doreen stood up. "I think I've taken up enough of your time, dear. You take care now."

Leanna hurried to her side. "Wait."

"Yes?"

"Thank you for the offer, but I'm not sure—"

"I understand. When you have time, read the directions on the card. It will tell you what to do." She stopped at the door. "Leanna, I promise that things will get better. They always do, ain't so?"

And with that, Doreen turned back around and walked out the door, her rose-colored dress swishing around her ankles as the tails of her white kapp fluttered in the wind.

Walking back to the kitchen, Leanna felt as if she was in a daze. She sat back down in her chair. Ate one of her cookies.

And then, unable to help herself, she pulled the card toward her and read the entire card.

AMISH WIDOWS CLUB
We're a group no one intended to join but no one wants to be without.

If you are interested in joining, call the number below. You'll hear a recording listing the next meeting place, date, and time.

At the very bottom was a phone number.

Hands shaking, Leanna flipped the card over, but it was blank. She dropped it again and stepped away from the table. Stared at the card.

She'd been invited to join a club of widows who didn't wish to get married again. It was shocking. Scary. And . . . maybe alluring?

Feeling her cheeks heat, she picked it up, shoved it in her bill basket, and then hurriedly cleaned up the kitchen and the living room. Went outside and checked on her garden. Walked into her bedroom and saw her dress for tomorrow's hostess job hanging on a peg.

Went into the bathroom and stared at herself. Saw her blue eyes and blond hair neatly arranged under a pristine white kapp. Examined her gray dress, the dress she wore to church and social gatherings for the last year.

Thought about Mervin and his rude behavior. And Leroy's visit last week. And Daniel, who'd tried to kiss her cheek. And Abram, who'd asked if her house was paid off. And Scott—who wasn't even Amish but had heard she was in the market for a new man.

Then she went to her bookshelf, picked up her favorite book, and sat back down in her chair. And realized that she wanted something more. Something more than just a good book to read. She wanted to stop grieving and making cookies for men she didn't want to marry.

She was tired of doing what everyone else thought she was supposed to do.

Making up her mind, Leanna Mast walked back to the bill basket, picked up the card, then walked to her closet. In the back was a pink cardigan. Once upon a time, it had been her favorite sweater to wear over her dresses. She slipped it on and was pleased it still fit.

Tucking the card inside a pocket, she walked out of her house and headed down the street. It was time to start living again. It was time to make a phone call.

Dear Reader,

I've never thought of myself as a great writer, but I have considered myself to be a dependable one. You see, I'm pretty good at turning in a book on time! From the time I "hear" the first scene of a novel in my head, I'm off and running. I usually write about ten pages a day, six or seven days a week. I enjoy it too. I grow to love my characters, smile when I think of a new plot point, and start to become so immersed in the story that real life and book life almost become intertwined. Though I often must rewrite and revise scenes and chapters, I rarely get stuck. If I do, it's usually nothing a couple of dog walks can't fix.

But then, right after I wrote the first third of *Unshaken*, everything that had worked for 100+ books went out the window. I froze. My mind went blank. And I could not for the life of me figure out what to do next. Facing that flashing dot on my computer screen felt impossible.

As each day passed and my looming deadline crept closer and closer, I started to get a little panicked. I began to procrastinate. I baked. I convinced my husband that we needed another dog. I read dozens of books. I walked and then walked some more. When I started cleaning out closets and cabinets, I knew I was in real trouble. I don't enjoy organizing anything. *Ever.* But, there I was, attempting to alphabetize our spices.

Things had gotten dire.

One night, when I was walking the dogs yet again and mentally preparing how to tell both my editor and agent that I was writing a horrible book, a neighbor asked if I'd like to come over for a glass of wine. She and her husband knew Tom was out of town and I was home alone. Needing a break from my thoughts, I happily accepted.

After we caught up about kids, vacations, and the weather, they asked about my book. Next thing I knew, I told them the whole, awful story. I told them how I was stuck. How I was experiencing writer's block for the first time in twenty years, and it was not fun. I even shared how all the characters in my head had ceased to cooperate.

When I finally stopped complaining, instead of walking me to the door, they decided to give me some help. Next thing I knew, Susan and Frank began to offer a bunch of new ideas. Some were good, even great. Others, not so much. But that didn't matter. What did matter to me was their kindness. These two very busy people took on my problems as their own.

While they gave me some new ideas that I was grateful for, what helped the most was the fact that they were invested in my story too. They liked Stephanie. They liked Hardy. They understood Bev and Carter. They even felt something for Timothy! Their time and encouragement gave me the confidence to move forward.

By the time I went back home, all those characters were talking in my head again. By eight o'clock the next morning, I'd abandoned all thoughts of spice rack organization and was back at my desk. Placing fingers on the keyboard had never felt so good.

I'd love to tell you that I made my deadline. I didn't.

I'd love to share that the book I turned into my editor was great. It wasn't. I've written, rewritten, and revised this book more times than I want to admit. But through everyone's care and help, it's become a book that I'm proud of.

Now that this book is complete, has a beautiful cover, and is in your hands, I have a feeling that I'll always be grateful *Unshaken* kind of shook me up. I often tell people that I like to write books about imperfect people facing seemingly impossible situations. Now I have a pretty good idea about what that feels like.

Thanks for picking up this book. I sincerely hope you enjoy the story.

Blessings,
Shelley

ACKNOWLEDGMENTS

Writing a story is a solitary experience. Writing a book destined for publication is a group effort. I'm so honored and grateful to have had a wide variety of people lend their enthusiasm, expertise, guidance, and time to make *Unshaken* the novel it is today.

First and foremost, I'm so grateful for my readers. Thanks for continuing to read my novels. Thanks for writing reviews, for becoming members of my "Buggy Bunch," for coming to book signings, for writing notes about books that mean something to you. Because of y'all, I've been able to have a job that I love. Please know that I write every novel with my readers in mind.

Of course, I'm so grateful for the entire team at Revell and Baker Publishing. They are truly an amazing group of men and women, and I'm still amazed that I get to say I'm one of their authors. Thank you to Laura Klynstra for inviting me on a cover model shoot and for graciously allowing me to share some ideas for future covers. Thank you to Karen

Steele, Brianne Decker, and Joyce Perez for their tireless efforts to promote my books.

I owe a huge amount of thanks to my editor Andrea Doering for kindly steering me in a better direction during the revision process and to editor Kristin Kornoelje for her suggestions, advice, and careful attention to details.

Once again, I'm indebted to my longtime agent, Nicole Resciniti. Not only does Nicole still champion my work, but she will still stop everything to either answer my call or reply to a text. Because of her, I'm not alone on this journey.

No acknowledgment letter would be complete without thanking my husband Tom, who makes dinner when I don't, cleans the house when I can't, and treats every one of my characters like neighbors and friends. He's the best guy I know.

Finally, I owe everything to God. He gave me the ability to take a bunch of jumbled ideas and turn them into a story. I'm so grateful to receive such a beautiful gift.

Shelley Shepard Gray is the *New York Times* and *USA Today* bestselling author of more than 100 books, including *Unforgiven* and *Unforgotten*. Two-time winner of the HOLT Medallion and a Carol Award finalist, Gray lives in Ohio, where she writes full-time, bakes too much, and can often be found walking her dachshunds on her town's bike trail. Learn more at ShelleyShepardGray.com.